SHOCK THERAPY

Subodh Ghose was born on 29 September 1909 in Bikrampur, Dhaka, now in Bangladesh, and educated at St. Columba's College, Hazaribagh. His early career was varied, to say the least. 'Starting as a schoolmaster', he wrote, 'I had the following occupations: performance on the horizontal bar of a circus; district board health inspector on the Haj Pilgrimage Service; sanitary inspector; bus conductor on the Ranchi-Gaya Motor Bus Service; confectioner; hotel-keeper; mica-mining prospector; vaccinator; poultry farmer; butter merchant; sannyasi... gypsy... union volunteer... political worker...'

In 1941, Subodh Ghose took to writing; his first few stories won him immediate recognition. His vivid and vigorous prose style and the formidable range of experience on which he could draw made a powerful and winning combination.

While he worked, rising to a senior level, on the editorial staff of the Bengali newspaper *Ananda Bazar Patrika,* he continued to write fiction; many of his stories were made into classic Bengali and Hindi films, so that his awards came from both the literary and film worlds. Several such stories have been included in this collection.

Subodh Ghose was prominent too for his editorials in the press; his last editorial appeared on 9 March 1980. He passed away the next day.

Shock Therapy

STORIES

SUBODH GHOSE

Translated from the Bengali
by various hands

Orient Longman

SHOCK THERAPY

ORIENT LONGMAN LIMITED

Registered Office
3-6-272 Himayatnagar, Hyderabad 500 029 (A.P.), INDIA

Other Offices
Bangalore, Bhopal, Bhubaneshwar, Calcutta, Chandigarh, Chennai, Ernakulam, Guwahati, Hyderabad, Jaipur, Lucknow, Mumbai, New Delhi, Patna

First published 2001

ISBN 81 250 1968 5

Typeset by
OSDATA
Hyderabad

Printed in India at
Baba Barkha Nath Printers
New Delhi

Published by
Orient Longman Limited
1/24 Asaf Ali Road
New Delhi 110 002

Contents

The Nectar

Mehndi shrubs fence a window of Chandrababu's house. Mala Biswas, Chandrababu's daughter, stands there all day. The townsfolk are quite familiar with the sight.

Why should a girl so often be seen at the window? Eyebrows are raised. This singular habit is enough to bring ill-fame to Mala. Her behaviour, too, fanned gossip at one time. The ripples of rumour receded as the days passed. Now she is just an addition to the backdrop of the mehndi fence, the lamppost at the gate and the makal tree.

Mala does not miss a single scene. She watches hawkers and follows with her eyes the policemen from the lines. Nor does she avoid their gaze. The mornings fill the street with students and officegoers. Weekly markets beckon more men. Mala looks on when a duststorm whirls away at noon or a shower melts the heat. Boys chat in groups on the road but she never leaves the window.

How does one describe this addiction? Is it an urge to watch everything, or is it the other way round — the desire to be watched?

Mala roams the streets as well. She quite often takes long walks. Her pockmarked visage, dark complexion, fat figure, strange glasses and umbrella and her servant, Ramjibon, are by now a familiar sight. Strangely impressive, also, are her sarees and the way she drapes them. Mala might just stop outside a gramophone shop and ask Ramjibon to inquire about some records. She can halt at Gurudas's watch shop and send the servant in for wrist bands.

Seclusion, probably, bores her and compels her to seek company. She does seek it but cannot cultivate people. At a gathering, for instance the jatra, where elderly women occupy seats behind a partition and girls huddle in rows of benches, Mala sits on a chair, away from all of them — and all alone.

Mala attended the annual function of the girls school. The large Santhali pendant of her necklace drew singular attention and snide remarks. But she seems to be above all that.

Autumn comes and brings with it the happy face of the town. The meadow beside Rani lake, the hillock of black rocks, telegraph wires, faraway neem bushes — all are blessed with the first glow of the season's magic sun, much like the hearty laughter of children.

It seems as if the town has been stirred from its slumber. And is playing with the prism of light. The season of loitering near the lake is here again. Harijan boys have again assembled near the deodar tree for a group drill. Ayahs are towing away perambulators. Basking in the repose of superannuation, Sharatbabu and Kantibabu, armed with their walking sticks, are striding along the gravelled road of the dam.

There is something in the breeze from the lake. It calls out everyone for walks; so they are coming in hordes. Entire families from Lalbagh are out for a jaunt. So is Mr Samuel with his pipe and golf club. And there is Mala, her long scarf flowing in the breeze. Mr Chowdhury, the missionary, is busy arranging a seat for his prayers.

On Cross Road the black hillock has stood for fifty years or so flanked by the karabi plant. It was never a sight to speak of, but today the walkers have deigned to halt here and scan the rock with rapt attention. Something is scribbled there, something that demands a hurried reading.

A hurried reading indeed! Nothing more than that. Because the words, to everyone's disgust, are profane. Addressed to a girl, they are as blasphemous as words can be:

> Purnima Basu. Beauty and quality seldom match so well. You seem to be averse to jewellery, and modesty is truly your adorning grace. I saw you just once, that too after an ordeal of six months. I know, you get letters from Vienna. How is their sender keeping? What about the other forlorn soul in Shimla? Aren't you a bit too tied up? And please don't yawn so often; it's rather crude.

Who could have scribbled such vulgarity? The entire town is aghast with curiosity and shame. Queries are heaped on queries. Who is behind all this? Who is Purnima Basu? Are the comments genuine? All minds and all brains are occupied in researching this single subject — in every household.

The waves of initial inquiry gradually subside. The identity of Purnima has been established. Her father, Mahitoshbabu, owns the house to the south of the old church. She is not a very familiar face. Her walled and fenced life of affluence has hindered familiarity of any kind. But the scribbler has torn apart the veil of seclusion and made her one with all.

But why should anyone bear a grudge against Purnima? Is he new to the town? Is it an act of vengeance? Whatever the cause may be no one appreciates such cowardice. Some people feel sorry for the embarrassment it causes Purnima's family. How terrible they must be feeling!

Their feelings could not be known but Mahitoshbabu and his family no longer come out of their fence of alienation for evening strolls. The scribbler has robbed them of that pleasure.

And what about Purnima? She must be aware of everything by now. Is she weeping? Has she refused to eat? Worries keep piling up as nothing is known for certain. Purnima might just be the opposite. She may have ignored all by her strong will power. Guesses keep racing against time.

Mr Chowdhury is distressed.

He takes his bath near the well at noon every day, without fail. His bald head, white flowing beard and fair, lanky figure are too familiar to all. Sometimes he washes his khadi dhoti himself after his bath. His stock of clothes is scanty. Without any ties in this world, the missionary considers the Church courtyard his only shelter. Feeble and frail, Mr Chowdhury is a rather strange and solitary sight in the noonday sun.

Rigid and truthful, harsh in the face of immorality, he could never stick to Government service. So often in the past has he messed up the revelries of youngsters. Once, as the municipal commissioner, he suggested a ban on cigarette shops. Quite naturally it was turned down.

Mild and timid on occasion, the missionary never budges an inch when it comes to the question of ethics. He knows and is certain that he symbolises decency and civility in the town. He can boast of treating sweepers to milk on Holi, taking away their liquor pots.

His distress is justified and so is his hurriedly lodging a report at the thana against the blasphemy inscribed on the black rock. He demands the scribbler's immediate arrest. And severe punishment.

The police inspector assures him of stern and prompt action.

Mala has read the words and read them with keen, clear interest. She knows Purnima, knew her much before the recent 'scandal'. They have often come face to face, and on every meeting Purnima refused to meet her gaze, closing the window with a bang. Mala could gauge her resentment, possibly aimed at Mala's dazzling green shawl.

The words have amused Mala. They have bulldozed Purnima's snobbery once and for all.

A fortnight later, mocking the cautious town, the black rock comes out with its second fusillade:

> Smita Nandy, who have you pledged to select as the man in your life? What are those faces in your album? But remember, the age of Draupadis is over. Will you ever cross 23? However, I am enamoured of your skill at make-up. Take my advice, stay a spinster and get rid of the album.

Once again the grapevine starts humming. What amazing audacity! And what cunning! One just cannot write the mischief-maker off as a stray loafer! He seems to be quite erudite — probably a young dejected lover.

In the evening at the office of the volunteer committee, the secretary, Nanibabu, sits in the candlelight with a worried countenance. A general meeting has been called today. All the members have come, one by one. All of them are students — Sotu, Priyotosh, Lokenath ....

Nanibabu says, 'This is an insult to all of us. Day after day some miscreant is taking us for a ride and hasn't been caught till date. And there doesn't seem to be any sign that he will stop soon. The whole town is on its toes, scared. Really ....' Nanibabu smiles a smile of woe. 'But I am confident he is not an outsider. A veiled face, a bit too elusive, but he has to be caught, somehow,' Nanibabu assures his companions.

Mr Chowdhury has not given up. He haunts the police station time and again and comes up with strange suggestions. When he demands an armed guard, posted near the rock, the inspector cannot conceal a laugh. It's too trifling a matter, he protests. The missionary is undeterred. He seeks prompt and severe action. What if it's a supernatural incident? 'Appoint a private detective then,' says the missionary, and threatens to rush a telegram to the Governor in case of further delay.

Even if the inspector does not take the aged missionary too seriously he does post a constable to keep a round-the-clock vigil on Cross Road. The words on the rock have by then faded out but as evening descends on the town it finds voice once again:

> Sudha Datta, what a sweet voice you have. Is it thanks to the carbuncle on your throat? Wear blouses with thicker collars. Why do you chatter so much in English? Leave the professor alone; he is married.

The constable swears that he never, even for a minute, took his eyes off the rock. But the poor man's job will possibly be on the line.

How audacious the invisible sinner is! The dumbstruck townspeople can't even dismiss him as a black magician. They are really impressed with the way he serves up delicious secrets. Is he a poet or a lover or a man of great humour? But if only they can catch him. Everyone — from the missionary, the volunteers to relations of the poor girls — will simply tear him to bits. Suspicion does its usual rounds: What is the Bengali manager of the carnival doing here for three months? What do the young chaps have to talk about so much at the watch shop? Why does Nando the mechanic read novels of late? Prashanto only runs a pan shop; what is behind his recent craze for music? Should he be spared since he is uneducated? The volunteers have stopped trusting the police; the police are suspicious of Matilal, who wears khadi. Matilal, too, is after someone or other. Everyone is tense; everyone is suspicious.

But is the black rock sleeping? What causes its reticence? Anxious, vigilant but eager, the town waits — its heartbeats regulated by the blasphemous scribbler. Words beckon its mornings, secrets wet its dust like dewdrops. Thirsty and hungry for a sinner's hand, the town keeps waiting ....

Fewer men visit theatres these days. Their roads seem to end up on the banks of Ranijhil. And they scan the rock in agony and expectation. Whose turn is it next? Who is going to be picked up next?

It seems the watchful sorcerer has heard them. Here is the latest oracle from him:

> Priti Mukherjee, you are not loveable, you are weird. What makes you hug other people's babies? I appreciate your problem. Take my advice, forget about the past as well as Giridih. And be careful in future.

What a fascination this scandalmonger has! The men are distressed, depressed and aghast but they can't keep their minds off him.

Sharatbabu and Kantibabu try to walk the other way. And talk about other things. One is upset, the other is mystified. They are about to broach the topic when the missionary walks past them; his flowing beard, upright visage and stern look at once draw their attention.

'Why did he give us that queer look of his?' Kantibabu asks, curious. 'He probably suspects us,' smiles his friend. The two old men nod in unison.

But what exactly is playing in the victims' minds? Have they overcome the blows? Some pray for their emotional well-being. Have they attempted suicide? Sudha Datta is the most talked about.

Concern cannot be done away with, nor fear. Who can vouch for human integrity? Even then such heinous attacks on characters cannot be supported, especially when all the girls come from rather decent families, concludes the grapevine.

Rumourmongers are working overtime. Purnima and her family are probably leaving the place for good. Sumita tried to consume poison. Priti's brother has sent goondas after the criminal. Sudha will be married off this month. Thus every household is on its toes these days. All eyes and all ears are set on the black rock.

All four of them — Purnima, Sudha, Priti and Sumita — are in the front row of the town cinema today. Mala notices them from her solitary seat at the end of the rear rows. What is the bond of companionship among them, she wonders. Her schoolmate Mukti Roy, is in the crowd from Senpara. She seems to know the famous foursome and is acting as a guide for her friends.

But those four, the cynosure of all eyes, are chatting away among themselves. They are, in fact, drowning other voices in their effusion and shrill laughter. A painting complete in itself, that's what they appear, feels Mala. Others just provide the frame.

Mala has drawn neither curious nor critical attention today. Even the bright lamp, her gorgeous woollen scarf and her queer, long earrings have dimmed in the dazzle of the four girls huddling together in the front row. For the first time in all these years Mala Biswas has not been singled out for public discussion. The galleries have settled down to watch the film. But those four are too happy, too chirpy to concentrate. Mala watches them, surprised at the glee that they seem to be radiating. They look anything but disgraced. Mala looks on, amazed.

Others, too, look on. Other girls whom the magic wand of scandal has not yet touched. But the black rock has more to come up with. Ranijhil and its adjacent fields are bustling with activity today. For the annual Anandamela. And suddenly the people notice — the rock has spoken again.

> Mukti Roy, how long will you hide your beauty from public view? What makes you so absentminded these days? Is that a book of poems in your hand? By the way, your most favourite poem of all is hale and hearty in Muzaffarpur. I simply prefer watching — especially your feet — and admire your gait. Remember, only your gait and not your face. Make-up can hardly hide crow's feet. Why don't you do something about it?

Mala, too, has come to the fair. But not the Mala the people are familiar with. She is dressed shabbily, without her glasses and without her shoes. Even the gorgeous blouse is missing.

Nuns from the Scottish mission are buying bouquets from Chandra's stall. Mala stops there for a while. She promises to buy a bottle of pickles from Malati's shop. Then she hurries to Ranu's tent, not because she loves magic shows but that square piece of ground holds a charm of its own. The crowd stares at the four familiar faces ... and at the latest addition to the black rock's list, Mukti Roy. Mala feels her legs giving way but she cannot give up her mission of watching the five women. Won't they even cast a glance at her awkward countenance?

Some kids call out to her from Anupama's tea stall. Mala obliges them by accepting a cup of tea. Anupama does not hide her irritation. 'Ranudi has beaten us hands down. She is fooling them with her sleight of hand.' Mala smiles and does not divulge the secret to the child.

She will never regain her place at centre stage. Mala feels lost and feeble in her strange, shabby dress. She belongs neither to the galaxy of Purnima and Mukti nor to the humdrum of Ranu and Anupama. She is alone, lonely and beneath recognition.

The volunteers have reassembled today. They wait, tense, as Nanibabu makes a sad face and says, 'Keep the secret to yourselves. We have traced the miscreant. He is our Chowdhury, the missionary.' Nanibabu's voice trickles down the dark line on the table. His audience is awestruck. Then Priyotosh finds his voice. 'What proof do you have?' Nanibabu keeps quiet. His eyes glimmer in the shadows of the room.

Here ends the responsibility of the volunteers. But rumours cannot be chained to the dark desk. They will spread to every corner of the town, generating disbelief, shame and hesitation.

Mala has withdrawn into a shell. So has the rock on Cross Road. The town too has lost interest in the story. Mala dares not venture into the domain of Purnima and her lot. They are to be gazed at and to be desired. They rule the days, they fill the nights. They turn filth into pure streams of light. For Mala, the window is the limit.

The mirror, too, tells the truth. It reminds her again and again that the world is no longer hers. Often, she wants to break the shackles within. But soon gives up in despair.

Mala is about to shut the window tightly when a storm cloud veils the moon this evening. Something crosses her mind and she calls Ramjibon for a walk. Tears come gushing. They kill the urge and unnerve Mala but as Ramjibon gets impatient she sets out for a stroll.

Long walks. Her favourite route around Ranijhil. She walks away as darkness gathers on the deodars and a duststorm ruffles the sky. After a while she sees herself in front of the black rock, waiting in the dark. About to prey on an an unsuspecting soul.

What a magic mass of stones and pebbles it is! How it has glorified a fortunate few and transformed disgrace into pride! And how partial it is! Why has it conspired against her?

Mala can silence the elusive scribbler once and for all. Armed with a piece of chalk she approaches the rock. The lightning is about to flash. Ramjibon will soon call out again and a bunch of lies, in their white splendour, is seen engraved on the rock:

> Mala Biswas, I bow to you. One, two, three, four — .... Let me not count the numbers. Who remembers the moths? Let Ranijhil devour your letters and rest awhile.

translated by Swati Ghosh

The Heart of a Lovesick Bird

'Dear brother, please pay attention to what I am writing.' So read Mira's letter from Madhupur. 'Try to understand me. For I fully realise the implication of my views. I know this is a good opportunity and you will be making a great mistake if you ignore it.

'You must have heard about an engineering firm called G.B. Construction Limited. It always gets government contracts to build big bridges. You have certainly seen in the newspapers the picture of a big railway bridge at Sambalpur. It was built by this G.B. Construction. The same firm is building the new bridge on the Lalki river, sixteen miles from your town. About one and a half crore rupees will be spent on the construction. The concern is also building some small bridges near Madhupur and the work is almost over.

'Saurav Sarkar, GBC's inspecting engineer, is now in Madhupur. But he will not stay here very long. Perhaps he will leave Madhupur within a month. He will supervise the work on the bridge over Lalki river. Perhaps he will stay in your town for three months and then proceed towards Sambalpur.

'Saurav Sarkar is the son of my husband's aunt. He was in Glasgow for three years and in Hamburg for two years. He returned to India after completing special studies in bridge construction engineering and training, and has become the inspecting engineer of a famous concern like GBC at this young age. He has a salary of one thousand five hundred rupees. He may have crossed thirty, but is certainly below thirty-five. But your Anima too is almost thirty.

'Saurav is yet to marry, but has given enough hints of his intention to get married. You should therefore realise that you can no longer keep quiet. You must show some initiative. I am sure Saurav can be made to marry Anima if you make a real effort.

'You have remained undecided for three years after your daughter became a graduate. But you could do nothing. If you could go to

Calcutta and stay there for some time, then you could have found a good match, but never someone like Saurav. In fact, you don't have the capability to get a bridegroom like him in a competitive area like Calcutta. There are so many girls there, more good-looking and educated than Anima.

'Hence this is a chance for you. You must temporarily keep your traditional views and ideas under the lid. One has to follow the rules of the day, otherwise one suffers a lot. Invite Saurav to tea and introduce him to Anima. She still looks pretty and I don't think Saurav will find anything to object to in her. God willing, Saurav will marry Anima.

'There is another thing. This is also an opportunity to get close to Saurav. Find a house for him within or on the outskirts of the town where he can stay for two or three months. Doesn't matter if the rent is three or four hundred rupees. Saurav wants the house to be airy with a lawn overlooking a garden. You don't have to engage any servants, but look for a gardener. Saurav will bring with him a cook, a servant, besides a chaprasi and an attendant.

'Read out my letter to my sister-in-law. She cannot expect a good match for Anima if she sits idle and doesn't make some real effort. She should also give up all her inhibitions about her daughter mixing freely in society. She must not get scared or hesitate to take the initiative. She must not object to Saurav's courting Anima. There is nothing indecent in it.'

As Nibaranbabu read out the letter, Suhasini, Anima's mother, listened to him with rapt attention.

Nibaranbabu: 'What do you think of it?'

Suhasini: 'I think Mira is right.'

Anima too had received a letter from Mira-auntie. 'I have already written to your father, but have to write a separate letter to you. You should think it your good fortune and something beyond your dreams if, God willing, a young man like Saurav marries you. Hence you must be a little bold. Don't think I want you to be a flirt. Behave with Saurav as a girl behaves with an educated and cultured gentleman. You should neither talk nonsense nor behave like an old grandmother. You will personally invite Saurav for tea. Saurav simply loves flowers. Send a bunch of flowers from your garden to him every morning and evening. Go out with Saurav if he invites you. Sometimes put on the Baluchar saree I sent to you from Berhampore last year. Don't walk hunch-backed with frightened eyes. Sing if Saurav wants to hear your songs. Remember, your future is in your hands. Perhaps everything will be all right due to God's grace.'

Suhasini: 'Anima, has Mira written to you?'

Anima: 'Yes.'

Anima turns grave —' She wrote a lot of nonsense.'

Suhasini: 'No, it is not nonsense. What she has written is correct. She has written to help you.'

Anima, however, remains grave and mutters: 'Strange!'

Suhasini: 'What is strange?'

Anima: 'You too are talking in a different way.'

Suhasini: 'One has to keep pace with the times. Besides, it is our good fortune to get a match like Saurav.'

Anima begins to laugh: 'Let this good fortune reach us first.'

Suhasini: 'Why not? If Saurav comes to like you ....'

Anima: 'Why should he like me?'

Suhasini: 'That is exactly what Mira wrote in her letter. Why don't you understand?'

Anima continues to look distraught: 'I still don't understand.'

Suhasini's face becomes a little sad. She too finds it somewhat difficult to gladly accept Mira's suggestions. It would have been a pleasant event if Saurav himself had come here to see Anima and selected her. It is not a good thing that the girl should run about to catch the attention of an unknown male.

It is, of course, true that a youth like Saurav is a high-priced offer to a man like Nibaranbabu. Once the latter was quite well-off, but no longer. He has only a big house and a lac factory. There is, however, hardly any market for lac. Nibaranbabu had to sell his car two years back. He is now in a position to spend five to six thousand rupees on his daughter's marriage, but none of the grooms who would be available at that sum, comes anywhere near Saurav in terms of qualifications and pedigree. Hence Mira's suggestion has to be accepted.

II

Nibaranbabu has lost no time in finding a good house for Saurav. The house, surrounded by eucalyptus trees, is located on the road leading to Hill Canary, away from the town. It has a lush green lawn beside which stand two square lotus ponds. Ivy creepers embrace the huge pillars near the entrance. There is also a row of tubs containing rose trees from Gajipur. Brindaban, the gardener, has already cleared the garden and removed heaps of dry leaves.

Saurav Sarkar, accompanied by his personal attendants, has also arrived. Nibaranbabu was present at the railway station to welcome him. Immediately after getting down from the train Saurav looks up at a smiling Nibaranbabu: 'I guess you are Nibaranbabu.'

'You are right.'

'Where is the house?'

'Here is Brindaban, the gardener. He will show you the way.'

Two taxis, loaded with Saurav Sarkar's luggage and servants, speed away, preceded by another taxi carrying Saurav and the gardener, Brindaban.

Reclining on a chair on the verandah, Saurav is reading a book when Nibaranbabu, accompanied by Anima, reach the house on Hill Road a little before dusk. Saurav looks really handsome. He is certainly not 35, maybe just approaching 30. Clad in white jeans and a twill shirt, his feet snugly enclosed in a pair of white leather slippers, Saurav appears to be a bright and smart guy. Nibaranbabu's eyes sparkle with great eagerness.

Anima is wearing a Baluchar saree, but she stumbles many times while walking down half a mile from her house. She has an unpleasant frown on her face. An unbearable and uneasy breathing seems to be causing her a great deal of pain. It is really a shame! Saurav Sarkar may represent some glory or fortune, but Anima's 30-year-old soul does not want to turn greedy. All this is really pointless, Anima feels.

Saurav literally jumps out of his chair as soon as he sees Anima and Nibaranbabu. Nibaranbabu smiles benignly: 'I have not come here to disturb you. Only, Anima has something to tell you.'

'Who?' asks a startled Saurav.

Nibaranbabu: 'Anima, my daughter.'

Anima also smiles: 'Even if you feel disturbed, you cannot refuse us. You must have tea at our place this evening.'

Saurav's eyes shine at the pleasant surprise: 'Why should I feel disturbed? Never. I will certainly be there.'

Anima and Nibaranbabu take leave of Saurav and start walking down the path which Anima had earlier traversed with great unease. But the feeling of uneasiness gradually vanishes from Anima's mind. She no longer has the unpleasant frown on her face. The Baluchar saree she is wearing also does not seem to be the sign of some helpless greed. On the contrary, she feels she has put on the saree in a hurry when she should have taken time and care to do so properly. Her frightened mind was expecting to see a dark cloud on the horizon, but she has come back after sighting the full moon.

III

Anima has not forgotten to send flowers to the house on Hill Road. The person whom Anima is always so eager to see, has twice walked down Hill Road to have tea at Nibaranbabu's house. Nibaranbabu is surprised and Suhasini highly pleased to find a shy girl like Anima talking freely to Saurav after such a brief acquaintance. In fact, Anima is no longer her earlier frightened self. A smiling Anima roams on the verandah and becomes somewhat restless as dusk sets in. She takes almost half an hour to complete her make-up, but still remains dissatisfied with her appearance. Suhasini too once noticed how Saurav talked intimately to Anima while taking his leave, how his face became shy as he muttered the words. Anima too got startled and listened to Saurav with a bent head. Her face had turned crimson as she nodded to Saurav's suggestions.

Suhasini can hardly suppress her temptation to inquire about the conversation. 'Did Saurav tell you anything?' she asks Anima.

'Yes.'

'What was it?'

'He asked me to go for a walk with him this evening.'

'O.K. Go, then.'

'I shall.'

Anima leaves the house before dusk. She knows that the invitation for a walk from the person staying in the house on Hill Road is meant not only for today but for ever. Mira-auntie's apprehension was totally uncalled for. She wanted Anima to get ready for a mediation, but nothing of the sort was necessary. And Anima did not have to be blatant or shameless to present herself to his attention.

The man with the pleasant smile has continuously stared at her with thirsty eyes and gratified her beyond all expectations.

Clad as usual in white jeans and a twill shirt, his feet wrapped in white leather slippers, Saurav is waiting near a eucalyptus tree on Hill Road to welcome Anima. Saurav's eyes are not dark, but intensely blue. At times Anima feels the eyes reflect the blue sky.

Anima smiles: 'It seems you suspect something.'

'What suspicion?'

'Perhaps you thought I wouldn't come.'

'Yes. For a moment I thought so.'

'Why?'

'I never had the courage to believe that I could get such a great reward within three days of my coming here. I could never imagine that a girl like you could accept an invitation from a man like me and ....'

'Please don't say that.'

'Why not?'

'I could never dream that a man like you would invite me.'

Anima and her love, Saurav, walk a long distance together along Hill Road. They don't forget to hold hands as they approach a solitary corner of the road. A stray crow flies away from the roadside karanja tree at the sudden sound of Anima's unfettered laughter. The path leading to Anima's house turns into a misty way as the evening sets in. Truly, Anima could never imagine that one has this overwhelming feeling of losing oneself in the company of the dear one.

'Let me escort you home, Anima.'

Anima turns her head towards the whisper and smiles: 'Shall we go now?'

'I don't want to, but there is hardly any time left.'

'Why?'

'I will have to go to the station now.'

'Why?'

'My boss may arrive.'

'What kind of boss?'

'Mr Sarkar, the engineer.'

'Who is Mr Sarkar?'

'Saurav Sarkar who happens to be a relative of your aunt staying at Madhupur.'

Anima's heart almost screams out in pain: 'What are you talking about? What a terrible thing to say!'

'What did you say?'

'Who are you?'

'I ... I am ....'

'Who are you?' Anima begins to sob.

'I am Mr Sarkar's steno-typist, simply a clerk.'

'Your name?'

'Don't you know it?'

'No.'

'Strange!'

'Maybe it is strange, but tell me your name. Come on, out with it.'

'I am Benoy Dutta.'

'Then you reached here before Mr Sarkar?'

'Yes, the staff always arrive before the boss. But Anima, now I understand the whole thing.'

'What have you understood?'

'You mistook me for Mr Sarkar. I am really sorry, Anima. Forget everything. Also ask your father to forgive me.'

It seems to Anima that her fate is taunting her in a strange pitiful language under the shadow of the evening. The voice of Benoy Dutta, the steno-typist, again becomes shaky with apprehension: 'I promise you that I will leave this place within a couple of days, as soon as Mr Sarkar arrives. Somehow I will manage the leave.'

'Please go away, leave me alone,' Anima blurts out. As Benoy Dutta slowly starts for the railway station, a tearful Anima also begins to walk, biting the end of her saree in sheer despair.

IV

A smile hovers on the corners of Anima's lips next morning as she goes through a letter written by Mira-auntie from Madhupur. It was a small post-card addressed not to Anima, but to Nibaranbabu: 'Saurav has gone to Calcutta. Perhaps he will reach your place after a week. Ask Benoy, Saurav's steno-cum-clerk, to be present at the station to receive him.'

'Whose letter makes you so happy?' asks Suhasini.

'It is from Mira-auntie.'

'What has she written?'

'She says that Saurav Sarkar is now in Calcutta.'

'What do you mean?'

'I mean Saurav Sarkar has not yet arrived here.'

'Have you gone crazy?'

'I am not crazy. I am becoming crazy.'

A visibly panicky Nibaranbabu suddenly rushes out of his room and stares at Anima: 'What happened?'

'Benoy Dutta, Saurav Sarkar's steno-cum-clerk, has asked for your forgiveness.'

'Who is Benoy Dutta?'

'He is the one whom we mistook for Saurav Sarkar and invited to tea three times.'

Nibaranbabu and Suhasini suddenly seem to have lost the strength to scream. They look like a helpless couple of unfortunates, victims of a cruel joke, and stand in silence with bowed heads.

Nibaranbabu's eyes become wet with self-pity. Tears also blur Suhasini's vision. Anima, however, suddenly starts laughing: 'I have to go out at once.'

Both Nibaranbabu and Suhasini look up to Anima's beautifully made-up face. She is certainly going outside. But where can she go? Why is she laughing so strangely?

Suhasini: 'Where are you going?'

Anima: 'I am going to meet the person to whom you wanted to send me by force.'

'What do you mean?'

'Let me find out whether Saurav Sarkar has arrived or not. Perhaps he has arrived.'

'No, you don't have to go now.'

'Why are you getting scared?'

'We are afraid you will make some mistake and talk nonsense.'

'I will neither make any mistake nor talk nonsense. I will act as per Mira-auntie's directives.'

Suhasini and Nibaranbabu stare at Anima for a while — they seem to have discovered a wonderful rule of the changing times. Anima, representing the new rule, looks like a butterfly oblivious of the flower on which it sat sometime back, getting its wings bathed in pollen. Anima's laughter too indicates a new energy of action. She seems to have forgotten her misplaced laughter of yesterday and made up her mind to seek something new.

A new apprehension overcomes Nibaranbabu and Suhasini. Is the girl going to face a new misfortune: being misled by a false hope?

'You look very worried,' says Anima.

'We can't feel calm,' replies Suhasini.

'Why?'

'Tell us the truth. Are you going to meet Saurav?'

Anima smiles: 'Yes, yes, yes.'

Nibaranbabu silently goes inside his room.

'What will you tell Saurav?' asks Suhasini.

Anima: 'I will tell him what I should, what Mira-auntie has asked me to tell him. I will invite him to tea.'

Suhasini heaves a sigh of relief with a little despair. 'All right.'

V

Saurav Sarkar is sitting on a cane chair on the grassy lawn. A well-built man, Sarkar is reading a newspaper with rapt attention, a smile bifurcating his lips as he chews on his pipe.

Ivy creepers swing around the huge pillar at the entrance as Anima arrives there and suddenly stands still. She seems to have suddenly regained her consciousness and becomes somewhat startled. But why? What for? Where and to whom does she want to take her disrupted desire? Has Anima really rushed to Saurav Sarkar as a lover with a secret hope and strange greed? Or, has she come here to meet someone else on the pretext of seeing Saurav?

No, Benoy has not yet left. Even now that scared and apologetic soul is sitting near a table on the verandah with a heap of files. He is hammering on the small typewriter, his head bent over his work. The sound of typewriting seems to echo the heartbeat of Benoy Dutta, a man solely concerned with his work. The man does not resemble the one who was known to Anima till yesterday.

Benoy Dutta looks up only once, but the calm and indifferent language of his eyes seems to convey that he has never seen Anima.

As a frown appears on Anima's face, Saurav Sarkar welcomes her: 'Please come here.' Anima's cautious eyes again get startled. She could hardly realise that she has come so close to Saurav Sarkar while watching the man on the verandah.

Anima's heart suddenly wants to scream out — why have you come here? Why is she feeling embarrassed when Saurav Sarkar has welcomed her with a polite smile? Perhaps Anima could never imagine that she would be welcomed in this way. She seems to have come here with a determined bid to make her father, mother and Mira-auntie aware of the fallacy of a bad dream. She has to undergo the test facing her. She will invite Saurav Sarkar to tea. And then her father, mother and Mira-auntie would know that Saurav Sarkar must have found the invitation quite funny and deliberately forgotten to attend it. He has no time even to cast a pitiful glance on the daughter of an almost bankrupt lac trader like Nibaranbabu with a meagre monthly income of Rs. 1500.

True, Nibaranbabu and Suhasini too had not realised the hidden meaning of Anima's laughter. Anima seems to have embarked on a false love journey to make everyone understand that the daughter of a man like Nibaranbabu will not gain anything even by worshipping Saurav Sarkar.

Saurav smiles: 'Please take a seat. You don't have to reveal your identity. I know who you are. Mira-di has briefed me about you all beforehand.'

Anima also tries to smile, but her laughter appears both distraught and pitiful. She feels more disturbed when Saurav looks at her with charmed eyes.

'I am so glad that you have come,' says Saurav.

Anima has almost forgotten the purpose of her visit and tries her best to recollect it. What does she really have to tell Saurav? What did Mira-auntie write in her letter?

Saurav Sarkar suddenly gets up from his chair and begins to laugh: 'Let us go and meet your parents.'

Anima: 'They have asked you to ... .'

'To do what?'

'You will come and have tea at our place.'

'Then I think we should not wait any longer,' Saurav Sarkar puts the tie dangling from his shoulder inside his trouser pocket and gets ready to leave, 'Let's go.'

A stormy breeze threatens to uproot the ivy creepers embracing the big pillars near the entrance. To Anima the stormy wind resembles Saurav Sarkar's outburst of happiness. After crossing the entrance Saurav Sarkar again gives vent to the happy state of his mind — 'This is good. I don't have any work for the next three or four days. It will be great relaxation. I can come regularly to your house for tea; if you desire, of course.'

'What did you say?'

'I said if you want me to go to your place, then I can ....'

'Of course, you are welcome every day.'

'Anima, it may not be possible for me to visit your place every day. Benoy, my steno-typist, is going on leave and will board the train tonight. So I can relax for three or four days before the new clerk joins .... What is it? Are you all right?'

Anima suddenly feels sick and puts her hand on the trunk of a roadside tree to keep herself still. Her head reels and legs feel paralysed, her vision suddenly getting blurred. Keeping her hand on the tree-trunk she tries to regain her balance.

'It's nothing,' mutters Anima and looks back towards the verandah as if someone has suddenly pulled the end of her saree. Benoy Dutta is standing still on the verandah and staring at her as if he has all of a sudden discovered a strange mist.

VI

'What Saurav has told us indicates that he has no objection to the marriage,' Suhasini says.

Nibaranbabu: 'I also think so. How can he make it more obvious?' Nibaranbabu and Suhasini are not talking in whispers, but speaking quite loudly as if to make someone hear them. Anima, of course, can hear them from her room, but does not show any curiosity. For she fully agrees with what they are saying.

Saurav has taken tea and talked with both Nibaranbabu and Suhasini for a long while. The elderly couple also clearly heard what Saurav's loving voice told Anima before he left their house: 'Mira-di told me something, Anima, but I don't want to reveal it today. I think I should be in no hurry to disclose it.'

Saurav leaves and Anima rushes to her room and does not come out even once to talk to her parents.

But Nibaranbabu and Suhasini are again surprised to find Anima coming out of her room fully dressed to go out. Where does she intend to go at this hour of the evening? Why is she weeping?

'What's happened?' cries Suhasini.

'I am leaving.'

'Where are you going?'

'To the railway station'

'Why to the railway station?'

'Perhaps Benoy will board the night train.'

'Let him go.'

'Why should he leave?'

'It is his wish. Why do you want to meet him?'

'I have got something to tell him. Otherwise, why should I want to meet him?'

'What is it?'

'I will bring him back.'

'Why?'

'Let him have tea here before he leaves.'

'Why should Benoy have tea here?'

'Because he is going to get married to your daughter.'

'Who told you so?'

'I am telling you.'

Nibaranbabu looks at Suhasini and then both of them stare at Anima. What does she mean? Was her laughter this morning false and her evening sob true?

Nibaranbabu: ' I have nothing more to say.'

Suhasini: 'I wonder how I will make Mira understand the whole thing.'

Anima smiles again: 'Write to her that God's will has prevailed.'

translated by Sattam Kumar Ghose

The Cactus

Mr Nag has a garden - and what a garden! one must exclaim - and a Durwan too, a tiger-like guard. But this guard Dalbeer is chiefly a night watchman. He has no duties in the daytime.

Mr Nag has his own duty roster for guarding his extraordinary garden: from 10 in the morning, Mr Nag himself can continue his vigilance almost throughout the day; during the short gap for bath and lunch, he makes over the charge to driver Satpal Singh barely for an hour and thereafter he is again back on his balcony chair - comparable to a kind of hunter's perch - with a volume of classics on his lap. Casually, he skips pages, in fact, not necessarily reading anything but perhaps because his eyes need some diversion, some rest.

Eternal vigilance is the price of this priceless garden. Virtually a botanical research field: for the variety of flowers, fruits, creepers and leaves, a multi-coloured spectacle. The ferns here are comparable to those at Shalimar Bagh in Kashmir. One marvels when a flower assumes the look of a fruit - and when a fruit hangs like a bunch of flowers. A Walt Whitman might like to scan some leaves of grass here.

Alpine flora, his favourite species, and then Julipars Casipio and rhododendron! Foreign tourists also queue at the gate to get an eyeful of that sight.

Mr Nag has his own research methods. Some ideas are, he found, rather too pedantic, too bookish. Who says that Calcutta soils are not conducive to the growth of violets and daisies? Drop in here in February, and get lost in the wide range of violets and daisies glistening in the morning dew.

Mr Nag recites Whitman: 'When lilacs last in the dooryard bloomed ...' and instinctively, his eyes shift to the lilacs in the garden, his baby flowers nursed so tenderly.

A hobby! Maybe, but what an expensive hobby! No, actually it is a research centre, a botanical sanatorium. Mr Nag, a retired judge, has spent his entire lifetime savings on this garden to ensure its all-round growth and richness - with the paternal care of a father for a meritorious son. Even today, half his pension is spent on this garden.

Mr Nag has no family - his wife died long back and his issueless existence found both comfort and meaning in the growth of this garden.

This garden is his family, one may safely say.

Look at that African Tulip! A bunch of red cotton. Mr Nag looks at it with all the affection on earth, as one might observe the face of a newborn baby.

His love for the garden naturally keeps him anxious and tense all the time. Disturbing birds are there, squirrels out on their notorious games, and wanton boys and greedy adults abound. But there is Dalbeer too - his Casabianca - and so Mr Nag can have peaceful slumber at night.

Mr Nag himself, too, is a picture of vigilance, with an airgun by his side. Look, two 'doyels' are leaping and chirping on an exquisite Damascacian rose - and instantly, the airgun booms and the doyels fly in fear. Content, Mr Nag flips pages of Whitman.

The night-time programme poses no particular problem. Dalbeer is there, his eyes a haunting cat glow in the darkness. A life-size electric torch is his main weapon. Just a very faint sound, and Dalbeer's torch flashes on the spot in seconds. A darkling owl shudders and sits quiet on the branch of a tree, eyes closed. Dalbeer throws a piece of stone and the owl shifts to a blind corner.

Winter, of course, brings some anxiety. Anxiety for a special kind of Himalayan orchid. This cannot easily survive the Calcutta cold.

Mr Nag has endeavoured hard - gone for all kinds of experiments, as if in an attempt to save a dying child. But, alas, ill-luck persists. The mystery remains unresolved.

His study tells him - the winter's touch will turn the green leaves of the chinar a fiery red like dazzling damsels. But that is not to be. The green goes grey, dries up and pales pathetically. A variety of fertiliser powders has had no effect so far.

This year, rather this winter, has posed a special threat.

Mr Nag is really worried.

An Arizonian cactus plant. It was planted at great cost, and after tiresome experiments. An adventurous move, no doubt. How far away is that Arizona desert! Its distance from Alipore, Calcutta, defies all sensible calculation. This cactus stands on the dry sandy vastness of the burning desert like a sadhu meditating, with its hands turned up towards the sky. How can that thing survive on this dam' wet soil of Alipore! Sheer absurdity! But that too is the focal point of interest for Mr Nag. He wants to play with absurdities to see how recalcitrant they are! Well, if somehow, by God's grace, his Alipur Arizona Cactus can survive the winter, then hurrah! - a splendid discovery will thrill all connoisseurs and botanical experts. The cactus will definitely have a longer span of life, and Mr Nag will feel blessed with a rare award.

The strictest possible care is needed.

Mr Nag has bought a piece of blazer flannel five yards long from New Market, to prepare a warm cover to foil wintry bites on his dear Cactus. Accustomed to playing with searching sunrays, his Cactus here matures gradually. So its bare body cannot withstand the cold winter of February. It would inevitably die.

So this special protection: a ghera-tope, a cover. Mr Nag himself places it on his lovely Cactus, examining thoroughly to see whether the flannel jacket has any opening or hole, makes sure his baby will not catch cold; only then does he go to sleep.

Dalbeer, his Casabianca, takes over charge.

Midnight.

Dalbeer on duty. Dressed in warm, thick, knee-length woollen overalls and a cap of warm rug-cloth. A torch and a small heavy rod - his two weapons. His boots give out a monotonous marching noise; his baton often cracks something hard in the otherwise silent night.

Dalbeer, the night watchman. Inhabitant of a slum at Behala, his daytime shelter. It charges him Rs. 40/- per month. Mr Nag pays him Rs. 250/-, but he can only manage to send home barely Rs.100/-. And that figure too does not always remain very definite. Dalbeer's home is Darjeeling. He came to Calcutta only two years ago. This is his first job in this metropolis.

At 33, he has a strong physique and short stature - his anthropological heritage. His eyes shine in indulgence at the hide-and-seek of some incorrigible squirrels, glow in anger at a sly bitch trying to sneak through the fence. A sharp marksman, Dalbeer throws the rod, and the wounded bitch runs away. Dalbeer roams all round in routine rhythm.

The cold is biting, and suddenly Dalbeer feels irked by a scene that he sees with his mind's eye, away in Darjeeling, where winter has a belligerent ferocity. His old mother is suffering. Is the stock of charcoal nil? Is there anything in the shabby hutment that can keep burning, that can generate some heat, just enough to put that lonely old woman to sleep? No, there is nothing that is certain to fuel the impoverished hearth. Last month, it was only eighty rupees that he had managed to send. It would not provide her the luxury of a burning fire. Impossible. Yes, there is every reason for this apprehension. She wrote to Dalbeer, asking for a little more to buy a rug that was absolutely essential for her to survive. A rug! That, too, was never to be, at least for the present. Dalbeer is optimistic. He may do something worthwhile in the coming month ... So, she must manage somehow, must manage to live till that time.

Dalbeer's concentration is a little shattered. A nightmarish feeling grieves him. He cannot brush aside something that appears like cinema slides on the dark screen of night, enough to move him with a touch of reality.

Yes, there is his mother, cold shaking like fury out of her frail limbs. No fire, no rug, no sleep. Just a struggle for existence.

She needs money. But money is not so easy to earn; Why doesn't she understand? Dalbeer tries desperately to find some logic behind his helplessness.

No he must forget all these things. On to duty. Some phantoms are hovering around.

'Hey - Khabardar - Khabardar!' Dalbeer shouts in a frantic bid to steady himself.

Dalbeer has one baffling hazard. There is an old, wretched maid, incorrigibly mobile for a octogenarian, who often succeeds in crossing the fence. God knows how!

Dalbeer knows her.

She is the female prototype of Wordsworth's leech-gatherer, one may well imagine. She, however, gathers only cheap vegetation that overgrows without care or protection - a sapling, some wild water plants, mushrooms and grassy leaves that are thought edible by the poor. She has an expert hand, doing her job with swift movements. Often, she seems to be just a shadow that flits past, barely seen.

She has a desire to invade Mr Nag's garden too - and at night. This is Dalbeer's headache. He is almost fed up with fighting a shadow. One day, rather one night, he must catch her, and then ....

But success is not so easy. Dalbeer's torch focussed straight on her forehead, she instantly ducks and vanishes. The gate, of course, remains closed. So the old mate plans to cross the wall by piling brick on brick. Sounds an impossible feat for an old hag. But her physical fitness - on a mischievous mission though — is really amazing. Dalbeer is almost in a frenzied state.

A thief - old, obstinate and untiring. She cares a damn for Dalbeer's tiger-like movements. Any day Dalbeer may find himself totally defeated by her. Dalbeer gets nervous even thinking about it. In the daytime, she plays some dirty tricks. A shower of abuse, vulgar and unprintable, reaches Dalbeer's ear as he smokes a bidi at the end of his duty, when the clock ticks 7 in the morning.

All sorts of dialect slang, which Dalbeer understands very well by now, overflows unceasingly from her mouth. Dalbeer - a devil incarnate, a bastardly slave, a bootlicker of a dishonest rich boss, and so on ... .

'I will break your head one day, you old hag!' Dalbeer shouts in Hindi and sometimes, in fact, feels like giving her blows. Passers-by, mostly on their morning walk, come to her rescue. 'Oh, durwaan, why lose your temper with an incorrigible madwoman? Let go of her.'

Dalbeer controls himself but harbours a feeling of revenge. Let the opportune moment arise, and then ....

Tonight Dalbeer is desperate. He must have a showdown. His nerves at least are on special alert, as it were, to nab the old hag. Catching her red-handed, he will take her to Mr Nag for the necessary ordeal - police or whatever.

Yes, this has really become a question of survival for himself. If the 'budhi' succeeds even once in stealing a flower or even a leaf from the garden, Mr Nag will feel one of his ribs has broken - and instantly Dalbeer will be fired. Jobless in Calcutta, he will be as helpless as Samson eyeless in Gaza.

So this danger must end. Dalbeer cannot stand it any more. It has almost got to his nerves.

'O Sakhbudhi, tum meri jan ki dushman ban gayi,' Dalbeer murmurs in Hindi. No peace till she is caught.

Tonight Dalbeer has smelt something. There is a chance - he believes, the old hag will make an adventurous move - and Dalbeer must make full use of it. Any moment, yes, any moment, she may come. Every minute is vital.

Dalbeer roams like a wild cat, hardly making any sound.

Round after round. Some more rounds. Tense expectancy makes him somehow tired too. No trace of the old bitch yet! Is his information wrong?

The job is so monotonous. Dalbeer, for the first time, feels a kind of strange boredom.

Again, after an hour or so, that memory invades his brain. Again, those cinema slides appear on the murky canopy of the sky. His old mother at Darjeeling has now become helpless. The money-order peon has failed her this month too. Dalbeer has to pay back a loan to a neighbour. It was already overdue.

'My mother may die in the cold,' Dalbeer is shocked at his own murmurs.

... And just at that moment, in the course of his momentary mid-winter night's dream, Dalbeer is further shocked at the sight of that old hag, who has, meanwhile, slyly managed to enter the garden, and now is moving towards some particular destination.

At last, Dalbeer feels the golden opportunity is here! He jerks himself to some rearguard action, follows the shadow in cat-like silence - step by step, halting at times, never allowing himself to lose the necessary pace to catch hold of her in time.

Let him observe first - what this damn spirit is up to! Let her dare touch something - picking or plucking - and in seconds Dalbeer will pounce on her. And then she will face the music. Mr Nag will —

But where is she going, after all? What is up her sleeve? She is not touching anything - no costly flowers, no fruits, not even some rare off-season vegetables that command a very high market price just now.

Dalbeer's eyes shine in the darkness, but now the surroundings look nebulous and hazy. The thief has come to a halt. It is near that Cactus whose life hangs in the balance - a gamble which Mr Nag is dying to win.

What is she doing? The thorny dry Cactus, a decorative piece of sandy landscape, what has it to do with her? It is not a flower to accompany some drawing-room verse; nor a fruit that invites a hungry bite. Then what ....

The misty moonlight helps Dalbeer to see things somewhat clearly. The old hag in a thin tattered sari is trembling. Dalbeer can almost hear her bones rattling. She has shrunk nearly frozen with the cold.

Suddenly, she snatches that ghera-tope, that makeshift heat chamber of the Cactus - that much-coveted flannel cover, now torn off. The Cactus stands denuded in the shivering cold, stripped of its garments and exposed to the icy damp that will definitely kill it.

But the old hag is in no hurry. She calmly covers herself with that warm piece of flannel. Her trembling has gone; she warms up visibly, signs of comfort that glare before Dalbeer's eyes.

But what about Dalbeer, the dutiful night watchman to Mr Nag whose allegiance was always unquestionable? Dalbeer now stands stupefied. He himself feels frozen, hardly able to move his fingers.

The old hag resembles his dying mother in Darjeeling! Her agony silently echoes his mother's lamentation, far away somewhere, ten thousand feet high.

Both of them — this old thief and his mother — are exposed to freezing death. They both cry, but nobody hears.

Bewildered, Dalbeer notices a feeling of satisfaction, writ large on the face of both; scenes and figures get mixed up. His head reels; he forgets that he must act.

The old hag now flees and vanishes as silently as she came. She nearly touches Dalbeer's shadow, unknowingly. Dalbeer, at shake-hand distance, stands motionless.

Suddenly, the full blast of a three-battery torch falls on his face from the first floor balcony. Mr Nag, in a dressing gown, has been roused from sleep by some unearthly sound, although Dalbeer has heard nothing.

'What is it, Dalbeer?' Mr Nag thunders from the balcony. Dalbeer has no answer.

Mr Nag comes down, passes through the garden passage in utter anxiety and halts at the cactus. The naked cactus has started to droop. Mr Nag is shocked beyond measure.

'Tum chor hai, you are a thief!' he points an accusing finger to Dalbeer.

'Nahi, huzoor,' Dalbeer fumbles.

'That old woman, that nasty thief, who is she to you?'

'Kaun budhi, huzoor, which old one?'

'My foot! That one whom you deliberately allowed to steal the flannel cover of my cactus. I saw everything.'

'She is nobody to me, huzoor,' Dalbeer stammers.

'A blatant lie! Don't forget I was a judge; I could detect all crimes. I know —'

'What do you know, huzoor?' Dalbeer, by now, recovers a little.

'She is your mother. I am sure of it.'

Dalbeer, too, was not prepared for such a fantastic castigation. A current passes through his head.

'Yes, huzoor,' Dalbeer's own voice now sounds like a desperate cry, his small eyes glistening with a burning sensation.

'Oh, you thief, don't you see, my cactus is dying?'

'It won't die, huzoor—'

'Shut up, you fool! Go and get the flannel cover at once. Run, you blockhead!' Mr Nag seems like a trigger-happy General.

'Nahi, huzoor!' Dalbeer is astonishingly stubborn.

'You want to kill my cactus?' Mr Nag is now in a murderous mood.

'Nahi, huzoor!' Dalbeer shouts as he takes off his own woollen overall, and then, with the care of a professional dresser, covers the cactus in the design of that 'ghera-tope', makes sure that it is safe, indeed, shrouded in a greater, safer warmth.

'Hum aur nokri nahi karenge - I want to leave the job, huzoor,' — Dalbeer softly pleads.

'But you are a thief, to be sure. I cannot let you go. You deserve a penalty under the law,' the retired judge is adamant.

'You are right, huzoor. Call the police, please.'

Dalbeer feels a delightful sense of freedom in anticipation of his arrest.

Jail signals him freedom, freedom from possible matricide.

translated by Uttam Ghose

The Axe of Parashuram

The collieries in this area appear to be doing thriving business. Markets and slums are springing up all around. Nayabad has a new lease of life with the arrival every day of more and more coolies, mechanics, clerks and shopkeepers. It is more than a marketplace now. Because it is too big for one police station, one sub-divisional officer has come here and opened his court. Since then Nayabad has been a sub-divisional town.

The first batch of the educated people who came to Nayabad consisted of a few lawyers, two doctors, and one overseer. One Bengali primary school was soon set up followed by a Municipality.

Long before this a beautiful church of the Catholic Mission had sprung up on the reddish ground. There were also the new buildings of a Christian convent for the native girls, an orphanage and a hospital for women, all coming into view between casuarina trees and looking as still as a picture.

Then came the winds of change blowing without a pause round Nayabad and pulling it swiftly like a night train along the road to its fated destination. But the one person who has been totally transformed in every respect is Dhania.

Dhania lives in a mud hut with a roof of khapra under an amra tree just behind the temple of Durga a little way from the Bengali colony. There is a goat tied up day and night on the ground in front of the hut. The boys of the Bengali school call it 'goat's lodge'.

Dhania is known as the mother of Tilak, and nobody has ever seen him. Nobody even knows the father of Tilak. But Tilak's brothers and sisters are born at regular intervals of two or three years. Each one appears like a blood-filled atom of joy and then is lost in the crowd. They are never seen again.

Dhania also disappears for a month or two. During this period she will be seen lying on a free bed in the Mission's Hospital for women with a small pale lump of flesh snuggled against her bosom. It is like a bird drawing its sustenance from the bodily warmth of its mother. As the bare scraggy body of the baby fills out, the folds and lines of its skin disappear slowly. The baby blinks and kicks and at the slightest touch moves its lips as if suckling.

But this little drama cannot go on. The fledgling one day flies and Dhania comes back to the 'goat's lodge'. Tilak's brother is also bundled off to the orphanage run by the Mission.

Dhania is such a queer character that even the nurses at the hospital feel confused. The lady doctor remarks in puzzlement: 'I feel really nervous. This woman is a challenge to the Bible and science. I know that the young ones of a bird fly as they grow up. But it is the first time that I have seen a bird flying away leaving its young ones.'

Dhania lives just on the outskirts of the residential area for the educated middle class. She has no relations, no society. It is like this till sun-down. After that she is of course in a different world.

From the road one can see a strange game going on every night under the amra trees - a game of whispers, no other sounds; muffled humming in place of songs, subdued laughter, faint light. Everything is so blurred here, nobody comes in or goes out. Nobody knows the shadowy figures except the police going on their rounds. But none of them makes any fuss about is. For each time Dhania's door opens, the police have a chance to earn more.

Dhania have always lived like this. But now the gentlefolk have started talking about her. It is because many of them just cannot forget her.

The boys returning home from Bengali School cannot help thinking of Dhania and her 'goat's lodge' under the amra tree. Their waking hours would be wasted if they cannot bring down some ripe amras by throwing brickbats and chew them on the way to the accompaniment of Dhania's loud cursing.

In the evening the lawyers and the doctors talk about Dhania in their clubs. They quip: 'Look, the woman lives alone, yet she seems to have no problem. A bit unnatural, isn't it?'

About ten at night, before joining their posts, the patrolling constables put a pinch of tobacco leaf into their mouths, and their faces brighten up. The boredom of patrolling throughout the night is relieved by a few minutes stay in the pleasant darkness under the amra trees. The faint lamplight coming through the half-opened door of Dhania's hut looks like an assurance of reward and fulfilment. The policemen never look up at the moonlit sky with such wistfulness.

But that is not all. Dhania's personality had cast its shadow far and wide - even on the sacred interior of the houses of Bengali baboos.

What is now going to happen is to meet a long felt need. Mothers of new-born babies just cannot do without Dhania's services, or else they would just forfeit their credentials as mothers.

It is common knowledge that mothers of small babies in middle class homes are habitually ill. Some suffer from post-delivery complications, some are about to sink with anaemia, and breast milk dries up in the case of others.

The lady doctor at the Mission Hospital who visits the ailing mothers in return for her impressive fees, observes, ' The mothers can be treated medically, but the babies need nourishment of a different kind.'

'What should we do, then?'

'You need a well-built, healthy-looking ayah to breastfeed the babies.'

At this the cheerfulness of the gentlefolk gives way to fear and anxiety. At last sheer necessity compels them to summon Dhania. The woman at the mud hut under the amra tree is now warmly received in the ladies' quarters of the houses of Baboos.

Dhania visits so many houses to breastfeed the babies on a part-time basis at the rate of six rupees per month for two shifts, one sidhe of rice weighing one pou and a saree at the end of the assignment.

Dhania goes out for work quite early every morning and evening. She is all smiles, holding a neatly folded clean towel, wearing her hair in a braid glistening with sweet-smelling lemon oil, and a light well-laundered saree over a red saya. As she walks, the silver rings on her toes make a sound like that of frying popcorn. She also wears a gold nosering that matches her smiling lips. Her cleanliness is more prominent than her make-up. She looks beautiful, but at first sight what strikes one is her smartness.

Dhania has got a part-time assignment to feed a three-month-old baby in the house of Mr Ghosal. As she comes in the maid leaves the place with a sneer. Mrs Ghosal is sitting on a cane stool looking terribly emaciated. The new-born baby is lying in the cradle in front of her. The maid delivers the news - 'Here comes her highness. What airs she has. I find it all so sickening.'

Mrs Ghosal asks the recalcitrant maid to take it easy. 'Don't be rude. I'm in trouble, you know, so I need her help. Why should we care where she comes from?'

Dhania meanwhile lifts the baby from the cradle and sits down, taking him on her lap. She tries to start a conversation with the mistress of the house, asking questions like 'How are you today?' but cannot go on for lack of response. After work she waits for a while and then goes away with her sidhe, a bundle of gifts.

In the afternoon women gather for a chat in the house of Narenbabu. Dhania goes there to breastfeed a grown-up child. The scrawny three-year-old boy cannot digest cow's milk. He goes around throwing tantrums. He keeps crying, tossing about on the floor, until he goes to bed, and he does not respond to kind words.

Dhania claps her hands standing on the verandah, 'Come on, my darling!'

The boy instantly stops crying and looks up at her like a charmed snake raising its hood. Then he comes running and throws himself into Dhania's lap. He plays with Dhania's bangles for some time and quietly snuggles in her arms.

After some time Dhania asks 'Where do I put him? Look, the boy has fallen asleep.' Suddenly a flutter is caused by some jokes among the women. Everybody teases Narenbabu's wife, 'Why don't you answer now? Don't you hear what the child's new mother is saying?'

Narenbabu's wife feels ashamed, and retorts in irritation, 'No, I can't talk to that woman. Puti, go and bring the child.'

At last Puti, the daughter of the Overseer - a stupid-looking eight-year-old girl - comes forward for the job.

Dhania waits for her remuneration. Everybody watches her from behind. Her feet look so clean, though she has come a long way on foot.

Someone blurts out, 'That shameless hussy has such well-shaped hands. The armlet has sunk into her flesh, look.'

As Dhania disappears by the back door, the curious eyes behind her get back their natural expression. The wife of the school teacher says with a shiver in a nasal tone of voice, 'I'm not going to wear a red saya from now on.'

In the afternoon Dhania smokes tobacco sitting on a cane stool outside her hut, talking affectionately to the goat grazing around and drawing appropriate responses.

But now there has been sign of Dhania for a few days. The door of her room is shut. Her goat is tied beside a drain in front of another hut in which lives old Prasadi Dom.

Eighty-year-old Prasadi was once jailed for an act of robbery and subsequently five times for theft. He spent forty-two years in jail. So he became a stranger to the normal way of life. And then one day he was crippled in an accident. A tree uprooted by a gale fell on him and he broke his hip bone. He has been unable to stand up since then.

Besides he is afflicted with the debilities of old age. Hunger is writ large on him. He and the goat are the two dependants Dhania looks after. After cooking the meal, Dhania takes a plate of rice to Prasadi, whose death is postponed due to this. This is the reason why one can see Dhania's goat tied in front of Prasadi's hut.

Meanwhile in the well-lit hospital for women, the nurses gather round Dhania's bed, requesting her to keep at least this new-born baby.

'No, I can't.'

The lady doctor replies. 'Everybody knows what you are. You can't hide it. Then why don't you keep your own baby?'

'No, lady doctor. I'm too poor to look after my child. He'll suffer so much and then will turn out to be a fiend. You see, I've no money to send him to school.'

'Stop talking nonense. Even the beggar women don't abandon their children. Are they richer than you?'

'Sister, they don't have to send their children to school. They bring them up as beggars. I can't do that.'

'All right, we'll raise funds for your child. Now take your child and go.'

'Well, in that case, one of you can easily take charge of the child and I'll work as an ayah for him.'

The lady doctor and the nurses do not feel like discussing the matter any longer. They shudder to look her in the eye, for in spite of their job to serve people for money they find Dhania's cold indifference so odd, even cruel.

'Take my adaab, I'm off now.' Dhania stands up. One nurse wraps the baby in flannel and takes him in her arms. He will be sent to the nursery. But Dhania does not take any notice of him. Wrapping her kansa plate and ghati with a towel and holding a hurricane lamp, she gets up.

Another nurse comes up with a register. The lady doctor asks, 'What's the name of the baby's father?'

'I don't know.'

The lady doctor is annoyed.

'You always give me the same answer. Why don't you tell us the name of the man you're living with?'

'I live with so many fellows, and I don't know the names of most of them. Forgive me, lady doctor, write any name you like.'

'You're in for trouble, let me warn you.' The lady doctor leaves the place in anger.

A mail train is heard leaving the Nayabad station with a shriek, picking up speed. The hospital building shakes under its impact. Wrapped in a red rug, Dhania walks down the stairs. The nurses keep staring at her and their eyes become misty with an unaccountable pity.

As she passes the gate the gatekeeper strikes the bell. It is nine p.m.

Years roll on. Yet Dhania's life under the amra trees does not lose its familiar tenor. The last time she was in hospital was only three years ago.

Nayabad Municipality has ensconced itself with great confidence. The new township has been extended in a planned manner. The car bought by the lawyer has the number '741'.

Thus years pass. Dhania is almost in her forties. Occasionally she is seen selling fried snacks, lighting an earthen oven by the road. The porters buy some of the snacks on their way back home. Dhania also makes one or two baskets of cowdung fuelcakes which are sold out. Her looks have lost their glamour as she is hard up for money. Rarely does she have a visitor at her residence. But Dhania is still proud of her health, her physical charms, so she is not afraid. She is sure she will not end up as a beggar.

Dhania has long ceased to be welcome to genteel society. The mothers are now in a better state of health, so they need not think of engaging anyone to breastfeed their babies. Besides there are now quite a number of rivals from the western countries - a variety of baby foods. Dhania is no longer called upon to preserve the life of a sickly new-born baby. Perhaps she is forgotten by everybody.

Schools and colleges at Patna are closed due to the Christmas holidays. The boys are back home. It is the season for hunting, picnics, carnivals and exhibitions. Nayabad is bustling with a new life. One day Dhania's oven remains unlit, for she is without money. The whole story of her eventful past unfolds before her as she thinks of the present.

She gets up to visit her old employers. She had a right to ask for tips from them. Maybe they would be glad to give a little charity, and some money would come into her hands.

But Dhania has now no access to the ladies quarters in Narenbabu's house. Mr Ghosal gives her four annas. Dhania finds that the whole place is full of boys and girls. The boys are rather tall. Dhania then visits a more liberal family. The mistress of the house gives her some 'sidhe' saying, 'Now clear off, please.'

At the gate of Dhirenbabu's residence Dhania waits for about an hour and then the maid appears to give her one rupee, 'Take this, Madam has given this, and now go, please.'

Dhania asks, 'Maid, where is the eldest boy in the family?' The maid flings a suspicious look at her and says, 'Look there, he is busy playing cards. But what business have you to ask?'

'My God, he is such a big lad now. He could not keep off my breast milk even when he cut his teeth. Do you remember how he bit me?'

'Don't make a show of your affection. Now go and don't come again.'

There were so many families like this. Dhania can easily approach them. But she has second thoughts. This is not asking far a 'parabi' or tips; this is like begging.

It is not evening. Yet, Dhania trots off in the direction of her hut. But her visits have their expected repercussions. Women's voices were raised against her, 'She is like an evil spirit that pops up all of a sudden. You can't tell when she will ruin our bachelor sons.'

The menfolk cannot ignore such complaints. Everybody thinks that such creatures of the immoral world should by no means be allowed to live near civilized and educated people. Their presence would always attract anti-socials.

The matter came up for discussion at the club in the evening and the proposal found general approval. Such immoral practices should not be allowed near Durga bari.

Dhania puts down her hookah as she hears the sound of the band. It sounds like the boys of the Mission Orphanage going in procession on a picnic. They are dressed in blue blazers, short pants, white flannel shirts, red socks and shoes, aged between five and sixteen, a whole platoon of healthy-looking boys. The ones playing the band at the head of the procession have a different uniform - white caps with white feathers and a green casuarina leaf pinned on them. The bagpipes, held on their breasts by small drum straps, touch their soft lips.

The soft light of the morning sun on Christmas Day has just broken through the mist and fallen on the roads and fields. The procession stops at a crossing of the roads. Bagpipes and drums blare three times and then stop. Little boys and girls, even old people, stream in and stand round them.

One white padre in white coat and pantaloon recites a psalm of David in Hindi - Amen! Voices of the boys - sounds of the wind in the forests - sounds of the waterfalls like the warbling notes of birds in the morning ... With a start Dhania walks up to the procession and leans against a tree.

The padres with long beards look so unkempt. Another padre with a cross glittering on his breast gives a sermon - 'Nineteen forty years ago this day the red sun appeared on the horizon in Bethlehem. The son of God was born to the daughter of a carpenter.'

It is so difficult to make head or tail of the sermon. Dhania moves aside so that she can see the faces of the boys more clearly.

'One day the son of God was seen going to Jerusalem wearing a crown of thorns to sacrifice his life for our salvation... .'

Dhania's eyes are meanwhile touching each face in the procession like an invisible kiss. She has contributed at least six of them to the procession. But there is no way to identify them. That ten-year-old boy beating the drum and wiping the sweat off his face with his shirt sleeve - maybe he is one of them. Or the next one. But who is not? They all seem her own contributions.

Dhania is standing wrapped in thought. The crowd has cleared off, the mist over the distant forest has disappeared, the procession is now passing through the fields, kicking up a cloud of dust. All earthly objects wear a pleasant look. Dhania stands erect and then wearily goes back home. A strange mixture of fatigue and pleasure pervades her body like the feeling after orgasm. She tightly covers her breasts with her sari and finds that her bodice is wet.

At the meeting of the Municipal Commissioners a note is prepared and sent to the police to see that the women engaged in secret immoral business be segregated and shifted to the market line. This is an irrevocable order. The police are entrusted with the task of making a list of such women and finding a place for them in the market area.

Dhania's hut under the amra tree is not spared - 'This can't go on any longer. You must quit or go ahead, or you must be a respectable person.' She spares no pains to stop her eviction. She is ready to sell her utensils to give the watchmen the money they want to buy their quota of betel. But the constables do not cooperate with her. 'Look, who is not afraid if losing his job? You must get your name registered.' The head constable snaps, 'None of your clever tricks this time. Give your thumb impression here.'

It is night now. Prasadi is sitting before the fire with his face between his knees. The fire in the dhuni has almost died down. Close by, the dog keeps barking. But Prasadi cannot hear anything. One of his toes was burned by a flying spark, but he does not feel any pain. He has been feeling shivery since the morning, but now even this feeling is gone. Dhania has been absent for a couple of days, so he has had nothing to eat.

'Uncle Prasadi!' Dhania breaks into sobs. Prasadi does not respond. She shakes him and holds up his chin. As the old man opens his eyes, she cries out 'Uncle Prasadi'.

Dhania's sobs have an electrifying effect on him, and his whole body trembles.

'You, Dhania?'

'Yes, I don't belong anywhere. They call me prostitute.'

'Don't talk nonsense.'

'Yes, uncle. They've got my name registered. From tomorrow I'll live in the market area.'

'Oh, never. You're like the goddess Lachmi to me.'

'No, I've no husband.'

'Cows have no husbands, aren't they Lachmi to us?'

'Don't say that. I am no cow.'

Dhania suddenly springs to her feet, 'Now I'm going. I don't think we'll meet again.'

Like a pampered child Prasadi casts hungry eyes all around. Where is that plate of rice wrapped in a gamcha that Dhania brings every day - the only source of his sustenance? Prasadi seems to utter something, but no word passes through his lips. A silent grief makes him sit as usual with his head between his knees. Once again he seems to hear the groaning sound of the sea he heard on his way to jail.

Dhania uncovers her head, drawing aside her saree, does her hair into a tight top knot, wipes her oily face with the end of the saree, and then her familiar smile spreads over her face. 'You're cross, aren't you, uncle?'

She slowly walks up to him, and takes the shrivelled body of the old man in her arms as if she were lifting a kitten. Taking off her bodice, she presses his head to her breast and runs her fingers through the old man's knotted grey hair. After an hour or so Prasadi falls asleep with a great feeling of contentment, his jaws tired and wet. Dhania lays him down near the dhuri.

The wide road in the south of Chakbazar has on both sides rows of two-storeyed buildings. Right in the midway there are two shops facing each other, one selling foreign liquor and the other country liquor. There are all sorts of shops on the ground floor selling paan-bidi, sherbat, attar, chaat and chameli oil. There is a shop that repairs old tablas and pakhawajes. Under a wayside tree on a concrete dais, eunuchs dance, clapping their hands. The windows on the first floors of the houses are all lit brightly like the screen at a cinema. This is where the women carry on their trade.

This new year one window on the first floor of a building is open. Dhania thinks of her life purified by fire for forty years with the base metal burnt out, and then puts on her make-up and dress. She lights the chandelier and makes a top-knot of her hair and covers it with a golden chumki-studded handkerchief. She wears a necklace of cultured pearls, a blue transparent silk saree without any undergarment. She sprinkles talcum powder all over her body and reddens her lips by chewing a roll of paan with strong jarda in it. She drinks at a gulp a mug of country liquor to warm her up and tightens her green velvet bodice. At last she stands still, resting her elbows on the window.

The winter wind at night is heavy with smoke and the smell of fried wafers coming from the sweet shop. Down below on the road there is a small crowd near the gaslight, staring at the window.

Though it is night, though Dhania is tipsy, though the gaslight has an uncanny pale lustre, she can recognise the boys. The lanky eldest son of the Ghosals is taking quick puffs at his cigarette. The son of Khajanchibabu casts furtive glances and makes some signals, waving a handkerchief. A drunkard also comes along with unsteady steps. Placing his two hands like binoculars over his eyes, the drunk looks through them for some time.

Dhania swallows the betel juice. Her ears have a burning sensation. She lets the end of her saree glide off her breast. Raising her hands and gripping the grille above she presses her breasts on the wooden plank of the window.

The crowd is dazzled at the sight of a colourful will-o'-the-wisp burning bright. The shadowy tempting outlines of two knees become quite visible through the transparent silk sari. It looks as if two planets were in perpetual bondage inside her bodice.

Dhania is now restless with - a burning estatic sensation. Yet she waits as calmly as possible. She will wait till dead of night, till the small hours - until the first visitor in her new life knocks at her door calling her by her new name.

translated by Dipendu Chakrabarti

The Harlot

The steps stopped at their door. Along with voices, happy and loud. And then came the knock. A man called out, 'Anybody at home?' Prasad leapt to his feet as if stung by a snake. The room was in a mess and his brain revolted. Scared and shocked, he whispered, 'Lata, this is exactly what I feared. Please, hurry up, get up for heaven's sake.'

Lata showed no signs of budging and clung to the pillow, a cigarette dangling from her mouth as usual. The bedside table was laid with all that made their evenings every day. A bottle and an opener. A silk saree was loosely draped around Lata's waist. She was ready for the evening.

Prasad pleaded again, 'This is not fair, Lata. Please clear the mess and save me from embarrassment. Think of your own honour, too. What's the harm in maintaining decorum? Just a matter of moments. Please don't make them wait any longer.'

Lata stood up. Prasad hurriedly put the beer bottle in the cupboard, hid two pictures under the bed and scanned the room for other proof of vulgarity. His eyes fell on the curtain, proudly displaying two nude damsels. He tore it from the string and despatched it under the bed again.

As he pleaded to Lata again, she retorted in disgust, 'This is too much for me. Why the hell should I keep playacting in front of guests? As it is I have to practise decency with even your servants. There's no great charm in being your mistress; you know that? To hell with your drama! The theatres will pay me so much more.'

Lata kept abusing Prasad and stood her ground. Prasad lost his voice. His appeals lost their voice too. Lata guessed his plight and with a bitter laugh said, 'Is that the way to keep a woman? It calls for some more courage, my child.'

Prasad relaxed a bit as she picked up a saree and went into the bathroom. He opened the gate and let in the guests. A big group - some young and some old, some ladies and some noisy kids.

At once the veil of gloom was dispelled. Dispelled by chirpy girls, bubbly boys, the familiar smell of perfume, essence and cheroot, the knock of walking sticks. Sounds and smells that this couple had banished from the house all these months. Once again the room started interacting with the large world outside. Prasad greeted them with a warm smile. He liked their manners as well. The initial hesitation of introduction evaporated in no time. Rakhalbabu piled up his woollens on the bed, chairs were brought in from every corner of the room and the ladies were informal enough to spread the carpet for themselves. Rakhalbabu spoke first, 'Ranajit, tell him why we are displeased with him.' A young man turned to Prasad, 'Really, you have to listen to our grievances. We are strangers like you in this alien place. We crave for the company of Bengalis and you seem to be avoiding us. Truly, we are deeply offended.'

Prasad nodded in apology. Abha, Ranajit's sister, quipped, 'Boys are so unthinking. You have found a friend. Now who will talk to us?' Prasad kept smiling, 'She will be here any minute.'

Lata came in a little later, draped in a traditional saree. She did not expect to confront an aged man like Rakhalbabu, but covered her head properly with the saree. Her parting shone red with the bright vermillion mark. So did her feet, decked in alta. Prasad's fears were blown away and at last he could concentrate on the conversation.

Abha requested Lata to sit with them on the carpet. Lata said, 'Let's go inside.'

The boys were having a gala time in the drawing room. The kids played, the elders interfered and the women enjoyed the mess thoroughly. For the first time in the past one-and-a-half months the little bungalow in a corner of Barakar colony throbbed with the simple joys of simple people.

Lata tried to entertain the guests by cooking tidbits for them but the ladies opted for just tea. She hesitated and then complained, 'See what a careless man he is. Doesn't even bother to ask what I will serve tea with.' Her guests laughed, 'Why are you being jealous?' Abha crept into the drawing room and confronted Prasad, 'She is angry with you. You are immediately called inside.' Lata had followed her and stopped Prasad in the shadows of the courtyard, 'I can't serve just tea. Can you go to the market and fetch some sweets?' Abha and the other girls heard her and protested, 'Please don't be formal.' Prasad then suggested. 'Open the biscuit tin.' Lata looked relieved.

The guests took their leave late at night. But before that they made him sing, playing the esraj.

Rakhalbabu put on all his warm coverings. His wife, the elderly lady, whose feet were swollen, adjusted her socks. Tarakbabu lit a new cheroot and got up with the help of a stick.

He had come with his daughter, Abha, three nieces and a sister-in-law. The kids were related to either Rakhalbabu or Harishbabu who, along with his wife, was down with gout.

Another exchange of small talk delayed their departure. Prasad saw them off with a lantern in his hand. Lata stood on the steps, hidden behind the shadows.

Prasad heaved a sigh of relief and took out the beer bottle in haste. Lata's energy was drained and she just dropped into bed. But Prasad looked excited. 'What's the matter? Come on, don't be a wetblanket,' Lata did not move, which made him more impatient. He pulled her by the hand. Lata sat up and grumbled in disgust, 'You fool, behave yourself, I tell you.' Prasad moved away, coaxing her, 'Go and get rid of the make-up. Let's open a bottle and have some fun.' Lata did not hide her apathy. 'What's the big hurry for? Is time running away?' Still, she went to the other room and did away with her carefully made-up disguise. She became her true self once again, and got into pyjamas and slippers. The unexpected evening was dropped behind like a crumpled saree.

Prasad was elated as he saw the familiar Lata. She ignored him completely and picking up a cigarette stood at the window. The darkness, broken only by twinkling dots of light on the bridge over the Barakar, engulfed her. The air was heavy with the stink of rotting flowers. Lata filled her mouth with smoke and then exhaled it slowly.

Something seemed to have struck Prasad. Bottles were rolling away on the floor. He spotted her near the window and muttered, 'So you prefer to be there. Let it be, let it be. Oh, I forgot. Full credit to you, dearie. You just fooled them today. What superb acting! Thank you very much. You saved my honour. I shall make you happy. But, but ... how dare you call me a fool?. You cheap whore, how dare you? I will simply ....'

He turned over the table and stood up, visibly angry. Lata stared at him, calm as before. She asked in her characteristic lazy but firm manner, 'What's all the excitement about?' She opened the cupboard and took out another bottle of beer. Prasad let her fill his glass and gulped the liquid at once. He stretched his hand out for a cigarette.

Prasad's fury did not impress Lata a bit. She knew very well how such macho displays could be done away with - a simple flirting and one or two jingles were enough to tame the man for ever. Prasad warned Lata again, 'Don't you dare cross the limit!' Lata nodded in agreement. Prasad retorted once more, 'Then what's the fuss about? Remember you are just a whore.' She didn't protest. He came out with the final broadside, 'You don't deserve even to serve Abha!'

It seemed something had stung Lata. Flickers from the fire of a horrible truth. Till this moment she had dismissed Prasad's ramblings as those of a drunkard; but his last words appeared to be bathed in truth. She caught hold of the chair Prasad was sitting on, her face drained of its normal colour. But then she retreated. She retired to the adjacent room, announcing that she was moving away, 'You can no longer keep me. I am going back to Tarakeswar tomorrow.'

The night wallowed in stillness for the next few hours. But it was not long before Prasad knocked at her door again. He was cautious lest Lata took her revenge. Such women should always be handled with cunning. Prasad felt that his honour was at stake and it was none of Lata's concern. Her world had no sympathy for Prasad's society which had banished her long ago. It she left tomorrow she might just defile him before that. She would trample on his honour and malign him if her own pride, dark as her character, was hurt.

Frightened and fretful, Prasad knocked again and again. His pleadings reverberated in the dark house. Lata answered after a long while, 'No, I am not leaving. You go off to sleep.'

'Chachiji,' Vikram called out from the balcony. He was the youngest son of the subedar and always armed with a top. Prasad opened his eyes to clear daylight.

The boy kept Lata company early in the morning and ate breakfast with her. The garden was his favourite haunt. Prasad kept to the bed, his head buzzing with bitter memories of the previous night. He could hear Lata dressing, opening the gate and talking to Vikram. The boy complained, 'Why do you sleep so late, Chachiji?' Prasad alerted his mind's eye. The servant was busy in daily chores. He would bring tea presently. And then the time would come to get up, watch Lata supervising the cook and serving lunch, and watch her again leaving for the temple with Mahabir. They were not a family nor a couple. But shackled by norms - by the regular practice of norms and maintaining decorum. Prasad would have loved to erase these lingering, monotonous moments and pull the evening closer, when Lata would be available in her own, familiar self. The wall between them that the day carefully built up could be brought down only in the evening.

Vikram left. And in came Lalababu's wife with her sackful of woe. Her son-in-law was looking for a job and the daughter was not particularly happy. Such stories hurt Lata, hurt her deeply. And Lata's familiarity with such normal people hurt Prasad today. He felt she was exceeding her limit. She was fooling the world with a fake identity, a made-up face - she was deceiving the eyes of this world. His conscience revolted against such blasphemy this morning.

Rakhalbabu sent a servant with a note for Prasad. He invited Lata to lunch at his place.

Something had weighed heavily on Lata's mind since morning. She could not figure out what was sending shivers down her spine. Not that she took bravado in men seriously but Lata felt a sense of weariness numbing her limbs. I don't have the energy, she thought, to face Prasad and abuse the shit out of him. Lata recognized the feeling. She was not afraid of Prasad's offensive; she was simply weak. And that made her wonder....

But then her soul protested. Did she care for this man? He was not the only man craving for her. That Marwari trader was still waiting for her. If at all she left, she would teach Prasad such a lesson that no one would dare insult a whore in future. Hearing Prasad call out for her, Lata shrank. She did not look up when he handed her the invitation note. Lata did not expect it and she was relieved. Yes, she would go. 'You are most welcome to visit them but don't forget what you are,' Prasad warned, sternly.

Their lives seemed to have reached a turning point. Poised on the crossroads, they turned over a new leaf, a strange and complex leaf, one might say. Prasad, too, began socializing, at times even with more zeal than Lata. He spent most of the evenings with Abha and her family. Lata, too, made her rounds of daily visits. Somehow she missed the chance to respond to invitations from Abha - she either fell ill or had other engagements. Prasad congratulated her; he was pleased with Lata's performance. She did not answer. Prasad spoke again, 'But remember, do not play the game too long.' 'But that will enhance your honour,' Lata said. Prasad hid his concern behind a smile, 'Really, what a game to begin! I dread the consequences at times.' Lata said, 'I will hardly lose anything. I will find my way out.' 'That's true, you have nothing to lose ... ' Prasad mumbled as he walked away.

Abha had visited them on one or two occasions. Though the warmth of the first meeting was lost. Lost, too, was the simple sharing of joys. Those were replaced by distant, stiff and formal conversation. Abha let the tea offered by Lata go cold and Lata did not feel like pressing her. Distance had also crept into Prasad and Lata's relationship. They had even stopped talking to each other. they no longer went out together nor were their nights spent in the frenzy of the old times.

Their neighbours often discussed Lata in their gossip sessions. Mashima felt she was a rather decent girl. The young daughters of Tarakbabu fully agreed with her and not with Abha who apparently disliked Lata as she was not up to the mark. Mashima retorted, 'What does Abha think of herself? How can she boast of her education? A widow - she should be ashamed of herself.' Nibha and Prabha enjoyed the outburst. Herself not of urban culture, Mashima was naturally not happy with Abha.

Lata was chatting with Lalaji's wife. And in the drawing room Prasad and Abha were talking to each other. Indifferent to what others felt, Prasad did not bridle his emotions. Abha was embarrassed and protested. Then they would go out together. Lalaji's wife was startled and asked Lata who the girl was. She strongly disapproved of such free mixing. Lata kept her cool. 'No one can take away my husband if my stand is clear. You need not be afraid.' But her companion was not reassured.

As the words echoed in her heart, Lata could hear a shrill, mocking laughter. She smiled at her protestations and her conviction.

That day the couple was invited to Tarakbabu's house. Prabha's husband had come to take her away. Lata had a good time with the boy and the other girls. While they were leaving Prasad noticed Prabha's husband touched Lata's feet. He felt the line should be drawn - here and now. On their way back Prasad came out with his agony. Lata kept quiet. Prasad said again, 'Your reputation is not at stake. Mine is. Your sin will ruin my reputation.' Lata would have loved to agree to what Prasad said. If her sins wrecked the citadel of Prasad's honour she would have rejoiced in peace. But was so much peace meant for her? And that itch of conscience denied her even morsels of peace. Was deception a sin? If it was she was a sinner. She wondered what she was making the sacrifice for? Was it to save Prasad's honour?

Lata heard the mocking laughter once again. Poor man, a victim of honour. Prasad resumed the dispute as they returned home. His tone was as incoherent as his words. He hovered around the truth. 'You need not pretend to be so chaste even behind closed doors. What are you trying to prove?'

'You do not need me any more.'

'How does that affect you? I will call you whenever I feel like it. But why have you stopped smoking? There's no need to practise purity at home.'

'I shall keep that in mind. I shall decide the course of my life.' Prasad had to swallow the insult. He felt he was groping in a blind alley. Only Lata knew the way out - and she would not care for a safe exit.

Lata behaved as if she was desperate. Abha's efforts amused her. Silly girl, how eager she was to steal a bad penny. Lata was composed, fearless. She had nothing to lose - not even her newfound reputation. With that she would sail away and defeat Prasad hands down. She would not mind if the days could be spent in this make-believe world. In fact, she enjoyed it. A strange world of half-truths - Lata could see herself mastering the art of surviving in it.

Abha was not keeping well these days. Prasad was at her bedside throughout the day. She developed hysteria with high fever. Ranajit was worried about this sudden symptom.

When both of them were back home Prasad, looking haunted by a despair he could not identify, spoke to Lata after so many days.

'How dare you malign Abha? Who gave you the courage?'

'I never talked about her - to anyone.'

'Even that's as bad as maligning her.'

Prasad sounded stern and convinced. Lata asked, 'What am I supposed to do?'

'I no longer need your help. But too much playacting is no good. I am grateful to you - you have played your part well. Let's draw the line now. Let's do away with it.'

Prasad had much more to say. 'If someone recognizes you, I won't have an inch in the world to hide my face. How long will you keep the keys to my name and honour? How long will you threaten me with your generosity?'

Lata stared at the tablelamp. She did not feel like answering back. Prasad concluded, 'You should go away.' Lata waited - stiff as a stone. 'I shall make full payment. I am ready even to pay an extra amount.' Lata at last found her voice. 'How shall I fend for myself after that?' Prasad lost his temper. 'Don't you remember how you harassed me the first day we came here. You even threatened to leave. I had to coax you so much, you bloody ....'

He was speaking the truth. Lata had nothing to object to. He was just stating the facts. And she had to face them.

Prasad cooled down in minutes. 'I no longer need you, really. I have lost the taste. Or the appetite. You can no longer serve my purpose.' He pleaded, 'Believe me, it's suffocating. Why don't you understand my predicament?'

'Do you really want me to leave?'

'Yes, but who will escort you?'

Lata stood up and screamed, 'I can take care of myself. You need not bother about me. I shall go away tomorrow morning.'

The night spread its stillness over Lata. She decided not to waste it by sleeping it off. As she lay on the verandah, Lata watched the pickles gather dew unattended. She smiled at herself. She sensed Prasad's trauma. His reputation was at stake. If anyone saw through the deception, if they knew she was Panchibibi from Tarakeswar and not a chaste housewife, his honour would be lost for ever. She herself could tear the veil apart.

On second thoughts, she rejected the idea. She preferred not to do away with the glory that Prasad's society had showered upon her of late. She could not shock Rakhalbabu nor Mashima. Let them live in peace. She could visualize Abha managing Prasad's home with all her domestic expertise. Lata would be nowhere around. No one would remember her.

What was Prasad doing? Lata gnashed her teeth in frustration. Would she test his 'honourable' mask once again? How would he resist her if she started flirting with him, right now?

But she could not muster enough strength to face that awful man again. From the core of her heart she abhorred the false, fake and futile nature of Prasad's 'honour'. Liquor could have done away with the bitterness but she was too alienated from drink these days.

The ground was slipping away from beneath her feet. Feeling feeble and worn out, she dried her eyes.

Darkness crept into her soul and revived her anger. The snake of vengeance started spitting forth its venom. Why shouldn't she, Panchibibi, also spit on Prasad's face? The face of civility? He wouldn't even dare raise his voice. The whore in her rejoiced in the humiliation that Prasad would be subject to the next morning.

Something struck Prasad. He could not be sure of Lata. If she would arise from oblivion ... Prasad came to Lata with a bundle of notes in his hand. The lamp in his hand dispelled the darkness from the narrow passage.

'I hope you are no longer annoyed with me. I have never harmed you, or cheated you, Lata.'

She took the notes. Prasad asked again, ' Why don't you say something?'

Lata covered her head with the saree, as if to avoid the blinding light. She said, 'No, it's not you, you haven't harmed me. Abha did this to me.'

translated by Swati Ghosh

The Fourth Battle of Panipat

Our class resembled an anthropological laboratory. Rarely were such odd samples of ethnic variety seen together. We had three princes with us. The first was a tribal lord's son, standing out with his pitch-dark complexion. The other two had genuine Kshatriya blood, were fair and wore pearl-set head-gear. We had others too — Cyril Tigga, Emanuel Khalkho, John Besra, Richard Tudu, Stephan Horo and a host of other faces. Yet the pride of placc or, so to speak, the centre stage was occupied by a handful of Bengali and Bihari boys who were much superior to the rest in intelligence and merit. We nicknamed the princes 'toads' and the Munda and Oraon boys 'tadpoles'. We never tried to make friends with them. The princes, too, ignored us. But not the tribal students; they craved for our attention. Tudu regularly came to be at my service at tiffin-break. I used to send him to Ganga Sahu's shop for some nuts. He was always eager to oblige.

Sahu's shop was quite far from school. Neither the distance nor the burning midday sun meant anything for Tudu. He would sprint like a free deer across the scorching fields. After handing over the packet to us he used to walk away. We admired his speed and tenacity. Tudu did not even tire and we appreciated it.

And he always took such compliments seriously. Flattered, he used to smile and keep quiet. We knew he was holding on to his breath desperately. We often forgot to share the nuts with Tudu. Even if we offered him some, he felt shy and refused.

Stephan Horo used to watch us intently. That strange gaze unnerved us. It was like a piercing arrow aimed straight at our hearts. But why Stephan? What was so special about him?

The other tribal boys were not of much importance in their temerity. We admitted that he stood out in the crowd, he was different. There were some efforts on our part to befriend him, which he dared to ignore. We wondered what made him so insolent!

Stephan somewhat impressed us that day. We were playing hockey, each armed with his own stick. Stephan insisted on playing though he did not have a stick. He kept asking for one for only a few moments but no one was willing to oblige. Horo said he would play without a stick and for one long hour he used his legs so well that our sticks looked weak and wan in comparison. Those tough legs could even break the sticks with brute force.

Stephan became a constant source of tension. Instead of admiring him, we started envying him. Even in studies he often made us look silly. He scored much more than Indu in a recitation and discussion of English poetry. This was too demeaning for us. It must have insulted the Bihari students too as they joined our slander campaign against Horo. Our charge was that non-Christian students were facing gross injustice in the school where all the teachers were Christian. They were being most partial towards Horo, who was a Christian.

The only sympathizer with our cause was our Sanskrit teacher, Pandit Baijnath Sharma. He comforted us; 'Such injustice is only too common in missionary schools. Wait till you get to the university. There merit will be the only factor.'

As we were promoted to the new class Stephan attempted another daring task — more incredible than playing hockey without a stick. He opted for Sanskrit additional instead of English. Our teachers were displeased. So was our headmaster, Father Lindon. Panditji was thoroughly amused. but Stephan did not flinch. Panditji told us: 'Now Horo will read Sanskrit. I feel sorry for the poor language.' We wondered why he looked so happy. But soon events took a strange turn.

Stephan stood first in reciting David's gospels from the New Testament. Our performance looked so mediocre that day. Father Lindon was all praise for him and pledged to make him a police officer once he was a Matriculate. Father was not boasting. He had contacts in high places. But we were not after such trivial ambitions. Why should we learn the New Testament by heart?

Stephan's behaviour at the bible class the next day came as a rude shock for us. He was sitting on the back bench but from there too, he drew the attention of Father Lindon. The father kept asking him all the questions. Stephan replied rather rudely, 'I don't know the answers, Sir.' He avoided the Father's shocked gaze and looked straight at his desk. Our teacher blushed in distress and disgust. 'What's wrong with you, Stephan? Why can't you answer a single question today?' We stiffened as Stephan said as harshly as before, 'I don't know, sir.' The Father was visibly upset and left the classroom in a huff. What was playing in Stephan's mind? Why was he so insolent? Did he feel he was very important?

The next blow was meant for Panditji. He had not been behaving normally for a few days. But this was the time to consult him on marks and totals, ranks and promotions. We expected him to be generous enough to help us score a lot in Sanskrit. If only Indu could get 85% in it! He had to come first and make fools of these Christians!

We had cornered Panditji in the library, at his place and even caught him on the way but he simply confused us with ambiguous answers. At last he came out with the truth. Stephan had bagged the highest position in Sanskrit. Indu scored a mere 32.

What treachery! Panditji tried to plead with us, 'Please appreciate the fact that Horo has mastered a language he had never read. And be happy that Sanskrit has charmed another alien. Call it the victory of the language.'

But we were not to be consoled so easily. He failed to feel our pulse, how our honour was hurt. Was it because he was a Bihari?

Someone up there must have heard our pleas and acted accordingly. When the results came out our faith in the power of truth was reestablished. Indu's name topped the list. Stephan was somewhere down below, scoring badly in all subjects except Sanskrit. We wondered what made him so unpleasant with the Christian teachers.

As days passed Stephan distanced himself more and more from everyone. Even from his tribal friends.

That Christmas we went for a picnic in the forests of Shilwara. As we were cutting dry branches for fuel we spotted Horo, loitering near the river, all alone. He had a catapult in his hand. He was the most unexpected guest but we were most eager to share the fun with him. He could even join the feast; the menu was long and delicious.

Horo approached us but his attention was elsewhere. He stared at a branch of the sal tree and aimed. In no time a squirrel fell, bruised. Stephan picked it up and put it in his pocket. Amazed, we asked, 'What will you do with it?' 'I shall eat it,' he shot back, his white teeth mocking our distaste. Still we invited him to join us. 'No,' he said, smiling sarcastically once more.

But what prompted this barbarous inclination in him? Tudu confirmed our fear. 'Horo is going off his head. Father Lindon has warned us not to go around with him.' Tudu had more to say. 'Stephan has made friends with an old Sotha tribesman. He meets him at the weekly market.' We could not gauge the gravity of the offence. Tudu was agitated, 'Horo has no right to make such weird friends. It is an insult to the Bible. He even shuns the church. Left the hostel for three days. He will be rusticated.'

'But where could he be?' Tudu whispered in our ears, 'He joined a feast in Buru, took draughts of country liquor. And ...' Tudu paused and divulged a great secret, 'Stephan has an affair with a girl, Chirki, from the Murmu tribe of the Morangi hills.'

We were awestruck, overwhelmed by the Munda's daring. At once in our eyes he transcended such trifles as Bible class, hockey matches or Sanskrit tests. We began to understand what alienated him from the humdrum that was all around. We could even visualize the lass from the hills — Chirki Murmu, her tresses flowing, peals of laughter shaking her all over and she imprisoning the wild spirit of Stephan in her jungle wilderness haunts! Horo would never come back, the world could never offer him so much.

Tudu kept complaining, 'Murmus worship heathen gods. He should never trust them.'

Stephan, however, stayed on at school. Often he attended classes, often he skipped them. Confined to a solitary room, he kept to himself. Sometimes he played tennis with Father Lindon. This was a rare honour even for a Christian boy. Others were only allowed to attend as ball boys. Father never deigned to play with a student. Stephan used to fetch water for the garden in the evening. Thus he earned free lodging and food at the hostel. Gradually he stopped doing that.

Tigga was asked to do the work. Poor boy, he also had to bring wood for the kitchen in the morning.

Tudu came up with more news. Stephan was not allowed to visit the weekly market. Instead, he had to read *Pilgrim's Progress* with Father Lindon in the afternoon. He was also treated with tea and snacks by the headmaster.

We were anxious, curious. We could faintly sense the turn of events but dared not reach a conclusion. Father Lindon, a member of the elite from Cambridge, was involved in a strange duel with an uncivilised, wretched elder of the Sothas. Theirs was the duel of eternity, betweeen barbarism and civilisation. The Sotha possibly wanted to avenge the injustice and brutality of ages. He would fight for their youth, forcibly converted by alien intruders.

Father would not let Horo go and so he was fencing off the boy's world. He would not allow Horo to hobnob with the Sotha at the market. His weapons were those that the urban ambience could offer - tea, tennis, biscuits....

We termed the duel the fourth battle of Panipat. We were waiting for its outcome. All were to go home on Good Friday. Tigga, Besra, Tudu, Khalkho — they left one by one with their sacks on wooden poles. They would traverse miles of forest paths on foot, as they could not pay for transport. but Father made quite a fuss as Horo was leaving. He was made to board the service bus and the missionary paid for the ticket.

We laid a bet on whether Horo would return. Indu was certain he would. Father had brainwashed him rather well with tennis and biscuits. But could such paltry bribes make him desert Chirki? Indu had no answer to that.

As school reopened we waited for Stephan to come back. He did, and we were disgusted with him. Who had asked him to return? But then Tudu's stories revived us. He churned out stories of Horo, Sothas ... and Chirki. He painted pictures of remote jungles where scarlet flowers blossomed as symbols of someone's love.

Tudu was Horo's neighbour in the village. The Christians there were generally shunned as heathens but our Tudu had spied on them and on Stephan. Father Lindon would never know the stories. Tudu couldn't even think of betraying Horo's trust. He adored Stephan and was pained more for that reason. Tudu recalled: Horo killed a deer that day with an arrow. Chirki washed his feet as he stood near the spring, all by himself.

Chirki fled from her village on a moonlit night. Horo was waiting in the dark and took her away.

Horo had been taken to the tribal ritual of beating drums despite being a Christian. He had danced with Chirki too. Loved and protected by the old Sotha, he was the darling of the tribe. He had also participated in the tribal festival of fire, burnt down trees and felled branches at random.

Tudu's voice faded away: Horo stood aside, healing his bruises in the cool breeze. And then came Chirki, took him in her arms.

We gathered on the grass near the hostel that evening, enthralled by Tudu's stories. And from the balcony floated in a flute song. The tune seemed quite familiar to Tudu and he started humming it, happy with himself.

'Who is playing the flute, Tudu?'

Tudu paused and said, 'This is Chirki's song. Stephan is playing it on his flute.' Then he explained the meaning of the lines: 'O my love, don't go away, I am so lonely in the forest ....' We sat there listening. We feel your pulse, Chirki, you are so much like our girls. Indu mumbled some poem....

We did not move. The song enthralled us and all of us, in our heart of hearts, consoled the girl from the hills: Rest assured, Chirki, you will get back your love ....

Our reverie was rudely ruptured by the noise of a scuffle from the balcony. Tudu sprang to his feet and soon brought back the news. He panted as he said, 'Father has broken his flute!' How we would have liked to help Horo! Why couldn't he resist the missionary? Tudu looked tense, he feared that Horo would take revenge.

To our surprise, Stephan remained cool and normal. Instead, it was Father Lindon who resolved to launch a crusade against the heathen tribals. He ventured into the forest once a week with constables or armed guards. He developed a good rapport with the police as well. We were concerned for this strange crusader. We were not used to seeing him agitated; it hurt us. Tudu came to our help again. He explained how the missionary was out to spread Christianity in the depths of the jungle and had built a mud church on the hills. He had declared war against the age-old domain of heathen beliefs and rituals.

But very soon his mission suffered a setback. The Morangis razed his church to the ground. The old Sotha chief led the mob. That day we attended the chief's trial. He was banished from the land. Stephan, too, was not the same. He just kept to his favourite swing from the banyan tree. It seemed the turmoil all around had robbed him of his strange peace of mind.

A few years later the storm that gathered on the horizon over the years surged forward. In the shape of the Non-cooperation movement. We plunged into the turmoil as the Jallianwalla Bagh massacre grieved and shocked the nation. We decided to boycott school. Along came all the Bengali and Bihari boys. But the princes and our Christian classmates remained loyal to the government; our protests and pickets had no impact on them.

We expected Stephan to throw in his lot with us. We wanted him to desert Father Lindon in this hour of crisis. That day as we were demonstrating at the school gate we saw him coming. We shouted slogans to greet him. But to our utter dismay, he forced his way through the crowd, pushed Indu to one side and jostled with Paresh. Like a charging bull he headed for the classroom.

Our eyes opened to the truth. Was Horo anything more than an unthinking slave of the alien missionaries? Would he ever learn to respect the heritage of a sovereign India, or know what is meant by one's motherland? Son of the wild, if only he tried to feel the country throb, in its forests and cities, its hills and homes alike!

Eight years later I joined the Lepo police station as the officer-in-charge. One morning some Birsaite Mundas came to report to me. This had become a practice with these men as they were the most disturbing elements in the forests. The law meant nothing to them, nor did did the police. They refused to pay taxes, they threatened to kill the court's messengers. They had even declared independence two years before. At that time missionaries and policemen bore the brunt of their attacks. In fury they destroyed several bridges and fought with the police in the jungles of Ormanjhi.

The last man to come up to my desk was called Runnu Horo. What a strange creature he was. His bare chest, disheveled locks, his primitive trinkets were overshadowed by only a pair of sharp, scanning eyes ....

I lost my voice for a few seconds. He was our Stephan Horo! As I called out his name he smiled and corrected me, 'I am Runnu Horo, Ghosh.' Was he a Birsaite, too? 'I am a follower of the noble Birsa,' he said. And then Horo elaborated, 'Birsa was our Gandhi. I never saw him; my father told me about him. They jailed him as if he was riff-raff, and he died in prison. Do you know who he looked like?' No, I had no idea. 'He was so much like Christ ...', Horo said and a little later spoke again, 'Our forests are no longer free from evil. The great Birsa knew all and warned us. Can I ignore him?'

Horo opened up a bit soon and started inquiring about long lost friends. His frail health disturbed me and I couldn't help asking, 'Why are you looking so sick?' He answered in an off-hand manner, 'I am suffering from tuberculosis.' As he was about to leave I asked him something that had been bothering me a very long time, 'Horo, where is Chirki?' He did not lose his cool as he said, ' Chirki has joined Father Lindon's mission in Hazaribagh, she lives in a convent there. She is a Christian.' His piercing eyes shone through a film of tears. I felt dumb. Stephan left like a fading shadow.

I never admitted to anyone how a sense of shame overwhelmed me that day. I felt as if our impartial stand had decided Stephan's fate in the fourth battle of Panipat. And exiled him to the wilderness.

translated by Swati Ghosh

The Sweet Cheat

That Sanatan and that Sudha!

Like father, like daughter, made for each other, if we twist the traditional sense a bit.

Events multiply, strange unexpected happenings — and this Sudha-Sanatan combine breaks down. The father collapses with obvious shock, and the daughter, with bent head, sheds silent tears, sobbing unceasingly.

Witnesses of the scene also have to share inexorably the sorrow of a parental sentiment — that age-old pang of separation that, perhaps, led to the death of king Dasharat when Rama went into exile.

Quite understandable, but the system, the tradition cannot yet change. The daughter must marry, must be allowed to go to another household, to persons with unfamiliar faces and features, and parents' tears will always drench the farewell scene.

Sudha's case, naturally, is no exception. The scene of departure is moistened, with neighbours, too, joining the ritualistic waves of lamentation. But, no, Sanatan has some real sympathisers. The groom's party also, quite often, appears considerably moved: the lone daughter leaving her father- yes, so sad!

But the neighbours could hardly dream of the anti-climax that awaits them. After less than a month, they are all irked by a totally unexpected outcome. The groom of just the other day as well as his relations, rush back to this locality, to Sanatan's house, only to find that they have gone with the wind! Yes, the Dad and his doll have vanished.

The police now make it clear; this is the third time that this fraudulent pair has made good its escape. Two persons - an elderly male and a young girl - have ganged up nicely to organize short-lived, temporary marriages, to enact a big drama, and then, on some pretext, the 'daughter' comes to see her 'ailing' father, never to return. The marriage becomes even more ludicrous than the children's game of dolls' weddings and ends without any fanfare. The 'groom' goes bankrupt, as ornaments, cash and other movable property have also vanished simultaneously.

Well, the police can cite two previous cases - one at Tarakeswar, another at Basirhat - the enactment of the same drama of deception. Both, only about four months back. And now, at Bhatpara. The intelligence report has it that the gang is identical. A professional pair of thugs to deceive the whole of society.

Police do their jobs here. The locked door of the accused is broken under the authority of the First Information Report. And the empty room seems a mocking rebuff. Sanatan and Sudha have already flown away on their magic carpet.

Neighbours who had shed tears only a few weeks earlier find it difficult to digest. 'Really, society is becoming like a zoo - nothing is impossible!'

Somebody retorts philosophically: 'Oh, no , a zoo is a much better place, sir. This can happen only in a society of those whom we call human beings.'

A gentleman like a political leader feels guilty in a different way. 'It is most shameful that such things should happen in our ward. All of us have been made a bunch of idiots by a fake father-daughter pair. What a black stigma ... oh!'

Yes, nobody had any shadow of doubt. That outburst from an old father, that polite sobbing from a simple daughter. Who could have guessed that big treachery was having a hearty laugh behind it all? Another question: are they actually father and daughter in real life, or just related for show?

No, the police confirm, that is not true. The male Sanatan is really the father of the female Sudha or, in other words, Sudha is very much the daughter of a father.

The police diary can give some more details: They - this fraudulent pair - do not stay at a place for a day longer than necessary. Theirs are all short-term operations. They assume new names, new identities, even a new caste, as required for a possible, covetable chance of marriage. The manoeuvre persists for a fixed period, credibility is established, the operation begins and ends — and they are gone. All to one blueprint.

Thanks to such a calculating brain, even the 'kepmari' gang may like to be tutored by them.

The gentleman who appeared with the bridal crown on his head only a few weeks back, looks more puzzled than angry. His face betrays a sense of loss. Which kind of loss — money, ornaments, or the sweet face of Sudha? He perhaps wonders how such a beautiful face can hide such a deceitful heart!

More tragic is the fact that he came to relieve a poor father of the burden of 'kanya-dan'. A resident of Naihati, he lost his first wife about fifteen years back. Now, at forty-five, he felt the urge for marriage not so much for himself as for Sanatan, a helpless father. But, yes, he perhaps also had to confess to himself, the sweetmeats prepared by Sudha did the trick. And her sweet face was also too difficult for him to ignore.

So this stationery shop owner from Naihati did not hesitate to take up the entire burden on his shoulders, to bear all that such a marriage, however simple, might cost. He also paid Sanatan, his nice father-in-law, a sincere 'pronami' of Rs. 2,000 in cash.

A beautiful bride cannot do without the beauty of gold, the beauty of a Banarasi silk saree, the beauty of other articles so very much associated with a beautiful marriage. And the marriage was really beautiful.

Today he is back here with the police, only to face a draconian beauty all round. Yes, Sudha came here about ten days back to console her father, and was to go back after two days. Her father himself was to take her to Naihati. ... But no news since then. And now -

Now it is no longer a mystery. This is their third successful operation.

The police diary can only give some theoretical satisfaction. At Tarakeswar they were Brahmins; at Basirhat, Kayasthas. At Tarakeswar today's Sanatan of Bhatpara was a Prasanna Chakrabarty and Sudha was a Sunayana. At Basirhat, the case involved one Sadananda Ghosh and his daughter Madhabi.

A father and his daughter. What are their real names; who are they? And why do they indulge in such a heinous game that plays with the sanctity of marriage, makes bridal nights an object of characteristic 'woman's frailty'? The bridal flowers, with drooping petals, shrink at such ruthless betrayal, as if in atonement.

Like father, like daughter!

The hopeless police go back, and that middle-aged shop-owner of Naihati learns a life-time lesson: how one can cheat in such a beautifully cruel way! He rubs his eyes, perhaps, for a clear view of the world.

... And right at that moment, the fraudulent pair are off to Ranaghat. Here Sanatan has become a Bijay Babu and Sudha changes herself to one Karabi. It is a small room in a by-lane, with a smaller window. Late afternoon. Twilight is saluting the approaching evening through a small passage. But Karabi has no difficulty in noticing a new face, no trouble in smiling indulgently at Ramesh, a local youth who, by habit, is quite solicitous about the well-being of the new arrivals - a poor father and his pretty daughter.

Once again, a net is spread.

That small room and smaller window.

But it is a sunny room, and the by-lane too enjoys fleeting moments of charity from the sun's rays.

Ramesh's bicycle bell rings like a calling bell. Karabi knows it is time she should come and look through the window.

'Why do you ring the bell in this fashion, so frequently?' Karabi sounds sentimental.

Ramesh has a hearty laugh: 'An astrologer predicted my wife's name would begin with the letter K.'

Karabi: 'But don't you ever feel that meetings like this - I mean, this talking openly through the window—will only fetch me scandal and nothing else?'

Ramesh, easy and happy, reeling on the bicycle rod, says,

'I can't help it!'

'What do you mean?'

'The day you first cast a glance at me, I discovered something.'

'A discovery!'

'Oh yes, I discovered that you are really my peace and happiness; frankly....'

'It is a luxurious whim for a rich man like you. In course of time you will find you are wrong. You will forget everything and you won't like me at all .... Then why drag it out unnecessarily ....'

'I am not a rich man,' Ramesh is firm in his answer - 'nor can I afford any luxury .... I came here to see you because I can't help it. No whims, believe me.'

'You are not a rich man then!'

'Not at all.'

'What is your job. I mean ....'

'Well, I am an artist.'

'Artist! What kind?'

Ramesh steadies himself. 'Have you ever been to Calcutta?'

'Yes, once, for a short while'.

'Have you seen pictures, I mean, films?'

'Yes, rarely though - '

'Haven't you noticed the big colourful banners, the hoardings on top of the cinema houses and city walls?'

'Yes, of course.'

'I paint those pictures, those banners, hoardings ....'

'Does it pay -'

'Yes, in fact, that is my earning - and by God's grace, it is not bad.'

'Does it fetch you about a thousand or so?'

'Oh yes, you may say so.'

'No, but tell me exactly how much you earn.'

'Enough to make you happy.'

Karabi now pretends a romance, typical of her - 'Enough! Yes, it is really enough to provide a hand-to-mouth meal twice a day, and a pair of sarees in a year. Enough, isn't it?'

Ramesh, uneasy: 'It is not so. I don't have to limit myself to a hand-to-mouth meal. And a pair of dhotis is not sufficient for me for an entire year.'

Karabi smiles expectantly - 'Then admit, you have enough money -'

'Yes, enough to keep you beautiful, enough to see that you don't suffer - but not of that type - you see -' Ramesh points to a distant three-storeyed marble house - 'Well, I am not as rich as that!' Ramesh pleads: 'You don't need so much either, Karabi.'

Karabi: 'How can the marriage expenses be met?'

Ramesh thinks for a few seconds; he has a little touch of despair in his voice: 'Is Vijay Babu —'

'Better not talk about him —'

Karabi, quite apt in the art of coquetry, masterminds her next venture. 'How much do you need, I mean for our marriage?' Ramesh appears serious.

Karabi finds her prey nearer. 'Even a shabby ceremony needs at least ten thousand rupees - to my knowledge - '

'Ten thousand!' Ramesh is alarmed.

Karabi's eyes, flirtatious and annoyed, are out to scrutinise Ramesh's monetary worth as a husband-to-be. 'Is it too much for you? Can you not afford to collect even ten thousand rupees?'

Ramesh: 'I will have to borrow it ....'

'What's the harm in borrowing; you will pay it back in time. But if there is a delay - Karabi stops. A deliberate pause. Eyes have to be shown tearful by now; credibility is the need of the moment.

Ramesh, anxious: 'What is wrong with you?'

Karabi - 'Do you love me, really?'

'Believe me, yes!'

'Then hurry - otherwise, I have no option but suicide - '

'For God's sake!' - Ramesh shouts - 'what do you mean?'

'An old wretch from Baidyabati, married once before, is my likely husband. He is ready to give ten thousand rupees to my luckless father - and what else can I do!'

Ramesh clutches his bicycle-handle with dogged determination - a soldier-like jerk runs through his veins. He rides on his bike and shouts: 'I give you my word - yes, ten thousand! Ask your father not to touch a penny from that old wretch.'

Karabi turns her face to conceal her triumphant smile.

Ramesh pedals by — 'And it won't be longer than a week, be sure!'

That by-lane of Ranaghat.

But a spirit of jubilation marks out that simple ceremony. Local fellows wonder how Bijoy Babu, who came here only less than a month back, invites almost all the residents of the by-lane. But by now everybody knows his miserable condition. So they protest, 'Oh, no, don't try and feed us, Bejoy Babu - it will be a sheer waste. Whatever little you have, adorn your only daughter. At least a little gold should be there, after all -'

Bijoy Babu feels obliged. Out of ten thousand rupees Karabi gets some gold ornaments worth eight thousand. The calculation is meticulous: the remaining two thousand rupees will suffice for the informal rituals.

Ramesh weds Karabi. The locality knows that Bijoy Babu has rendered himself penniless for his daughter's marriage. A loving father can afford to become bankrupt for his daughter's happiness - so ... how can they protest?

Karabi dresses herself with ornaments bought by money that Ramesh has provided. But that is a secret.

Now, that old scene again. Enactment of that past drama, perfected through industrious repetition: Bijay Babu breaking down with suppressed shock and Karabi sobbing with polite artistry, last performed at Bhatpara, earlier at Tarakeswar and Basirhat, and today at Ranaghat.

Yes, the same scene. The neighbours, too, feel the pangs of separation. How sad!

Ramesh and Karabi leave for Baghbazar, Calcutta.

The bridal night at Baghbazar has no special lighting or decoration. It passes off almost unceremoniously, though a very limited number of friends and relations, who love Ramesh, gather and try their best to make good the impoverished festival by zest, jokes and laughter. An all round enthusiasm fighting hard against material want. Left together late in the night, Ramesh and Karabi observe each other's face from the other's point of view. This room is small but, Ramesh feels, nothing bigger is necessary; Karabi removes her bridal veil, looks up, heaves a sigh of relief, slightly disappointed - as her deerlike eyes manifest — the room is really small; a bigger one would do better!

Ramesh: 'Would you allow me one thing?'

Karabi: 'First tell me what it is.'

Ramesh: 'I want to portray your face on my canvas. It won't take much time. See what magic my brush can perform in two days!'

Karabi is curious: 'I really can't understand.'

Ramesh: 'This canvas will preserve another Karabi here, equally lively, particularly those captivating eyes of yours, you see ....'

Karabi: 'Well, go ahead, I will have it on my return.'

Ramesh: 'Return? Where are you going?'

Karabi: 'To my father, at Ranaghat.'

Ramesh: 'Oh, of course. But you are not going there so soon, I mean, not in a day or two -'

Karabi: 'Yes, but if father himself comes, then - '

Ramesh: 'Will your father come now?'

Karabi: 'He may come anytime, maybe tomorrow - from what I know of him ... he is so upset ....'

A little pause. Then Karabi again feigns a painful outburst - 'Oh, nothing cheers me at all when I think of him. He must still be weeping.'

Ramesh tries to console her: 'Naturally so, you are his only child. I can feel his grief, really, but ... let's see - let your father come, and I will talk to him.'

Karabi: 'Talk! About what?'

Ramesh: 'My request will be - I will myself reach you to Rangahat after a month or so. Hope he won't press me.'

Karabi: 'Father won't agree, I am sure. And, let me say, don't press him either; he will be hurt.'

Ramesh feels depressed: 'But don't you feel I will be hurt?'

Karabi: 'Why? Why should you be hurt - anyway?'

Ramesh: 'If he comes tomorrow and takes you back, well ... it will be really difficult for me to stand, you see -

Karabi now throws a piercing look at Ramesh, trying to grasp it. What a fellow; now her husband wants to assert his legal rights!

Ramesh: 'If he really does so, then I too may accompany you. No harm if we both stay at Ranaghat for a couple of days and then come back together.'

Karabi: 'Don't you have some self-respect? How can you go without an invitation?'

Ramesh: 'Won't your father ask me at all? In all probability, he will - '

Karabi: 'No, he won't.'

Ramesh: 'Why? That is something wrong.'

Karabi's voice betrays a surreptitious quivering; 'How could I know, why do you ask me?'

Ramesh: 'But you yourself can plead for me with your father.'

Karabi: 'Plead what?'

Ramesh: 'That he should ask me to go with you.'

Karabi: 'How can I be so shameless? Is it not too much for a daughter to ....'

Karabi doesn't finish her words as she finds Ramesh's face turning unusually grave. Any shred of suspicion?

Karabi: 'Why do you look so grave? Do you suspect something?'

Ramesh: 'Suspect! What should I suspect?'

Karabi: 'You may think I have no feeling for you.'

Ramesh: 'I would perhaps die before I could think so.'

Karabi shudders. A strange pin-prick of hurt, never known before. A ripple of electrical currents, hitherto unfelt, dances to the tune of her heartbeat. She feels a little out of breath.

'Why will you die? Death is not so easy for a man; don't you know that fortune smiles on him whose wife dies soon -'

Ramesh: 'I don't believe that.'

Karabi: 'Just imagine, I am no more. You are talking and smiling to your new wife after some time, in the same manner as you do now.'

Ramesh: 'I can't stand such jokes, Karabi.' Ramesh gets up and takes her hands in his. A touch that seeks a kind of reassurance. 'You are very much here, very much real.'

Ramesh murmurs: 'I have not much experience, but I am sure no one else can boast of a better wife than mine.'

Karabi is further alarmed. Again that strange heartache!

Ramesh: 'How can a husband live without such a wife? It makes no sense, no meaning.'

Karabi cautiously takes her hands out of his grip, moves to a distance, sits on the bed, bending her head. Why does it feel strangely awful to look straight at the face of this man?

Evening has approached unnoticed. Karabi, suddenly anxious; 'Will you not eat today, and make me starve also?'

Ramesh: 'Well ....'

Karabi: 'I mean, I find in you no urge to bring some food from outside. Nor to ask me to cook something.'

Ramesh jumps up, amused and delighted. 'Will you cook?'

Karabi: 'Yes, I will, it is a question of just one night, let me record my labour for one night here.' Karabi smiles.

Ramesh: 'This is exactly what I was longing for.'

Karabi: 'What?'

Ramesh: 'The hotel food the last few days tasted so repulsive I am really hungry for your cooking. I mean, your cooked food.'

Karabi: 'Really so, you are longing for that?'

Ramesh: 'I am crazy for it'.

Karabi: 'You had better control your craziness.'

Ramesh: 'Craze, Craze, Craze, I will remain crazy for you throughout my life.'

Suddenly a gust of romance fills this small room, spreads to the adjacent kitchen. The rolls of smoke melting away in the evening air, the sweet clash of utensils, and the smell of some delicious food cooking - all bring home the point that Ramesh has a home. His wife has just shed her bridal dress, as it were, and hurriedly domesticated herself because her husband is in a hurry, he is hungry. She cannot rest; she must rush. The 'anchal' of her new Basanti saree is tied around her waist, hands drenched in yellowish cooking pastes, a lock of hair falling over her forehead, constantly disturbed by the evening breeze, could not, however, disturb her at all. She is a wife, totally serious about her new assignment.

Cooking ends. Asans are placed on the floor. Ramesh sits down as Karabi dishes out vegetable pulao for him. Its smell has already boosted his appetite for food; its maker has increased his appetite for a sweet home and a sweeter wife.

But Ramesh sits still!

Karabi: 'Now, please start.'

Ramesh is still silent.

Karabi: 'Why do you look so grave now?'

Ramesh: 'I am haunted by a new craze.'

Karabi: 'New craze!'

Ramesh: 'Yes, I don't like to eat alone, I mean, in this fashion.'

Karabi: 'What do you want?'

Ramesh: 'Come, let us share the dish together.'

Again that electrical ripple — this time through her veins, specially over the entire body, every 'local sign' is touched to the core. Nerves intertwine into a labyrinth, difficult to tear off. Karabi never dreamt of such things ever.

But she has no option. They start eating together.

Ramesh: 'Well, these are rare moments. From next week, I have a lot of work, great pressure, so much backlog in my work. God knows when such a chance will occur again.'

Karabi: 'What chance?'

Ramesh: 'This, this eating together.'

Karabi: 'You work hard, eh!'

Ramesh: 'Yes, no help. Sometimes even when I have high fever — our taskmasters know no mercy.'

Karabi: 'Now, I have become another burden - you will labour hard and die - '

Ramesh: 'Not at all, I am in high spirits. Till now I earned just for myself. Now for both of us. I feel enthusiastic, Karabi. I could never stand to see your face grow sad even for a moment.'

Karabi: 'You have already borrowed a good deal. Haven't you -'

Ramesh: 'No worry. I have my overtime plan. The entire debt will be clear in two years.'

Karabi discovers another self. Her head bends, as if in conscientious surrender.

Ramesh notices something: 'What's wrong? You are not eating at all?'

Two drops of sparkling tears fall on her hands.

Tears are no stranger to her. But never tears of this type. Heartache, hitting her brain, her brain sending currents that softly squeeze the eyes, shedding warm dewdrops.

'What is this, Karabi?' Ramesh shouts.

Karabi rubs her face, stands up, washes her hands and face, and now confronts Ramesh squarely.

'Listen' Her voice sounds mysterious.

'Do you really want to live?'

'What do you mean?'

'Then call the police at once, immediately - and hand me over to them, please hurry up -'

'Karabi!'

'I am no Karabi, I have no name, I am nothing -' Karabi, eyes closed, recites as though uttering some theatre-dialogues on stage before a bewildered face: 'I am a cheat, a fake, a criminal.' Perplexed, Ramesh clutches her desperately - but Karabi goes on.

'I am the dangerous daughter of a dangerous father. Marriage is only a sport to us - it is by such a show that we play and earn, and run away. I have not come to stay with you. I will leave you soon - as soon as my father arrives.'

The words are clear and distinct - and have no ambiguity.

Ramesh perhaps cannot understand a single point. He is witnessing a captivating drama. How nicely Karabi is performing her role. A brilliant feat.

Ramesh tries to recover from this hypnotism. Yes, he can grasp little of this undreamt of outcome. He at last attempts hard to read his death-warrant. But - But can such a beautiful face be so ugly, actually?

The face of a thagini.

Karabi: 'I know, you won't call the police. You are so innocent, so mild, so foolish.'

Ramesh sits grim, speechless.

Karabi takes off her ornaments - one by one - and places them on the bed.

'All that I can do, - is this. At least Rs. 8000 of the loan you can pay back!'

Ramesh does not move an inch.

'Now please, let me go.'

'Where - ?'

Karabi cannot answer.

'You would like to go back to your dangerous father?'

Karabi has no answer.

'You must speak out.' Ramesh, excited beyond measure, jumps out of the bed.

Karabi seems more excited now - 'Tell me, you won't allow me to go?'

Ramesh: 'No, I won't.'

Karabi: 'Then, hurry up.'

Ramesh: 'What is the hurry? Why?'

Karabi: 'Right now, take me away - anywhere, any place in this world.'

Ramesh: 'Well, but why?'

Karabi: 'Oh, you fool, don't ever allow that dangerous shadow to touch us. It may, yes, any time.'

Ramesh: 'Dangerous Shadow!'

Karabi: 'Of my dangerous father - he will come in the early morning. It is already late.'

Again two pairs of restless hands prepare for a new journey. Nothing is left. The empty room of a Baghbazar lane can cast a similar rebuff at any demanding trespasser.

The dangerous daughter, turning into an obliging wife, now has vanished with her harmless husband, never to return to her life-long partner in dubious games - her father.

Yes, the thagini cannot deceive this husband. She has changed.

But no, this is wrong. She is still a 'thagini'.

Next morning, when Bijoy Babu, journeying by the early morning train from Ranaghat, enters that Baghbazar lane, he too has an experience, the first of its kind in his life. The big lock on the door is an unbelievable sight for him. Peeping through a crack in the window, Bijay Babu sees that room mocking him in its nudity. A peal of silent laughter roars into his ears - deafening, unbearable.

His suffering did not last long. The police handcuffed him with great alacrity, and before the jeep is to whisk him away he too learns the lesson of his life: 'Oh Thagini, can a daughter cheat her father in this way?'

Is she a 'thagini' still?

Translated by Uttam Ghose

The Incense

When it comes to Mr Tainbrooke the whole of Sheikhpura is unanimous — that there are officers and there are officers, but there is none like Mr Jerome T.L.Tainbrooke. This sub-divisional town is in love with this man who almost single-handedly raised funds and organized grants to revamp the local hospital. He is a man on the move. Now you see him at the Milad gathering and the next moment he is attending a recital from the Gita. And he never forgets to leave his shoes at the door. It is difficult to find a fault in him.

Tainbrooke is the latest star of the Indian Civil Service and he is not a shooting star. To top it all, he is an Indologist. You can regularly read about his research in New York's Samson Institute's journal. His erudition about things Indian was first revealed in his famous thesis — 'The influence of Celtic minstrels on the Pantheism of the Rig Veda'. To throw light on such an abstruse subject using both proof and conjecture is no easy task. And Tainbrooke measures up to it. He can read the Devanagari script, write in Bengali and deliver a lecture with aplomb in Hindi. His grandfather, Captain Tainbrooke, was a close friend of Mark Twain. From this wise grandfather Tainbrooke had picked up invaluable information about India. Had India not been swept by chauvinism, people would have also noticed this aspect of Tainbrooke's versatility. While being transferred from Jagadishpur, Tainbrooke had said in his farewell speech: 'I might be wrong in realising, I might be wrong in knowing, but I know the soul of India in my own way. And I love this soul of India, resplendent as it is, like the milky Kanchenjunga.'

A long time ago Tainbrooke had found a censer in a field near Rajgir. It resembled a lotus and was made of sandstone. He kept it on a tall tripod and every evening a bearer would pour a handful of incense in it and let it burn. Tainbrooke could smell an oriental magic hidden in the fumes.

Junior school boys were playing football when a hoodless Tourer swung off the road and noisily parked by the field. Tainbrooke jumped out of the car and joined the players. Anadibabu, the games teacher, was on tenterhooks. He stopped blowing the whistle for a while. He thought of David Hare to console himself. The game began to hot up.

Karalibabu's son, Balai, was a constant source of tension. He kept trying to trip up Tainbrooke, time and again. Anadibabu blew the whistle at him regularly but that did not prove a deterrent. This brat had stolen the games teacher's peace of mind. But at the end of the game, Tainbrooke singled out Balai for praise. That did not stop Anadibabu from taking the boy to task — he let him off with the severe warning that such audacity would not be tolerated in future.

The people of Sheikhpura got another glimpse of Tainbrooke's brilliance during the Durbar Day celebrations. His speech moved all and sundry. From the members of the Bar library and the Taluk Committee to the clerks, shopkeepers and parish priests, every citizen of the sub-divisional town went back with glowing memories of a lecture that drove home every point, word for word.

Tainbrooke says in his speech: 'I want to remind every Government servant, especially policemen, that they are not demigods. They are the servants of the people. The police must always remember that they are not the heads of society. They are its two hands. It is their duty to follow orders. On this auspicious day, I have this inkling that somewhere on the firmament a cloud of trouble is gathering. We will soon face testing times. It is likely that a storm might blow over this small, happy town of mine.

'When the storm comes it is important that the relationship between the public and the Government does not sour. That is why I sound this note of warning to the police. If they transgress the limits of law it will be considered treachery and they will be punished for it.' While the speech is in progress most people stare at the district superintendent of police, Raibahadur Jankiprasad, with a feeling of curiosity and revenge. The DSP remains impassive.

Sheikhpura remains as cheerful as its school playground. Even if Tainbrooke doesn't manage to come daily he joins the game at least thrice a week. Anadibabu is much relieved. Tainbrooke and Balai are on the same team - thus leaving little chance for a confrontation. The schoolboys have become Tainbrooke's favourites. Every afternoon they wait eagerly for the sound of his car.

But storm clouds gather. Disaster seems to be looming large over Sheikhpura. Twenty-one members have resigned from the local board. Three hartals have taken place. Rajganj colliery goes on strike. A meeting takes place at the Jain dharamshala. A thousand people march, demanding swaraj.

But Tainbrooke remain unruffled. Not one man is arrested. Nowhere is Section 144 clamped. The police wait at the thana. Tainbrooke has ordered them to stay there.

Sheikhpura is on the boil for three months. And Tainbrooke has done just one thing. He spreads the message - 'I appeal to the public that whatever problems or differences they have should be resolved through discussions. Democracy is the highest form of living and the touchstone of democracy is discipline. Let us not destroy that.'

The agitation runs out of steam. Probably it dies on its own because it did not meet any opposition. Tainbrooke is overjoyed at the success of his social experiment. He forms a peace committee. Somebody suggests that the DSP be a member of the committee. Tainbrooke overrules him.

But the morning choir has not stopped. The storm seems to have disappeared, leaving a trail of musical anger. The silence of a Sheikhpura dawn is broken by the sound of music, the sound of protest. Tainbrooke is waiting for the songs to subside. Days pass. The peace committee tries to gather information but nobody can unravel the mystery of the morning choir. Nobody knows its members, where they come from or where they go. Many men, young and old, keep awake the whole night, they wait with impatience - will they sing today? When they doze off at daybreak voices are suddenly heard and fade as suddenly. No one can be seen.

The songs will never stop. A story is doing the rounds of the city - a few kilometers west down Gaya Road is the Doomrichowk dak bungalow. Then five leagues down the right across the old Karbala is the Bahera forest. To the north of the forest runs a river and by its side is a huge banyan tree. Opposite the tree travels the PWD road. Here bus drivers rest awhile and the radiators are filled with water. There is also a police outpost. Under the shadows of the banyan tree stands a milestone.

The tragic story begins at this spot. Here a hundred sepoys lost their lives. The legend goes that one Mr Carlyle tied the sepoys to a cannon and blew them up right under the tree. The town believes that no human voice sings the song. It is the voice of the sepoys so it comes down Gaya Road, roams the city and stops before sunrise. Tainbrooke hears the story. He pacifies the peace committee and assures them that he will put an end to the musical mirage.

The November night nears the dawn. In the pink and purple glow of early morning the municipal lamp throws some light. The long road lies asleep, wet with dewdrops. The sal branches doze in a foggy slumber and hidden behind the shadows and the landscape in the mist stands Tainbrooke like a watchful sentry in the barrack of an unreal realm.

And then he hears the march of music. Mingled with the gentle morning breeze it seems to approach the town. The words are too faint to comprehend clearly. Small streams of sound seem to merge to create a waterfall of melody. Tainbrooke can hear it approaching, approaching fast:

'There rises the new sun of the new era. Arise and awake, my brothers and sisters of Hindustan. Bathe in the rays of the morning sun.'

The choir is on its way. Tainbrooke listens, holding his breath, to the mingled voices of some young souls lost in the joy of singing. These were familiar voices of joy and despair and Tainbrooke can feel their pulses in the faint beams of the newborn day. He waits and listens, stiffening his jaws in suppressed excitement and tension.

Tainbrooke waits for some time more. The song seems to sweep every place, knowing no direction. Reaching the field it swells up into a war cry and then stops. After a long while it comes back, but from an altogether different corner. Like a spiralling wind it blows over the paddy fields across the railway tracks towards Darjipara.

The legend goes that Aurangzeb poured molten lead on the root of a banyan tree after uprooting it, thinking this would prevent the growth of any sapling. Tainbrooke possibly knows the story. That day he detains all the students after classes are over. And then he flags off a march by the students that will go to every corner of the town till ten at night. They are promised a feast in the school at night. Tainbrooke gives them some money for refreshments.

Balai is put in charge of leading the procession. He lowers his head to a drooping branch. His stare is vacant. A terrible blow of insult seems to have stopped all his frolic. He stands like an ailing man minutes before losing consciousness.

Balai begins to sing in a most expressionless manner for the first time. 'I am a little lamb of Jesus.' Tainbrooke is the composer. Like birds lost in the wilderness of a strange horizon, Balai's companions repeat: 'I am a little lamb ...' Balai yells in the queerest of voices as if he has bitten his tongue: 'My joys are endless ...' Again the boys echo: 'My joys are endless...?

The procession sets off. As a well-meaning parent hides his affection behind rigid discipline, Tainbrooke watches them go away and then retires to his bungalow. He is confident that a day-long toilsome march on the path of righteousness will make the boys tired and compel them to abandon the wrong way.

To top it all is the ten-rupee tip. The thought assures Tainbrooke more and helps him relax.

As evening descends Tainbrooke picks up the district gazetteer. The Indologist in him will excavate the truth in the vengeful archaeological myth of Sheikhpura. After turning over pages he stops at a point. He stares at what is printed there: The East India Company used to have its tanks under the pipal tree, eleven kilometers from the Dumrichowk bungalow, at the spot where the milestone of the town stands at present. The local people believe captured sepoys were executed there during the Mutiny.

What a cock and bull story! Tainbrooke abuses the thick-headed Government surveyor who recorded this rubbish. A trader's brain cannot rule a colony so many centuries later. He ponders over it for two hours and then makes up his mind.

He rewrites the paragraph — Brahmadatta, a monk, who belonged to the fifth century A.D., had his ashram where now stands the milestone of the town, under the pipal tree, eleven kilometers from the Dumrichowk bungalow ... Tainbrooke stops for a while. He frowns and stares at the vacant air. An abominable mirage floats wherever he looks. It blocks his vision and he knows what it is. Gandhi, it is Gandhi, everyone's Gandhi, the undaunted, indomitable, half-clad Gandhi.

Gnashing his teeth, Tainbrooke picks up the pen again and in a moment's passion puts these words on paper: An evil aboriginal ruler robbed the land of its peace and prosperity. The Kshatriya king, Debopriyo, by his service pleased the ascetic Brahmadatt who cursed the tyrant to death.

Inspired and happy, Tainbrooke types out the new historical truth. Then he fits it perfectly into the original paragraph, checks whether there is any gap and then sinks into his seat, totally exhausted. And excited. It was like throttling a gushing spring. He prepares for the rest of the night with a cup of coffee and a book. Contentment seems to have drained out all his energy.

Outside, the dark night spreads its veil — its heart throbbing in grief. The marchers, meandering through the mango grove, are on their way back. Their mumbling voices, weary and worn out, are singing a distorted song. The hissing sound of their breathing reminds one of a hurt snake gnashing its poison fangs.

Tainbrooke shivers. For a minute has vision of the soul of India becomes blurred — it does not resemble the snowcapped, serene Kanchanjanga. Instead, it looks like the cowardly and malicious Balai.

Tainbrooke cannot take his eyes off the window. A cruel and heartless sense of disappointment gnaws at his nerves — they will come. They will troop in again tonight. Those formless, shapeless, strange figures will sneak in tonight, hugging the shades and unlocking the doors of slumber — they will drown the world in their frightful chorus — no one can stop their surge ... .

The incense stick weaves myriad dreams in the air. Smoke crawls freely out of the window. Something keeps buzzing in Tainbrooke's head, and makes his limbs ache. In a strange fit of passion he rings the bell. The orderly rushes in. Looking flushed, his eyes bloodshot, Tainbrooke screams at the top of his voice: 'Run and call the DSP. Call the subedar too. Alert the Eastern Rifles. Cordon off the town. We will keep vigil throughout the night. They have to be hunted down tonight. And they will learn the final lesson ... .'

The crisis of democracy ends with the legal battle between Balai and the King Emperor. No one known the details for certain. No one dares enter the court premises. They are too heavily guarded. One can only catch a fleeting glimpse of Balai, getting down from the prison van. Balai has his head bandaged, a rope around his waist. The DSP, Janakiprasad, towers over the crowd. Standing erect on the verandah he feels his belt while the veins on his forehead bulge out in arrogance. Watching the crowd swell outside the gate, he shouts all of a sudden, 'Disperse.'

And then stretching his hand towards the police picket at the gate he commands: 'Charge.'

translated by Swati Ghosh

Shock Therapy

Basil, the son of Mr Watkins Moore, was, to put it in the language of the times, 'off his rocker'.

Old Watkins Moore had been an officer in the Indian Army. Now retired, he lived in a small town in Chhotanagpur. The bungalow, rather unimaginatively called 'The Retreat', was nevertheless rather picturesque, sited on top of a low mound and surrounded by eucalyptus trees.

Old Watkins had a standard reply to all questions about why he had chosen this god-forsaken place to retire to: 'This bungalow reminds me of our manor in our county. You know; we belong to Yorkshire, famous for its gallantry; and we Mores of Yorkshire are old blood, blue to the last drop. We have been lords of the manor for the last five hundred years. The price of chivalry on the field is no longer privileges from the King. So today the family coffers are empty. The country is overrun by fishermen calling themselves officers; and the measure of courage is the distance to which one can row a dam' boat; so they are paid more'; then, with a pause:- 'but that kind of work is not for the likes of us or ours; the ingrates back home seem to have forgotten that we once fertilised the tender soil of our native shire with the bones of Normans and today - we are paid less! - I hate these colonies; dam' the foreigners and dam' their bloody foreign ways.' The old man would then relapse into a fog of nostalgia from which he would emerge only to emphasise - 'I'm going back, I want to go back, my good old Yorkshire calls to me - before I breathe my last. For once, I want to fill these old lungs with the air which so many generations of my ancestors had breathed. But ... the pension is too small. My son Basil will come out and then ... after I have seen him safely into the service and happily married, I want to go back home.'

Basil finally arrived; even the news of his impending arrival created something of a flutter in the little community facing life bravely among the heathens in this forgotten corner of the world. Mrs Walters sent a cable to her daughter Clara in Mussoorie, and was rewarded by the arrival of the dutiful daughter on special leave from her school. Mrs Stokes, not to be outdone, ensured the presence of her daughter Sylvia, till then away to Kurseong; and Mrs Lane, who had entertained hopes equally high, called her daughter Anna back from faraway Ooty.

Even the ordinary people of the town, the other side of the 'civil lines', soon came to recognise Basil. A better-than-average hockey player, he alone ensured the triumphant march towards the Trophy of the European team - the Panthers. On the ultimate day, it had appeared as if Basil was playing against the opposing team.

But there had been another side to this 'success' story - something that had caused old Moore to shed tears in private and pray to his god - 'O Lord; let me not experience the ultimate ignominy of being shunned, not at this stage in my life, when I am so near to closing my innings honourably.'

For in a few days the old man had understood that Basil was not quite, quite. A trifle mad, in fact. This fact however had not yet become public knowledge.

The other day old Watkins had been totally flabbergasted by the sight that had greeted him when he had stepped out into the garden to have a peaceful after-breakfast pipe: Basil was courteously offering a cigarette to the native cleaning woman.

His initial shock replaced by a deep anger, it had at last seemed to that old fire-eating veteran of countless wars that the morning sun had lost its brightness; his fingers automatically searching for a non-existent revolver in a non-existing holster, the old man had found himself picking up a flower-pot instead and then, had managed to control himself enough to emit a deep-throated roar - 'Basil!'

Basil had approached his father with a smile as fresh as the morning sunshine - 'Morning, Dad.'

'Come with me.'

The pair's departure, which represented a walk to the gallows, had actually culminated in the drawing-room. Seating Basil on a couch, old man Moore had expressed his opinion of his son: 'Do you realise that you are quite mad?'

'No, I don't. Dad, you are not well. Your eyes are bloodshot.'

'Quiet! Do you or do you not want to become acceptable?'

'Certainly I do.'

'Then never repeat such a performance, and be there at the Walters' for tea this afternoon.'

'All right.'

'And you will behave like a true Englishman.'

'Yes, Dad.'

All the invited guests were there on time at the Walters'. Mrs Lane was there; so was Mrs Stokes. And so were Clara, Anna and Sylvia, appropriately dressed and coiffured. The only one missing was the chief guest - Basil Moore.

Old Watkins was becoming nervous. Rather apologetically, he looked at the assembled matrons - 'I saw him getting dressed, he should be here pretty soon.'

Basil arrived a little later - perhaps ' made an entrance' is a better phrase - dressed in a blue shirt, red jacket and yellow plus-fours; and playing a mouth organ.

Watkins Moore wished for invisibility; he emitted a kind of croak 'Heavens!' There was a chorus of quickly hushed ladylike expressions, and Clara, Anna and Sylvia through some kind of unspoken empathy left their chairs and moved closer to their mothers. Old Moore gathered up his last remaining reserves and looked at his son - 'You've made a mistake. Basil; this is not a Fancy Dress Ball.'

Mrs Walters: This is not a club for clowns!

Mrs Stokes: This is not a gathering of gypsies!

Mrs Lane: This is Society!

The only response to this collective expression of disgust, shock and ostracism - from the side of the Object - was a charming smile and another shocking statement - 'All of you are feeling very hungry, aren't you?'

Clara, Anna and Sylvia left the room. The sound of the high heels expressing, with each collective tap, the rejection by a trio of young hearts of this apology for a young man from home.

With a leap rivalling that of a young goat for a particularly choice piece of greenery, Basil followed the retreating females out of the room. The next event followed almost immediately - high pitched screams leading to, one supposes, a few ladylike faints.

The gathering in the drawing room moved out as one body; Watkins attached himself to Basil's collar with one hand, and, with the deftness that had characterised his exploits on the battlefield, used the other to give a clout on the head to Basil with the bowl of his pipe;- 'Have you lost your senses?'

By this time the pitch of matronly voices had been climbing steadily. A melee, as the French, those lovers of emotional scenes, say. Mrs Walters was fanning her near and dear one with a dainty lace handkerchief but was nevertheless sufficiently conscious of her social responsibilites to glare at Mr Moore and, putting sufficient venom in her voice, to utter - 'Take your gypsy son away immediately.'

Old Moore was still holding onto Basil's collar. The old man had strength enough to shake that young person like a dog and repeat, almost as an echo of Mrs Walters - 'Swine! come home with me and we shall see.'

Old Watkins had, however, a bit of self-respect left. While going out of the house he fired his parting shot at Mrs Walters. - 'Gypsy! A scion of the Moore family a gypsy! You Walters and Stokes and Lanes... half-caste mongrels all!'

Basil laughed heartily - 'You are right, Dad! Totally daft, all of them.'

Dark days were upon old Moore. Basil appeared to aspire to new heights of madness day by day. Every argument of the old man, all his requests, had no effect. Basil had taken to walking the streets of the town, and old Watkins to imprisoning himself in his bungalow. He had no face left in society. All that he had left was to listen to the daily bulletins of Basil's exploits, and gradually lose what mental balance he had left.

The only regular visitor was Reverend Jacques. He was the only person who persisted - 'Don't give up hope, Mr Moore, your prodigal son will return home one day.' The opinion of Society was much more explicit - 'A rogue and a scoundrel! A deepwater fish. Be careful.'

The next year Basil again played in the hockey tournament, but this time for the local native club, Tarun Samity. Tarun Samity won the Trophy. The European Panthers lost and old Moore had another round of invective thrown at him by society.

Basil had now grown close to the members of Tarun Samity. The Indian members congratulated themselves for this favour bestowed upon them by a white man. The club secretary, Dhiren , an advocate by profession, arranged a feast in honour of Basil.

Basil had no inhibitions. At the feast, he gorged himself on 'khichdi'. Dhiren's uncle, the retired subjudge, watched this scene with a great sense of appreciation and respect - 'Only rarely does one come across an Englishman with such a large heart; I used to know an Englishman in the Jute Mill, he had great respect for prasad after a Satyanarayan puja.'

Dhiren's uncle advised Basil: 'Mr Moore, join the Army or the police - An upright Englishman like you must become an officer — it's the only proper thing to do.'

Basil whispered into Saroj's ear - 'Tell me, is the old gentleman slightly off?'

'Oh, no! he is Dhiren's uncle.'

Basil had suddenly turned unmindful. He made no reply to the many questions addressed to him by the many guests and family members. He was busy looking up to the first floor windows where a number of young female faces were to be seen. With his head on one side, he looked exactly like a cock.

This turn of events was not to the liking of the members of Tarun Samity. They had or perhaps assume that Basil's warmth of emotion was limited to the male sex. Dhiren, who had also observed Basil's behaviour, concentrated on his food.

Suddenly, Basil turned turned full face towards the window in question and emitted a piercing whistle.

Saroj was rather grave for his age and punctilious about social niceties. After the dinner he took Basil aside -

'Why were you staring at the ladies in that kind of uncivil manner?'

'Ladies?' Basil was surprised.

'Yes? At that window.'

Basil smiled charmingly. Then lowering his voice he whispered — 'Why were those girls looking at me in that way? What did they want?'

'Again you use the word girls. I am talking of those ladies of the household.'

Basil appeared to be ashamed of his behaviour. Touching his hat to his chest, he said:

'I am sorry. Please excuse me. Please call the ladies so that I may apologise for my behaviour.'

'No, leave it.'

'Please, I beg of you - call them at once.'

'Do be quiet, Basil: you don't know about our customs; that is why you are making such a suggestion. Hindu ladies do not present themselves before men who do not belong to their families.'

'Really?' Basil tried to digest this one - 'They do not show themselves to any outsider? Who do they marry then?'

Saroj's only reply was a short expletive in pure Bengali, a language as yet foreign to Basil.

The bad taste left by this incident was, however, removed over a period of time, due primarily to Basil's behaviour. After all, how could one dislike this open-hearted individual? Free with his money, fat contributions to the club chest, and petrol for the jeep on hunting expeditions. In fact, Basil was much less egotistic than even a fair-skinned Bengali. The adjectives applied to Basil by the rest of the European society were understandable as necessary in order to keep their own, rather their veneer of, aristocracy untarnished.

On the day of Saraswati Puja at Saroj's, Basil arrived uninvited. Blowing a cloud of smoke towards the idol of the goddess, he smiled appreciatively.

Saroj, a god-fearing young man, was not very happy. Outwardly he tried to appear affable - 'How nice of you to come; but don't approach the goddess with your shoes on.' - 'I am loking at your idol.' Basil gave his considered opinion: 'Nice looking girl. I like it.'

Saroj, took Basil aside- 'Be very judicious, my friend. Don't say anything concerning religion. No Hindu will stand for it.'

Basil was immediately apologetic - 'All right, I take back my words. I don't like your idol; will that do?'

Tarun Samity was staging a play. Basil was the man who contributed the most - both in terms of money and labour. Worked like a coolie when the stage was being erected and cleaned up all the gas lamps.

Basil turned up when the greenroom lights had just come on. Crawled in, in fact, through a gap in the canvas flaps - 'Where is the heroine?'

Biren and Rebati had just started shaving. It was Saroj who replied to Basil - 'Those two, they will act the female roles. They are not dressed yet.'

Basil stood there as if shell-shocked. Then made a face - 'Idiots! you think I am mad? Just you wait.'

In a few moments Basil had put out all the gas lamps and then he himself vanished. Saroj promised himself that he would have his own back. Twice he had pardoned Basil but there are limits!

Slowly, Tarun Samity started realising that somewhere there was a mistake. Dhiren was the worst sufferer. Basil would call him out in the small hours of the night, go and hide himself amongst the flowers in the garden. Attempts had, of course, been made to make Basil see the error of his ways, but to no avail. Dhiren's uncle had issued an ultimatum - 'If that white-faced monkey comes here again and creates a nuisance, he and his friend Dhiren will both taste the wrong end of my wooden slippers.'

In spite of all this, Basil turned up at Dhiren's in the middle of the night. Dhiren's uncle came out of the house to have a final showdown.

Basil, as if unaware of the undercurrents, immediately inquired after the old gentleman's health in rather expressive language - 'How are you, sick dog?'

Dhiren also came out. Almost apoplectic with rage, his uncle turned to him: 'Dhiren, this fellow is a grade one bastard. Did you hear what he said just now?'

Basil took out a flask and a small tumbler from his pocket. Uncle gave a roar - 'Hold it ! You want to drink. Go and do it in the station toilet. Not here. Now get out.'

Basil was quite unmoved - 'Come on Uncle, why get upset? This is called holy water. Even Dhiren likes it.'

Uncle's burning eyes turned to Dhiren in reply.

Tarun Samity realised then that Basil was neither as simple as he seemed nor was he possessed of the spirit of pure rebellion. There was a kind of ulterior motive to whatever he was up to. It was not safe for any gentleman to be seen in his company. He was interfering in matters of religion too.

Everbody therefore became conscious of his own self-respect. The close relationship between Basil and Tarun Samity was breaking up.

That year, in the hockey tournament, Basil played for Bahadur Club. Bahadur Club - whose secretary was Akshay the bidi-seller, whose manager was Latif the mechanic, and whose President was Prankumar the greengrocer. Most of the players were drawn from the ranks of the bus cleaners.

Society (even the Indian one) raised its nose and commented - 'God! such degradation.'

The memory of the warm welcome that they had once extended to this person of lowly tastes shamed them.

That Basil had fallen, was a fact. No objection seemed to be able to stop him. It was as if he was creating a world of his own, out of his own stupidities, his own destructive desire to lower himself in the eyes of others. His soul seemed to be possessed of an other-wordly concept of pleasure. Eagerly almost, Basil continued digging down into the forbidden strata of society, a man in search of a touchstone whose existence he was not sure of and whose nature only he perhaps knew.

Basil's routine these days began with tea at Haripada's tea stall in the mornings. He had taken to smoking bidis. Afternoons he spent playing the tabla at Latif the mechanic's. Evenings were spent at Akshay the bidi-seller's, lying on a bench listening to gramophone records and whistling to the tune of the foreign music.

Sometimes, a good samaritan, looking at an Englishman in obvious distress, would ask, 'Where do you live?' Basil would reply gravely - 'Benares.'

No matter where he spent the day, late evenings would always find Basil at Prankumar's house. Prankumar, the hooligan from Calcutta who had turned over a new leaf, gave Basil a human reception. He and his family - that is, his wife Champa and son Keshto.

The first day, the two friends had parked themselves on the outer verandah with a bottle of country liquor produced by Prankumar. Champa had observed this alien from a distant planet through a crack in the door. Basil also had been surprised, his thoughts torn apart by the intermittent tinkle of glass bangles. Time and again, his eyes had tried to penetrate the secret of the half-closed door.

After finishing the bottle, Prankumar had called out - 'Champa, serve the food.'

Champa did not belong to the strata of society where it was not proper for women to meet unknown males. Earlier, there had been gambling sessions on this verandah. Often, as in such sessions what would begin amicably, would degenerate into fisticuffs. On those occasions it was Champa who had the job - performed quite willingly - of pulling her husband out of that session and breaking up the gang with her favorite broom. But on this day Champa was unnerved. She was unsure of herself, and knowing herself to be so, was almost shivering.

Prankumar called again - 'Serve food quickly.' So Champa had to come out with bread and curry on two plates. Seeing her come out of the room with her burden, Basil stood up quickly with his hat in his hand. Prankumar, more pragmatic than many others, said - 'Come on, sit down. No need to make a fuss.'

Basil sang three songs. One after the other. Inside the room, Champa gave silent vent to a great deal of mirth.

Basil returned home late at night to find old Watkins in a semi comatose position on the sofa. Basil knelt down beside his father, and with his hands on the old man's knees said softly - 'Dad.'

'Who, Basil?'

'Good news, Dad. Today I met an Indian lady.'

Old Moore widened his eyes. 'Heavens! you have made a mistake, dear boy, a big mistake. There are no ladies amongst the Indians. You have seen Satan's shadow.'

When Basil was about to get up old Moore spoke very sweetly - 'Listen Basil, I have to talk to you. An appointment offer has come for you from Army Headquarters. Tell me, what shall I reply?'

'Write to them that Basil Moore is a madcap.'

'Get out. Away with you!'

'Don't feel sorry, Dad. I have thought this matter over and I am now confident that I am totally mad.'

Prankumar's home became Basil's regular evening haunt. It was as if he waited the days out only for those evenings. Prankumar had given him free rein. Of course, there had been talk. Nevertheless....

When Prankumar had a bit too much, Basil would just begin to feel warm. He would shout in a hoarse voice, 'Kishto! Kishto!'

Champa would have no choice but to come out and talk to him in a low voice - 'Don't shout. You know how people talk.'

'All right. Send Kishto then. I want to pet him.'

'No, I won't. Go home now. It's late.'

One evening in such an atmosphere Prankumar had, as usual, had a bit too much, enough in fact to make him a little morbid. 'It's a dog's life. I don't want to live any more, I want to commit suicide.'

'Okay!' Basil was matter-of-fact. 'Go ahead and die. I shall take charge of your wife and child.'

'Bloody f——' Prankumar picked up the empty bottle and and hit Basil on the ear with it.

Basil could only hold his head in his hands. Champa rushed out of the room and took the bottle from Prankumar's hand in a split second. 'Now you want to be hanged, or spend the rest of your life in jail, maybe?'

Drops of blood were falling on the sleeves of Basil's jacket. Champa called softly 'Sahib'. Basil did not reply.

Champa stood quietly for some time. Then, putting her hand on his golden head she called softly again, 'Basil? Sahib?'

Prankumar tried to raise the bottle again. 'Right before my eyes?'

Suddenly Basil stood up and said: 'Excuse me. I shall never say that again. Goodbye.'

Next morning nobody saw Basil in the town. His associates, of course, came to know what had happened the previous night. Akshay, Latif and many others caught hold of Prankumar. All of them were angry and even hurt: 'You had to hit him so badly just because he is a trifle mad? And you of all people! Drinking away his money every evening! You should be ashamed. If a tiger forgets his strength and mixes with a flock of sheep, do the sheep have to show their own strength by butting him?'

Champa told Prankumar very clearly: 'Wherever he is, go and bring him back. He must be badly hurt; you have hurt him and now you have to make amends.'

The local police inspector turned up with a constable - 'You had the gall to hit the son of Mr Moore ; if you think you can get away with this kind of hooliganism you are greatly mistaken, my fellow.' And the inspector caught hold of Prankumar's ear.

Suddenly and to everyone's utter surprise, Basil, with his head bandaged, turned up on a bicycle - 'And who the hell are you?'

'I am Rai Bahadur Maheswari Prasad Singh, Inspector of Police.'

'Look here, Mr Policeman. If I find you butting your nose into my affairs I shall personally ensure that you don't have a nose left.' Basil accompanied his statement with a gesture involving his shoe-heel and the earth, much to the amusement of the onlookers.

The police inspector, thwarted and insulted, could barely control his anger - 'All right, if that's the way you feel. I was here at your father's specific request and I am now thinking that it would not be a bad idea to report everything to him.'

'Yes, you had better go and do that.'

A totally unconcerned Basil walked across to Prankumar's house, parked himself on the verandah and shouted - 'Kishto! Kishto!' The door opened a crack and one had a glimpse of the *pallav* of a saree and a female hand.

Latif suppressed his amusement; he raised his voice for everybody's benefit - 'Come on, friends, out. Our job is over, we are not needed here any more.'

Akshay added - 'Yes, let's. This is foreign wine. A bit too sweet.'

Prankumar had changed. He had become quite detached from his family. After the incident he had been pursued by the devils of his own guilt. Somehow, it seemed to have made him softer. Not only had he stopped protesting, he had practically stopped speaking to anyone.

The change in Champa was also noticeable. She could now be observed dolling herself up every evening, a labour of love that kept her quite busy. She had gone to the extent of changing her style of doing her hair every day. Even Prankumar had observed this and had commented on this - 'You want to put the memsahibs to shame.'

Holi, the festival of colours, arrived in the small Chhotanagpur town with its usual bagful of nature's springtime bounties.

This one day in the year it was a time to find some pleasure in all one's pain; nature cooperated - the full moon rising in majestic splendour over the heads of the tall firs, a perfect counterpoint to the last rays of the setting sun over the vast fields - fantasy taking over from reality for a few brief hours. In the peculiar irony of life, men and women experienced a tightening of nerves, an anticipation of pleasure as painful as the world from which they sought to escape.

There was a cloud of coloured powder over Chowkbazaar. The mad beating of drums accompanied by equally possessed dancers; roads and footpaths coloured by the ejections of countless water-guns filled with coloured water. The natural results were represented by the frogs who had left their natural habitat of roadside drains, quite unable to stand the attack on their sensitivities made by hundreds of drunks throwing up at regular, and irregular, intervals.

About five hundred enthusiastic onlookers were encouraging the efforts of a few clowns. The centre point of attention being mad Basil, riding an ass and with a biscuit tin on his head. Basil punctuated his incessant circling on his peculiar mount with drinks of raw liquor from a bottle and handfuls of chocolates. The low-caste boys who made up the majority of the audience, showed their appreciation of Basil's antics by throwing handfuls of coloured powder on him, with maniacal shouts of joy.

Champa had busied herself cooking a number of novel dishes - this day of all days. She was also dressed for the festival. A check saree and stole with silver sequins. Broad silver belt at her waist and silver bells on her ankles. The whole ensemble enhanced by a broad silver necklace around her slim neck. 'Her normally large eyes were enhanced by lines of kohl.

Champa was aware that Prankumar would not return home that day. Every year of her marriage it had been the same. The two days of Holi he seemed to vanish into thin air.

This year, however Champa was expecting quite a different man: the sound of steps on the verandah - Basil with a handful of coloured powder. 'Champa' - Champa shivered. Today Basil had called out to her directly, taken her name. His usual practice was to call for her son Keshto.

'Champa, today is Holi, *Holi hai*.'

Champa had to come out of the room,. Basil painted her face with the coloured powder in his hand. Champa wiped her face with the pallav of her saree and stood there silently.

'Champa.' Basil's soft words were belied by the false courage reflected in his somewhat unfocused eyes.

'Yes, Basil.'

'I ... I want to tell you something.'

Champa was afraid. But this was a fear that lessened distances, not increased them. Physically, she stood rooted to the spot, unable to move, as if her legs had lost all power to move. She made a last effort - a request, begging almost - 'No...no. Please don't.'

'I have to, don't you see?'

'No, please don't tell me, Basil.'

Basil's head kept falling forward but Basil had not moved away; Champa's fears had also not deserted her; but she summoned up enough courage to say, wiping her face once again in the age-old concession of women - 'All right; tell me another day.'

'Good night.' Basil emitted a tuneful whistle and lumping himself on the seat of a passing rickshaw majestically stated, 'Chalo, the Retreat.' Then, in his exuberance, he could not restrain himself from letting go in his normal bass - 'There is a green hill far away....'

Normally all festivals are succeeded by the onset of a feeling of anticlimax, ennui, almost. For Champa, the only sequel was a fever, only the fever. She was unconscious from the very first day. Prankumar, to his eternal credit, did not spare any effort in getting her medical attention. He sold her jewellery - the same jewellery she had worn on Holi day - when his money ran out.

A week passed. Returning from a hockey match. Basil saw the civil surgeon Dr Mitra coming out of Prankumar's house. Basil barred his way. 'Well, surgeon; and who are you treating? The patient or your wallet?'

'What, what did you say? You have the guts to complain about my course of treatment?'

'That, my dear pill-roller, is my abiding sorrow; instead of putting you in jail I have to be content with making complaints.'

'Mr Moore, you should learn to speak properly. We doctors can only treat a patient. Whether the patient becomes well or not is God's will.'

Basil quickly spread his hat in front of the doctor - 'Please, doctor, return the fees that you have taken; I would rather give them to God.'

Prankumar came out and took Basil aside. Not to be silenced so easily, Basil emitted his parting shot — 'Take my advice, surgeon, take a job in a veterinary hospital. Animals don't complain.' To Prankumar he said - 'Listen, my friend, stop depending on these swine; these people are very smart. I'll go and bring an apothecary; they know less and therefore cause less damage.'

The darkness of the evening found Basil roaming the streets of the town. Finally, a faded signboard written in English drew him to the verandah of a house.

'Kaviraj,' Basil called.

Latu Kaviraj came on the verandah with a kerosene lamp throwing its sooty light on the pallor of his face at the sight of the Englishman.

'I don't keep alcohol.'

'Can you treat fever?'

'Fever? Even the sound of my pestle is good enough for a cure.'

'Can you cure in a day?'

'I can cure in an hour. But I shall need to be paid well.'

'All right, come with me.'

'Extra six annas for reading the pulse.'

'All right.'

'And the best medicine will cost you seven annas.'

'All right, all right., but make it quick, man.'

Latu Kaviraj had, however, sensed something in the urgency. He continued standing at the same spot with much wringing of hands and running them through his thin hair. He finally gave vent to his greed - 'Sahib, why don't you come out with some advance?'

'What madness!' Basil dropped a four-anna coin on Latu's outstretched hand and, almost pulling him as one would a recalcitrant child, brought him, tired and out-of-breath, to Prankumar's house. Champa had become comatose; her body was losing its warmth; the death-rattle was in her throat.

Basil spent the evening in the liquor shop. He drank his fill and then went and lay down on the sacks of vegetables in Prankumar's shop - himself as incapable of any volition as those necessary adjuncts of Prankumar's life. In the depths of the night, passers by heard mad Basil's croaks and whines and sighs and told themselves — the man is really drunk today.

The small procession with Champa's body anticipated the sun on its way to the cremation grounds. Prankumar with Keshto on his lap, Akshay, Latif, and the various other members of the Bahadur Club and finally, Basil - hockey-stick in hand and a bit of straw between his teeth.

The file of human beings wended its unsteady, snake-like way towards the river, thin and emaciated, a mere trickle of rippling liquid, completely outdone in presence by the broad sandy banks, now slightly damp with the early morning dew. The men of the cremation grounds were building the funeral pyre, were cutting sandalwood into small pieces. Akshay, Latif and Basil, the list of friends, unrelated to the dead or the living, sat on a dune a little distance away, watching the proceedings.

Champa's body was lowered from the cot on which it had been brought to the grounds. They waded into slightly deeper water for the ritual bathing. After dipping the body in the water a few times it was laid down reverently on the sand. Somebody suggested - 'The dead should not wear bangles.'

Immediately, somebody took a piece of stone and beating at Champa's wrists with it, took off the bangles.

Misirji, the priest, said, 'Now rub the body over with ghee.' Prankumar took a handful of ghee and started rubbing it all over Champa's feet, chest and head.

Misirji encouraged him — 'Go ahead; it's necessary; but you have to harden your heart a bit for these things. When the soul leaves the body, what is left? The Atman leaves only an earthen doll for the rest of us. There is no shame.'

By this time Basil had stood up and the hockey-stick in his hand was looking more and more like a weapon; the wind had made wings out of Basil's red tie. Latif said, a trifle urgently - 'Sit down, Basil. Sit and watch.'

'No, I won't sit. Terrible. They will roast her now.'

Misriji had already started his litany -*'Om devaschagni mukha sarve hutta shanang grihitra ....'* Prankumar was diligently rubbing ghee on the body, the head was getting a shine from it in the morning sun. A clod of earth was sticking to her raven hair. The check saree, now wet and loose, was spread out on the sand.

Suddenly a burnt brick hit Misriji in the chest. The force of it laid the old priest out completely. Latif and Akshay shouted together - 'Hold him, hold him, all of you!' Basil, the strength of madness in him, was not to be stopped so easily, however. He had jumped right in the middle of the crowd, his hockey-stick like a flail, and was laying about him, seemingly completely out of his senses. Prankumar was the first one to catch Basil - by attaching himself to a fistful of Basil's hair.

Basil was lost. As if unable to recognise his erstwhile friends, he could only display a deep desire for revenge - in his shaking hands, in the fire in his blue eyes, in the deep creases in the flesh of his cheeks and the skin of his forehead.

By this time, many had armed themselves with bamboo sticks. Within a couple of minutes Basil had lost his hockey stick. Latif and the others came and pulled him off. They took him quite a distance from the scene. Akshay, tired and sweating, wiped his hand — 'The foreign devil - more dangerous than real ghosts.'

By this time the small group was quite distant. Latif let go of Basil. 'Go home now, my friend.'

Basil walked along the snaking wound of the river. The midday sun raged over an erring world. Leaving the scavengers, a flock of crows intent on washing themselves in the shallow waters, Basil walked on over countless bodies of dead snails and scallops.

The ground sloped upwards towards the foothills in front of him. Behind him stretched a vast expanse of paddy fields. Nearby, silent under the shade of eucalyptus trees, lay The Retreat.

Nobody to watch him here. No one to look at him, no one to touch him. Basil lay down on the grass and closed his eyes. The sun traced its predetermined way through the skies, noon changed to afternoon, afternoon to early evening. Even the birds in the paddy fields wended their way home. Basil did not feel anything, did not understand, was not conscious of the passage of the day.

Waking was an experience. It seemed that the turret of the castle was in front of his eyes, a huge star seemed to be growing by its side. The darkness behind was growing banks of fog on its chest over an imagined vista of distant moors. A lark, flying towards the distant hillocks, left behind the notes of his song like a tangible reminder of his own state of mind. Basil walked on.

Basil was walking through vineyards, crossing fields of daisies; somehow, today of all days, the air seemed to be laden with the mild smell of orchids. Basil was walking through a dream, in a dream-world, a world of fantasia made real by his footsteps alone, a flight of magpies disturbed by his flying feet. Crickets playing their music from hidden corners of the worn out bricks of the old abbey.

Basil was now near the dyke. Standing on the bridge, he heard the country church orchestra play Brahms through the distant sounds of a spring. In front of him was the sandstone rampart, backed by the huge gates of history - looking at him as if with the undiluted love of affectionate progenitors.

Basil could understand very clearly - a change, a change had occurred. His veins had finally fought free of a flow of poison — as if a personal ghost had been laid to rest. He understood and, understanding, breathed more freely. Filled his lungs with the new air, welcomed a new world inside himself.

translated by Bappa Chakravarty

Homecoming

Singapore and the jungles of Johore Bahru, one thousand five hundred miles away, have been bombed. And the backlash, a thousand scared live-dead bodies, broke on the platforms of the Howrah and Sealdah stations like a smelly, confused wave. Looking at this scene of human stupidity and naivete, Dhrubesh was dumbstruck. He had come to Sealdah station to put an old aunt on the train. Everyone was escaping - the young, the old, the men and the women; from what, they had not understood: a crazed collective expression of naked childlike fear, half-dead, pallid, lost faces - coughing, shouting, choking.

Fear makes everyone run. The deer run at the sound of the hunter's gun. Over the grasslands, around the bends of a small river, Imprinting their hoof-marks on the riverbanks, they look left, they look right, and with surpassing grace, they vanish like some airy creation of nature, leaving one to wonder at the deep intimacy and warmth of that collective feeling of fear.

Could there be a greater contrast than the expression here, on this platform? A special train had just come on to the platform. Before it could come to rest, the maniacal crowd fell on it in a body, like a stone from some giant's catapult. Broke into pieces at the doors of the compartments; and the shouting, jostling ugliness began again. The upper class compartments were no better. Dhrubesh was taking his aunt towards a second class compartment when suddenly a man with a suitcase on his shoulder fell on him. A sharp jab from his elbows was enough to make Dhrubesh's old aunt sit down right there and, before Dhrubesh could ever think of counter-action, the man had vanished into the crowd of passengers.

At home the maidservant gave notice. She wanted to go back that very day. Insisted on being paid for the month. Dhrubesh accepted defeat with bad grace. The maidservant had overheard a number of 'bhadralok' voice their considered opinions: 'The Japanese have arrived, dressed as women. They were seen last night hiding in the mango groves. After that they have gone and hidden themselves somewhere else.' This was enough for the maidservant.

Harbilasbabu was Dhrubesh's uncle - a distant relationship. Harbilasbabu was rich and a landlord. Walking down the street in front of his house in the evening, Dhrubesh suddenly decided to pay a visit. On a big rug in the drawing room, Haribilasbabu's four sons-in-law were reading detective novels, each clutching a bolster. Harbilasbabu himself was concentrating on the plans for a new house.

Dhrubesh was a little surprised. 'You are still here?'

'Why? What has gone wrong?' His uncle was equally surprised by the question.

'The war; there have been bombings in Singapore; people are running away!'

His uncle continued looking at him. The four sons-in-law raised their heads slowly. They did not seem to have heard Dhrubesh; rather their white, calm eyes seemed to be looking at Dhrubesh's words, as if what we had said was part of the printed words they were reading, remote, phantasmagorical.

The servant brought some honey and ayurvedic medicine in a stoneware bowl. Uncle licked at it and calmly instructed the servant about his dinner menu.

Dhrubesh made a last desperate try. 'Everybody seems to be worried about this war.' Even this had no effect. The pairs of white eyes continued looking at him. Mummified eyes, cold eyes, dead eyes from a thousand years, suddenly raised from their earthen coffins.

Dhrubesh left. It was no use. These people did not care. If this world of atoms and molecules suddenly turned into an unimaginable entity, a cosmic whirlpool, even then his uncle would not forgot to realise the monthly rents, would continue to instruct his servant about the nightly dinner menu.

While coming out Dhrubesh saw Lakshmi Muhuri, the clerk, sitting with his books and papers in the office room. Dhrubesh approached him - 'What are your plans, Lakshmibabu, now that the war is almost at our doorstep?'

The only reply from Lakshmi Muhuri was a kind of croak, 'If I have to die, I shall die here!'

Dhrubesh was no longer interested in talking to this creature. This man was already half-dead, resigned to his fate. He had lost even the energy to fly away.

In this atmosphere of fear and tension, Sanatanbabu's drawing room was occupied every evening. The daily congregation of friends continued to assemble early and disperse late. Gambling and politics. Sometimes politics overruled gambling and sometimes it was the other way round. Given the natural inclination of the members, however, it was really chance that was the major participant.

Dhrubesh is an irregular member of this club. Rarely does the topic of war crop up. Always Sanatanbabu's reaction is the same - 'I'll give it to you in writing, nothing is going to happen. These people who are running away - they are all crazy, I tell you.'

Dhrubesh would pick up the gauntlet. 'Why? The Japanese have already come so far, and you think they cannot come here?'

'No, I don't mean that.'

'Then you think they will be defeated at Singapore?'

'No, not that either.'

'Then what ?'

'I am just telling you that nothing will happen - absolutely nothing will happen.'

Sanatanbabu was secure in this belief. he did not care for rationality; his happiness lay in his total faith in his own opinion.

History teacher at the Annadacharan Memorial School, and a salary of forty rupees. This was Dhrubesh - walking the battlefield of life laden with his personal burden of a hungry, deprived, lower middle class family like other people; ordinary problems. ordinary deprivations, magnified and made extraordinary only through the merit of being personal to him.

This was not, however, all that there was to the man called Dhrubesh. He belonged to history. That was his life. He had been spawned by it. Its world was populated by the continuity of sorrows and happinesses of this bounteous earth, like birds inhabiting a virgin, untouchable jungle. The contradictions of this world surprised him incessantly and its tensions led him to greater levels of appreciation of the *fact* of history, of the historicity, as it were, of each separate event since time immemorial. Consciousness touched him, as it had touched man, those aeons ago, Consciousness that had turned a creature into an instrument of his own volition, changed, nay transmuted an animal into the arbiter of his own destiny.

There are of course many other teachers in the school. They teach students the Grand Strategy of getting through examinations. They are reputed, and they are paid better. Dhrubesh Dutta tells students the story of the Skull of Sialkot - the pages of history remaining unread in that bit of bone, the story of our ancestors. Who was he? He was a soldier, he had fought animals with his stone spear, standing before *his* cave, and died defending what he thought belonged to him - establishing with his personal sacrifice the right to possession, the right to think aggressively. A sacrifice that, after thousands of years, makes us *men*, possessed of the consciousness that leaves us free to act, for ourselves. That is why Dhrubesh Dutta never gets tuitions. Careful parents dislike freethinking schoolteachers.

Rama was putting Tutu to sleep. A little earlier, her neighbours, Dinubabu's family, had come to meet her before going away. They were the last people in her block to leave. They had stayed on for quite some time but had also, finally, lost courage.

The ladies had left, leaving behind Dinubabu with a servant; mainly because Dinubabu had a job, and a good one at that. His wife had said to Rama, 'We are leaving, Rama. Haradhan the astrologer has said that whatever is going to happen will happen within three months. That's why I have decided to spend some time at Deoghar, and postponed Bina's marriage.' Rama had replied. 'So you people are leaving me all alone,' and Bina had whispered,' 'Are you not also planning to go away, then?'

Rama had smiled, 'You want me to be frank? I really cannot bear to be parted from him.' Her words had reached the ears of Dinubabu's wife. She had said, with no attempt to disguise her anger, 'People do go when they have some place to go to. Who does not want to be with the family? When times are bad, it's much more sensible to lessen the burden a bit. A few days' separation has never destroyed love or affection, if the feelings are strong enough.'

And they had left. That last statement of Dinubabu's wife had been both clear and pointed. Rama really has nowhere to go. This essential truth was known to her, and to them.

Rama had lost her mother early. As she was an only child, her marriage had left her father free to leave this materialistic world and become a sadhu - a personal goal that he had fulfilled within a week of the marriage ceremony. Perhaps Rama's attachment to her small family was so strong because there were no outside distractions, no other emotional attachments. She had never thought about what might have been, confident in her own commitment, her love, for her family. Today, the cruel truth behind all those statements completely tore apart that tenuous fabric, so lovingly woven.

There were no bombings. But the schools closed down. All the students left for what their parents had decided were safer abodes. Dhrubesh lost his job.

If truth be told, this mishap left Dhrubesh extremely depressed. Rama and Tutu - their welfare, their expectations, were uppermost in his confused mind. Rama - totally immersed in her family - her only occupation the building of a gilded cage. Tutu is only six months old. In these six months Rama has perfected her plans to make a man out of him, from his diet to his education and including his marriage. Dhrubesh's sorrow is that the lifeline to this fantasia, his job, is no longer there.

'I am jobless.' Dhrubesh went out of the house, leaving behind three simple words like the irrevocable pronouncement of a particularly insidious, cruel fate. Rama, her hand on Tutu's small body, shivered repeatedly, as if it had suddenly turned very cold.

There is no longer a job to go to; but this is not the only truth in Dhrubesh's life. The smoky evenings in that small Tollygunge flat are as a backdrop to him; scenes jump before his eyes - bayonets flashing in the Libyan desert, a thousand footfalls in the hard snow outside Kharkor, white waves in the wake of a fast warship, the crankling of tanktreads all over Europe, the roar of bombers in the night skies - to Dhrubesh all these are the components of an extraordinary orchestra, playing the dawn of a new age.

He feels, he thinks; there is a clash between personal good and collective good. This fire of rebirth is at once the funeral of nationalisms, the mechanics of economics, the blind haughtiness of feudalism, old methods of exploitation. To him, this is the beginning of the end of imperialisms. The fat on the body of empires is melting, Dhrubesh feels; he is overwhelmed by a curious sense of romanticism, of adventure, of a *new* feeling, a novel realisation. This feeling possesses him, rolls over him like a wave.

Rama brought a cup of tea and put it down in front of Dhrubesh. Her face was sombre. All of a sudden a plane flew over, very low.

Rama jerked up at the noise. Both of them looked at Tutu. The child was smiling and waving his tiny limbs.

With a spontaneous laugh Dhrubesh took little Tutu up on his lap. The gesture lightened the atmosphere and also perhaps the depression that had afflicted both of them for the last two days. 'Are you not thinking about the future? ' Rama asked in a wifely tone.

'Of course I am.'

Rama had no other question to ask. She was not satisfied, though. If she had been sure that Dhrubesh was actually looking for a job she'd have had no complaints. But she knew her man. The war had somehow obsessed him; all he'd look forward to would be the war reports in the newspapers. She remembered distinctly that at the time of the Spanish civil war, only a few years before, he would wake up in the night, a man possessed - in delirium almost. There were nights when he would not even sleep - would walk the night away.

Dhrubesh went out, with no word as to when he would return, maybe one in the morning. On his way to no particular destination, he met Nitish. That very serious young man was carrying a huge bundle of posters under his arm. The sight of Dhrubesh occasioned a whoop and a holler almost akin to that emitted by a posse when finally the outlaw is lassoed.

'Dhrubeshda, you really are something, we have been looking for you for days, and you simply vanish from the scene. How do you expect us to cope with everything?'

'What is it? What are you young fellows up to now?'

'You have to come to the public meeting that we are organising at the park tomorrow evening, Also you shall have to give a speech.'

It was as if Dhrubesh had found what he was looking for. The opportunity made him happy. He told Nitish - 'Of course I shall speak; but I warn you, I shall say what I feel, I may not say what you want me to say. If you have any objections, tell me now.'

'All right, say what you like,' Nitish smiled, with the inner joy of an organiser who has managed to get hold of a last-minute speaker for free.

Rama's world is a small one. A small house in the poorer section of Tollygunge. Married for only a few years, her love for Dhrubesh is much more than that for herself. Finally, the entry of Tutu into her small closed world opened up new vistas, gave her the chance to dream anew, experience again the painful pleasure of anxiety for a newly acquired possession, sleepless nights made memorable by the pure joy of motherhood. Tireless, constantly trying to dissolve her self into that of her little world. She was satisfied.

Then came the blow. War. Joblessness. Worries of a different order. Such a large world, well known saints and sinners, huge dimensions of greed and destruction, a world large enough to absorb the body-blow of a world war. Let that world reap its own fruits, wallow in its own destructive actions; why couldn't an unkind fate leave her small world, with its minute joys and sorrows, alone? Rama had all the blind complaints against the war of a bird whose carefully built, delicate nest is destroyed by an unthinking, malevolent storm. Why couldn't those hundreds of thousands of soldiers have fought amongst themselves without touching her small world? Even a mention of the war was enough to sour Rama's mood. To her, this war, this destroyer of homes, was a personal enemy.

For Dhrubesh, the war was a concerto played fortissimo, on the joy of re-creation. The war was the harbinger of a new age. It seemed strange to him that people around him, the thousands populating this city, were unaware of this cosmic revolution in the affairs of men, this re-birth and re-definition of societies akin in their far-reaching effects to the births of new planets, the creation of whole new solar systems. This tremendous contradiction, and the realisation of it, overwhelmed him, possessed him, enveloped all his waking thoughts and senses. Dhrubesh would walk miles along the streets of Calcutta, spending his mornings and evenings reading the posters, studying the speeches of political leaders, listening in on public meetings, watching processions. This search for the *waking* people, the *conscious* people, that small breed of men and women who had realised that this World War was the precursor to worldwide social change, occupied all his consciousness.

The whole day he would look for a job and, in the evening, tired and emotionally weary, would lie down on the grass of Curzon Park - his senses dulled, his body a mere repository for a mind tired as a bird is tired after fighting the bars of its cage through which, it knows, the sky beckons.

Memories crowd him sometimes; shimmering images of a small village in far off Chittagong - Birajpur. Dhrubesh has not been back for a number of years; the home of his childhood becomes overgrown with weeds - shelter to snakes, scorpions and porcupines, in his fading visions; the peace of Birajpur melds into the workaday problems, sounds and crowds of Calcutta.

Birajpur - where time stands still; where the whips of clock-hands do not force life into ignoble paths - the small waves of the canal rise slowly and subside equally slowly - setting the measure for the slow rise and fall of the blacksmith's hammer; giving the signal to the tired farmer to take it easy on the plough. An orchestra of life that never exceeds the pace of the allegro. Dhrubesh remembers the narrow road by the side of the pond, the tide-water in the canal as of a maiden's eyes bidding good-bye to her lover; the supreme sensual pleasure of youth, physically experienced by jumping off from the narrow wooden bridge into the waters of the canal and feeling at home with the fishes, swimming for no particular length of time, and to no particular place. He does not remember anybody from the village, but still, after so many years, people from that almost-forgotten corner of the world write to him.

'We have heard that you have grown up, got yourself a job, have even married. Would you lose your self-respect if you came back home even once? Please do come. Summertime is best, and you can eat ripe mangoes - do bring our dear daughter-in-law with you. Everybody wants to meet her. Yours etc., your uncle from the house to the north.'

No matter how hard he tries, Dhrubesh cannot remember who the writer is, this person from a faraway memory, closer to him in affection than many others who came later!

The students of the village school write to him - 'Please send us a Message for our new school magazine. It's handwritten, and we shall await your Message most eagerly.'

Dhrubesh wonders, where do these people get his address from? From where do they collect all the news of him? Perhaps they cannot accept the idea that Dhrubesh - a member of the tiny world of the village, *family*, as such - can get lost in the crowds of the wide world beyond. As if the umbilical chord of tribal ties has continued down from the Stone Age right to this affectionate little village in Chittagong - a final whiff of scent from an almost dry blossom.

No, Dhrubesh chides himself, this has not been proper - it has not been *right*, this forgetfulness of his. He is secretly ashamed.

The public meeting in the park was well attended. The crowd overflowed beyond the railings. Hundreds of red flags, unconscious symbols of a coming storm.

Dhrubesh stood up to speak. 'Friends. Today we gather together as on a stormy night. This climactic event of the century has imposed the most difficult of duties upon us. This meeting today - is symbolic - of non-combatants gathered together under the tent of a great soldier.'

Somebody from the back made a poisonous, sarcastic comment. There was a roar of laughter from the crowd. A couple of volunteers requested with folded hands: 'Please, please don't behave in that way.'

Dhrubesh's calm voice prevailed over the disturbance; firm with his resolve, he continued, 'We are all soldiers. We are all Indians. Turn the pages of history and discover for yourself how many times we have been invaded. We have never compromised with the enemy, never come to terms with destruction. We respect that history of our country, that record of continual struggles. We have not forgotten that the Huns could not finally prevail upon us - the quivers of the Kushan archers were burnt by the revolutionary courage of the Indian people.

'Hail to the Hindu religion' - Dhrubesh's words provoked a great roar from one section of the assembly. Dhrubesh continued, albeit with a bit of disgust in his voice - 'No, never;. I never meant that — say Hail to the people, to their struggle.'

This was enough to generate a commotion. A group of disgruntled persons turned around and shouted abuse; amidst more commotion, they left.

'Friends. Think where we stand today. The hosts of the enemy are about to descend upon us like a poisonous flood. Every atom of this earth is scented with the breath of a hundred generations; where shall we go?' Again some people raised voices - 'Hail to the new Asia!'

Dhrubesh lost his temper - 'Hail to the new man. Hail to the God of the world's people. I feel sorry for those who are only thinking of Asia, they have the wisdom of the one-eyed deer — and they sow the seeds of their own destruction.'

This was the last straw. From all sides there were sounds of protest. Dhrubesh was hit on the hand by a brick thrown from one side. This served, however, only to encourage Dhrubesh. In his excitement he stood up on the table and continued to shout,'No amount of hooting or brickbatting can deter me. I shall stand here and shout before you people - those who want to attack my country are my enemies, in no way can they be anything else. They are the new poison of the twentieth century. Their warehouses are full of wood for our funeral pyres. They are coming. Like the Babylonian plague, they will destroy kingdoms and societies anew. They mouth empty promises of freedom and they carry steel handcuffs wrapped in silver foil.'

After a physical bout with the volunteers, the protesters finally left the meeting.

Dhrubesh's voice was now breaking down from the emotional strain - 'Please listen to me, my friends. We had lost the courage of our convictions. Today we get a chance to shed our fears, to break the shackles of our meaningless anxieties. I see reflected in your eyes the light of that torch. This is freedom, my friends. This is our only sheet anchor in our journey through the darkness of the night.' The clapping was like the sound of lightning all over the assembled crowd. A new wave of consciousness seemed to sweep the gathering.

'How dead is dead? Shall we be as dead as the steps of the burning ghat? Living with the wounds of every stranger's footsteps, living in silence, living in stealth and degradation? How many aeons will it take for us to come alive, for us to *be*? Friends, I stand amongst you here and I see the face of the future. This wild dance of death will calm down; our sacrifices will make that new dawn brighter and show the way for the procession of the Free Man.'

After he had walked away some distance from the meeting, Dhrubesh looked back. He could still hear the confused sounds of the assembly and then. 'Long live the revolution! *Inquilab Zindabad*!' The shouts broke like millions of tons of water from a tornado. A thousand fists, the symbol of the collective resolution of a people.

Those whom the people respected, those to whom people were accustomed to run for a few words of comfort and wisdom, these were the people who were spreading their views all over the newspapers every day - 'We have nothing to do with this war. This is a war between Britain and Japan. India is neutral.'

In a small restaurant off Dharmatala, Dhrubesh was privy to the opinions expressed by both known and unknown people - there is nothing to be done. Protest and contrary opinions only made the interlude bitter. Dhrubesh sometimes felt like asking them, 'Who does India belong to ?'

Finally one day he did ask the question; after much soul searching and getting the better of his common sense and conquering the fearsome possibility of that contrary answer, he took the plunge.

It happened exactly as he had feared. The cafe crowd was unanimous in its opinion - 'How can we call this our country? Have the British left us with any right to do something for our country? We can do nothing - there is nothing to be done?

Dhrubesh came out of the cafe. It seemed to him that the whole city was already destroyed - ugly in its brokenness. The houses had the look of ancient ant-heaps; the people like aimless worms, intent only on feeding on dirt and garbage.

His head finally started spinning from all the aimless walking in the midday sun. It was still a couple of miles to Tollygunge. Seldom had he felt so depressed. People were looking for the peace of the graveyard; the messages of history had not become the truths of life for these apologies for Man. They were in search of the easy way out. The deadly disease of impotence, dressed in empty promises, in the bright colours of nothingness, was upon them. Dhrubesh saw a headless stone colossus crushing the earth of his country under its misshapen legs.

Rama had lost her patience; it was past one-thirty in the afternoon and Dhrubesh had not yet come in for lunch. These days he did not speak unless spoken to. Rama could well imagine the seriousness of effort that was behind the stated purpose of searching for a job.

Dhrubesh entered. Rama said, 'How many battles did you win?'

Dhrubesh did not reply. He took a towel and went for a bath. There was no water in the bathroom. Dhrubesh went out to have a bath by the roadside; there was a tubewell with a handpump on the footpath outside the house.

It was Rama's fault that there was no water in the bathroom. However, today she did not feel the cruelty of this mistake. If the lord and master was only worried about the universe then she was not, she thought, to be censured for being what she had become. She could serve rice in a plate; she could not grow rice in it.

Rama could stand everything except this attitude of total unconcern. She was a daily witness to the growing poverty of her family. If Dhrubesh had spared one iota of the energies that he invested in thinking about the war, for the affairs of his family, then perhaps matters would have been very different. In the last two months, he had not exchanged a single decent word with her, let alone a word of love.

Dhrubesh came back from his bath and entered the kitchen. His food was there, covered. He would, of course, not have been surprised had there been no food at all. Rama sat and watched the whole sequence. Dhrubesh finished his food, went and lay down on the floor, covering his face with a newspaper.

Rama approached him slowly. She did not want to have a fight with him, but she had determined to speak her mind.

'Are you listening?'

'Yes.'

'You don't look at your son any more. What is this that you are doing? All right, you fight your wars outside these four walls, but the war within these walls is destroying me. Don't you have a single thought to spare for the future of your son?'

Dhrubesh said - 'Would you be willing to work?'

'What work?'

'There is a cook's position in a zamindar's house in Benares. Board and lodging, and a salary. Then you can forget about me and take charge of Tutu yourself. You can manage very well without me, but you cannot manage without your son.'

The words hit Rama like a fistful of hot gravel.

'What kind of a husband are you?' She continued staring at him. Her eyes were smarting from the heat of her burning home.

Dhrubesh turned his face away.

A month passed; and with it the last of the reserves had also gone. The milkman had refused to give credit. Perhaps, with the secret knowledge possessed by businessmen, he had already discerned that she would be unable to pay at the end of the next month.

She sold some jewellery. Dhrubesh was getting ready to go out for the evening. He did not wait for a cup of tea. He was aware of what was going on.

He was at the door when she called out from outside the room - 'Listen, on your way home bring one yard of flannel for Tutu.'

This was another blow - this reminder of his responsibilities. Thinking of the fate of the universe is not the proper occupation for a person who has lost the ability to buy a yard of flannel for his son. She wants to drive this basic truth home. She has adopted this strategy after much thought. Maybe it will work.

The day was a repetition of many other days. From Sanatanbabu's drawing room to small offices, he had run the gamut of insults that was due, or undue, to him. A feeling of insult, helplessness, the pain of being a misfit, washed over him.

A few people in the cafe off Dharamatala whispered, 'Spy, a spy.' Nitish said, 'Dhrubeshda, we hear you make fun of us these days? You have said that we are all like wooden puppets?' Not only Nitish, but many others have also started saying things about Dhrubesh. Some overtly, and some behind his back. To some he was a lickspittle of the British - and some others had him classified as an obvious bourgeois. Still others, gifted with X-ray eyes, had discerned in his heart the feelings of a Nippon-lover.

It did not matter - this barrage of criticism; but what was really depressing, what dampened all his enthusiasm, were all these symptoms of degradation. From the scholars to the houcmaid, everyone's thoughts were running along only one channel. What will happen after the war, who will profit in what way - this was the only subject for consideration. Everyone had made lists of their burden of duties and demands to be attended to after the war - Dinubabu's wife would have to get her daughter married. The Patriots would have a fight after the war - with those who won the war. The business magnates were eager for the war to end so that they could expand their business.

After Dhrubesh's departure, Rama had cried to herself. Not because of her poverty, not because of Dhrubesh's unconcern.

Rama had cried because today, she had discovered her own selfishness. She had devoted all her attention to Tutu - no other matter in the whole of the world came even remotely close to Tutu and his needs. Why did she need Dhrubesh? So that he could break the stones in the path along which Tutu would grow? Was that his only role in her life?

She looked up at Dhrubesh when he returned. Looked at him carefully. He had grown thin. Maybe she would have continued looking at him. Instead she went inside and came back after a short while carrying a glass of sherbet.-' Drink this.' Her voice was soft.

She cooked the best food she could, given her circumstances. She had the feeling of being whipped by her own countless cruelties towards him. She had to wipe her tears a number of times.

Before he went for his bath she was standing there. She insisted on scrubbing his feet. Sat by him as he ate, and fanned him as he tried to sleep after his lunch. She looked at his face - the cheeks sunken, the bony jaws prominent.

With a long-drawn-out sigh, she continued fanning him.

He did not know why his mind was so peaceful today - as if a shower had washed clean the dust of many days.

Another evening in Calcutta. The soft grass of Curzon Park caressing his tired body. Calcutta's life a dim flow of sound in the lights and shadows of dusk.

With a shout, a boy jumped the railings and entered the Park - a newspaper vendor. The bodies slowly rose up, each from the dark grave of his mind. The boy was shouting - 'Chittagong is bombed, Chittagong is bombed.'

There was a rush to buy the newspapers. Dhrubesh also got hold of a copy, ran to a street light, spread out the sheet and read.

A few lines of fact. The enemy is here. They have bombed Chittagong. People have died, people have been injured. It left Dhrubesh choking, his throat constricted with an unknown fear.

They have come. The enemy. Their ugly shadows are on the waters of the Karnafuli river. Malevolent sparks of darkness against the purity of the morning sky.

Dhrubesh was shaking. He gritted his teeth .... Who are these people? Those who set fire to his country's earth?

In his mind, all the pages of history became smudged, the names meaningless. These was only one name - Birajpur. The burning waves of the little river were calling to him.

Rama woke up in the middle of the night. Dhrubesh had not returned. The lamp was dim, the small flame glowing bluish.

Tutu was deep in sleep. Rama opened the window and looked out. The city was blacked out, as if submerged under a deep sea of kohl.

There was no sorrow, no rejection, no anger - only a few drops from calm eyes; drops that dried as soon as they appeared. Everyone was at home; only he was not there. Let him go, she thought. She would not have been able to hold him. She knew this. She knew it from the core of her being.

He wouldn't stay. He would not have stayed. How could he? He belonged to History. Perhaps, after so many months, he had found the rudder which would propel him to his own private goal.

Rama had closed her eyes calmly. She opened them to find the morning sun upon her. A pair of Spitfires sped by overhead. Tutu smiled and waved his limbs. She picked up the child and held him close. His future would grow with her.

Her eyes were closing of their own accord; her head bent forward in the age-old gesture of submission, the salutation of her heart.

She bowed to those who staked their lives to save the honour of their homeland. The red-blooded ones, the handful of young men who stood in the way of the dark shadow of the enemy's progress. Those few who checkmated death on the dusty board of Birajpur: she bowed to them. She was certain, the enemy's mad juggernaut would stop for a moment, near that small wooden bridge, and an unknown schoolteacher of history would kiss the earth of his ancestors, an earth coloured by his own blood - a kiss that would herald a new age.

translated by Bappa Chakravarty

Eyes

The fog in Shillong is like the town itself, quiet and lazy; predictable in the ways in which it comes and goes, the directions it takes and then melts into the surroundings.

This characteristic, however, was not shared by Aparajita, the niece of Mr Nag, although she, too, belonged to the same town and was, in her own way, as much of an institution as the fog in Shillong.

For, while her beauty lent as much grace and charm to that venerable town as the beauty of its misty environs, her own nature, quite unlike the aforementioned laziness of the fog, was completely unpredictable, as if the mist had suddenly decided to become playful and developed a regrettable (to those concerned with this particular fact) impish tendency to deliciously vacillate on the most important issues (again with specific reference to those directly concerned) of life.

Aparajita had descended upon this sleepy little town a year ago and had continued there since. Nothing indicated whether she would, or would not, continue to titillate that town indefinitely.

Mr Nag's pleasant little bungalow was in Laban, a discreet and private neighbourhood built on a slope a little distance away from the noise and business of the main market. The gate was like a green Arc de Triomphe in miniature. The green was punctuated by the smiling faces of a hundred white roses and Aparajita reflected that smile: in the mornings for Kinshuk, and in the evenings, for Hiranmoy. Twice a day, she smiled equally perfectly, causing great debates to rise as to the direction that her maidenly fancies would finally take.

The daily spectacle, however, was thoroughly enjoyed by Meera and Heera, the two daughters of the professor of mathematics staying in the house opposite. Their tinkling laughter made light of the serious business of meeting two extremely serious suitors with charm and grace precisely tailored to the matter at hand.

Aparajita, of course (in spite of her apparent vacillation), was not a silly girl. She understood that Meera and Heera's giggles were underlaid by an unstated jibe, as if, being the daughters of a mathematics professor, they had precisely computed an equality because of which Aparajita was quite unable to vary the extent of her smiles - morning and evening - even an iota. Perhaps they thought, to put it in the language of laymen who do not understand the mathematics of the maiden mind, that Aparajita loved both her suitors equally well.

In the evenings, Hiranmoy would stand at the gate and say, 'Good night, Apara.'

In the mornings, standing almost precisely at the same place, Kinshuk would whisper - 'Good day to you, Jita.'

Meera and Heera would give way to their mirth and quickly hide behind the window curtains. They had, perhaps, calculated that Aparajita had divided herself into two parts - Apara and Jita, and selflessly given them away to two different people.

Meera and Heera were, however, quite mistaken. None of these ideas were true. If the truth be told then (and in this the chronicler of this little drama claims the superior knowledge due to his status as historian) Aparajita loved only herself. She had not fallen in love - in the deepest sense of the word - with either Hiranmoy or Kinshuk. She was, however - looking inwards - unable to deny the truth that in the final analysis, she would have to choose one of them as her partner for life.

Her aunt, Mrs Nag, had asked her at least ten times during the last three months, 'Why don't you finally choose?'

She knew that her definitive answer would mean her getting married within the week to the chosen (not necessarily approved) one.

Truly, Aparajita's mind was in a whirl. Hiranmoy and Kinshuk, both were equally acceptable in terms of their looks and personal qualities. However, there were sizeable differences between the two of them. Aparajita's mind was unable to decide whose love would make her life most meaningful. There is a great difference between the noonday sun and a moonset; yet if somebody is unable to decide between the two of them, no great blame can be attached.

Who knows, perhaps Meera and Heera would go through their daily round of merriment only to pierce her mind with the needle of shame at this indecision; but they were unaware - as was the rest of the world - that Aparajita's mind was not as the soft earth: it was made, if a comparison be attempted, of soft stone. Aparajita could feel another level in their laughter - a level of jealousy and frustration. Meera and Heera were no ugly ducklings but after the arrival of Aparajita no one looked at them twice. It had been Aparajita all the way.

Shifting Mr Nag to the rear seat of his own car - Aparajita would herself take the steering wheel in the evenings. The car would vanish in the direction of the golf course. After a long and hard ride, the return journey would paint a very light shadow of tiredness on the youthful face - a picture perfectly in harmony with the falling dusk, made all the more desirable by an unruly curl from the coiffured hair. Aparajita was very conscious of the dozens of admiring eyes following all her arrivals and departures.

Aparajita had never framed the major question in her life as, whom to love, Rather, because such a question had never appeared to her as the most important question, she had turned the whole thing upside down. The simple truth to her was that she would love the person whose love she would like to have. The apparent circularity of this solution - if such it is - never bothered her.

Which of the two? Whose love would she love to possess? In this, Aparajita, her uncle and aunt, Meera and Heera, and many others in Laban, all were equally confused. Neither Aparajita, nor Meera and Heera, could decide whom Aparajita would finally choose.

The daily routine at the vine-covered gate was a physical expression of this question, and it included every single thing - even the smile. As if, she wanted to know which one of the two would give her the respect and affection for which her twenty-five year old, charming self was yearning. The noonday sun or the setting moon, whose light would make her look the most beautiful?

It would not be out of place here to put our (the reader's and the author's, the latter having generously decided to include the former in his confusion) house in order. It would, perhaps be appropriate to describe Hiranmoy as the setting and Kinshuk as the noonday sun. Hiranmoy was quiet, and Kinshuk somewhat more of an extrovert. Both of them had come to Shillong from Calcutta but a few days had revealed to the people of that town that both seemed to be made of money.

If money be the criterion then there is not, of course, much to choose between Hiranmoy and Kinshuk. Hiranmoy is Jute and Kinshuk is Iron - if one goes by share values then both of them would probably turn up equals. Hiranmoy owns five houses in Behala and Kinshuk, seven at Dumdum. Hiranmoy is the Director of a bank and Kinshuk that of an insurance company. Both of them own their own bungalows in Shillong. Hiranmoy, in fact, stays close to Aparajita's house and Kinshuk, a little further away.

Hiranmoy's bungalow is practically made of glass and sited on the top of a small hill in Rilbong. Kinshuk's house, boasting very pretty woodwork, is in a private street, off Dowkey Road. Hiranmoy owns a sedan, and Kinshuk - a tourer.

Hiranmoy's face is quite handsome except for his eyes, and Kinshuk's face is attractive only because of his eyes.

As in the lives of all human beings, in the case of these two also, there are two major flaws.

Hiranmoy's eyes are made of stone - he is blind; and Kinshuk is a divorced man. One's eyes are clouded by darkness; the other's mind has a dark wound.

When she had first come to know of these flaws, Aparajita had classed them both as untouchables. She had found this face of truth to be almost unbearable. Afterwards, of course, the calm mute appeal of the darkened eyes of the one, and the blatant desire in the sharp yet dreamy eyes of the other had made her realise that these flaws were not really flaws, but the very personal sorrows of two essentially good men.

When Hiranmoy came to meet her, walking confidently with a small brown spaniel on a leash, gold-framed dark glasses perched on his Roman nose and a smile on his face, who could ever imagine that behind those gold-framed glasses there was the impenetrable darkness of two blind eyes?

And Kinshuk! Aparajita had noticed that even when Meera and Heera walked by dressed in all their finery and looking for all the world like a pair of fairy queens, he never even noticed them.

The laughter of Meera and Heera really scared her sometimes, made her depressed. As if that laughter was a physical external expression of her innermost conflicts. Piercing her armour to expose her inner weakness - the weakness and indecisiveness that made her unable to choose even after being in the company of both men for so many months.

But for how long? Suppose after some time neither the Sedan nor the Tourer turned up at her gates? What, then, would happen? Perhaps, on that day Aparajita would have to hide her face for all time to come, in the mad joyousness or the waters of the Mushmai waterfall at Cherrapunjee. Even if she didn't want to, the sting of their laughter would drive her to it.

So she was afraid. Especially when she worked at her own (oh, so desirable!) image in the mirror, she felt sometimes that she was being cruel to herself. This had to end.

Her aunt suddenly came into the room - 'Have you decided?' Almost equally suddenly, Aparajita reached a decision - 'I shall tell you today.' The only outward expression of this momentous event was a compressing of the lips and the delicate touch of a tiny handkerchief to a beautiful brow. Her aunt was, however, happy. Almost simultaneously there was the honk of the tourer at the gate.

The drawing room looked almost as if it had been deliberately designed for dramatic interludes. Kinshuk sat down on a couch and Aparajita occupied another, in such a way that she could look directly into his eyes.

She looked at him silently for a while, her lips quivering from some emotional upheaval within her and then finally, she could control herself no longer.

'Kinshuk, why you want to marry me?' Perhaps he was not quite prepared for such a question, but it was nonetheless very sweet to his ears.

'Cause I love you. Such a simple answer does not deserve a question, Jita.'

'Why do you love me?'

'Because I want to be happy.'

'How will you be happy?' Her questions, it seemed, were searching in the darkness for comforting answers. Kinshuk laughed.

He got up, walked over to where she was sitting and let her feel the burning desire in his dreamy eyes.

'Do you truly not know why, if I marry you, I shall be happy?'

'No, I don't.'

'Then let me state the obvious - because you are beautiful.'

It was as if Kinshuk had declared a win on her behalf. A priest was at the altar of her beauty. Aparajita could see her own beautiful face reflected in those dreamy eyes. His eyes came a little nearer to her face. She could now clearly see the thirst of the noonday sun in those eyes. She raised a slow hand and as if with the promise of things to come, turned her face.

Looking at the blush on that beautiful face, Kinshuk smiled again, 'All right, but Jita, do you believe me now?

'Yes ... yes, I believe.' With this gift of belief Kinshuk left.

Evening came, with the promise of events to come, Aparajita was in a kind of a daze. All she could think about, was Kinshuk. She would do her last bit of duty by the shiny sedan and its blind occupant - she would bid him adieu.

There was the sound of the sedan. Hiranmoy, with a smile on his face, followed the brown spaniel into the drawing-room.

'Is Apara here?'

'Yes, I am here. Please sit down.'

Hiranmoy sat down. All that remained was to phrase a small, simple sentence and see him off for the last time. She mentally prepared herself.

The ways of the human mind are, however, not very predictable; and as far as Aparajita's mind was concerned, the author has had earlier occasion in this narrative to refer to some of its less robust qualities; so that she delayed uttering that last sentence and in delaying subjected herself to the calm faith of the pair of stone eyes.

'What hope carries you here, Hiranmoy?' Whether she betrayed her mind or her mind betrayed her, she would never know.

Hiranmoy said — 'I do not come here with any hope, Apara. I do not have courage enough for that.'

'Then what do you come to see?'

Hiranmoy laughed - 'I do not come to see anything, Apara; in any case, how could I?'

Apara's eyes felt as if there was some dust in them. Those beautiful eyes did not feel beautiful any longer.

Aparajita - 'Please do not mind, Hiranmoy, but I would like to ask you something.'

Hiranmoy - 'Yes, do.'

'Why should I marry you? How will I gain?'

'You are quite correct, Apara, You will not gain anything ... I shall be the gainer; but ....'

'But what?'

'I shall never see that beautiful face of yours, but the world will, and the world will say that you are ....'

'Yes?'

'That you are extraordinary ... extraordinarily compassionate ... extraordinarily human ...'

It was as if all her twenty five years she had been waiting for these words - *greatness*, the sum total of Hiranmoy's words, greatness, the intense thirst for it, sparkled for a moment in the two eyes of the complex riddle called Aparajita. The whole world was at her feet - she could see the image as on a frame - mesmerising her, overwhelming her.

Hiranmoy said, a little shyly - 'Don't you believe my words, Apara?'

She stood up. Without even a trace of hesistancy in her voice she said, clearly and strongly: 'I believe only in you.'

Hiranmoy took his leave of her and she turned back inside the house. Her aunt asked - 'You would like to say something?'

'Yes?.'

'What?'

'Hiranmoy.'

The marriage ceremony was not over but Aparajita had already prepared herself for the homage to be paid to her greatness. She could imagine the wave of adulation - 'There is no other example of such sacrifice, such unsurpassed greatness.'

Instead, she could hear her aunt's friends — 'What has she done? Marrying a blind man?' She could hear others - 'How could you, as her guardians, marry such a beautiful girl to a blind man?'

She could feel her ears burning. By that time, however, she had put her hand in Hiranmoy's, she had accepted him as her husband and this fact was there in black and white in the Registrar's book.

She could hear Meera and Heera's laughter: 'Now they will look into each other's eyes.'

'Blindly,' whispered Heera.

Before the marriage ceremony had ended, so had her visions of greatness. What was left was a terrible realisation - she had been a fool, a complete fool, a person completely ruled by the whimsical mists of her mind.

The ritual vermillion was put on her forehead by one of her aunt's friends.

Afterwards? Within the next twenty-four hours she realised that the vermillion mark on her forehead was burning through her skin. To her feverish mind, it was more like a live coal which was insidiously burning its way through her life itself.

She had already resigned herself to the fact that she could expect nothing from the world. Perhaps, the only thing that had kept her going through what she now considered to be more of a farce, was a last curiosity as to the bungalow in Rilbong - she wanted to see, a bit morbidly, how great that house would make her. It was the only thing that had made her travel in the same car with a blind man. Otherwise, she now told herself, she would not have come at all.

There was no mist, the pines did not whisper, only the fading rays of the evening sun in a clear sky. She stood there silently, a tangled bundle of nerves and conflict.

Her silence was in sharp contrast to the tremendous expression of happiness and a shout of sheer joy that almost blew out of his throat as Hiranmoy cried out,' Come close, Apara.'

She stood close to him, His blind efforts to locate her physical presence, the waving of his arms in the empty air, shocked and terrified her. Somehow, it was quite repugnant. As if the paws of a blind animal were searching for a victim. With so much light around, here was a creature of darkness - looking for her, hunting for her, enveloping her.

She said : 'What did you want?'

Hiranmoy was gratified that she had spoken. 'I just wanted to tell you that I have got rid of the nurse.'

'Why?' She had to make an effort to suppress the sharpness in her voice.'

Hiranmoy smiled. 'From now on, I want only the touch of your hands on my things, nobody else's.'

'What, what did you say?' Aparajita could no longer suppress the rejection in her voice. As if the house at Rilbong had suddenly displayed all its cruelty and sadism by accepting her only as an unpaid servant. This, this was the man who had first told her that she was extraordinary. All his wooing and praying had been for this, to make himself into her Lord and master, and he was now calling to her to become his slave for the rest of his dark, unlit life.

Hiranmoy said, 'Apara, where is your hand?' Involuntarily, she retreated a step. Hiranmoy shook his head from side to side, and then asked, 'Are you sitting down or standing up?'

Aparajita : 'Why?'

Hiranmoy smiled. 'If you are standing, then do sit down.'

She did not. What difference would it make? That man would never see her, could never acknowledge with a single glance the beauty of her postures. Even if she shivered all over, this man's personal darkness would never even quiver.

'Apara, I can tell you something but you may not believe it,' said Hiranmoy suddenly.

She taken aback - 'Leave aside the believing part, you can say what you want to.'

To her feverish mind, it seemed that his face reflected the ugly pride of a product of darkness.

'I am not sorry that I cannot see you.'

In one second her last remaining commitments, her curiosities, all were destroyed. Some fool had thrown a missile at her delicately preserved world-mirror, breaking it into a thousand meaningless fragments. The vermillion streak on her forehead burnt its way through her skin, her bones, through her very being.

Her eyes became pools of hatred. She crushed her lips with her teeth. 'Are you telling the truth?'

Hiranmoy smiled. 'Absolutely.'

She clutched her handkerchief in a hand grown cruel through her resolve, and in a burst of delirious energy, wiped the vermillion mark - her physical commitment to an alliance that she now despised from the depths of her soul - from her forehead.

Hiranmoy's blind eyes continued to look at her. No words passed his lips. She felt that even if she had committed suicide at this very place he would have continued to look at her in that way.

The evening wended its way from the half-light of dusk to the darkness of the night. Aparajita continued to stand at the verandah railings. The evening breeze had started its mild walk through the woods. She could hear the whispering of the pines echoing her sighs as she looked at the ruins of her so vaunted life. Now nothing but an unclaimed and unclaimable heap of rubbish piled before a pair of blind eyes: she looked at this picture of herself with her eyes, eyes that were smarting from the pain of not-belonging. She was as a broken winged bird, lying helpless before the hunter who, through his blindness, could not even acknowledge her death - a death that he had caused, a death of her self respect and of her pride.

The verandah lights came on. She could see Hiranmoy walking the length of the verandah with his spaniel. Aparajita continued to look at him with eyes filled with hate. The stone eyes would never understand, would never see, that the evening breeze had brought a glow to her young cheeks, the whiteness of her neck, the champagne-coloured saree, and the way it clung to her figure - the allure of the thin gold necklace with its small locket which shyly sat on her bosom. All that those blind eyes could do was pour an inky darkness over her beautiful body and face. She would never hear from those lips - 'How nice you look, Aparajita, how beautiful, how desirable.'

The person who had first whispered this sentence to her, the person who would have continued saying this to her for the rest of her life, that man was perhaps, even now, looking at the hills and wondering why Aparajita had plunged a knife into all his hopes, all his desires. Those eyes, his eyes, in which Aparajita had one day seen her own likeness, were now gone from her. She had been fooled, defrauded by the insincere statements fronting a dark mind, and the apparent calm of a pair of stone eyes - and she had thrown a handful of dust into the only pair of eyes that mattered. She had the feeling that the dust that she had thrown had come back into her life with all the viciousness of a curse of the gods.

Throughout the day, the sibilance of the whispering pines changed, but her resolve remained. She was a guest in the bungalow at Rilbong. She had to be very careful. She would not allow that creature who thought of himself as her husband, to touch her. She had to do this, for after a few days, she wanted her freedom.

This promise to herself had led to her writing a letter. It was necessary. She wanted Kinshuk to come and see that it was Jita who was alive; Apara was dead. She wanted to him to listen to her faith in his dreamy eyes, to see her belief in the noonday sun. She wanted him to forgive her, her whim that had led her to this, and to reaffirm that she was still loyal to him. And then — And then a wait for a few days, maybe a few months until the court gave her a release - freedom from the monstrous darkness of this house in Rilbong.

Rilbong to Dowkey Road is only a few miles. The letter reached swiftly, and swiftly also came the reply. Aparajita held the letter in her hand, her mind mad with joy and expectation.

She would go into Hiranmoy's room when he went out to walk on the lawns with his spaniel. She would write with his pen, - 'Come to me, come to me for once. Yours, Gita.'

Her fever would subside with the completion of the letter. She would touch her bosom with the pen and look out of the window, her passion spent. She would sigh, and the fading sound would make Hiranmoy look up from his walk down the lawn. Then he would continue on his perambulations.

The bearer would come and take away the letter. Aparajita would rise slowly, put the pen down and go into her own room - look into the mirror. She had neglected herself: a saree that was not quite appropriate, unbrushed hair, a picture of self-degradation.

That evening the pines no longer whispered, they cried out as if in pain. The wind, passing down the long verandah, around the cornices, and through the half shut windows, whispered eerily. Aparajita's ears, however were tuned to a different kind of music. Kinshuk had replied. He was coming. This evening she would gaze upon those dreamy eyes again. She had dressed for the occasion.

She spoke to Hiranmoy. For the first time, on her own, after coming to this Black Hole, although there was a lot of hate that she had to suppress.

'I think we can expect a gentleman to call on us this evening.'

'Who?'

'Kinshukbabu.'

A little surprised, nevertheless with an expression of gladness, Hiranmoy replied, 'Which Kinshuk? Oh, the one in Iron; has a house on Dowkey Road.'

'Yes.'

'You know him?'

'Yes.'

'He is in Shillong, then?'

'Yes.'

'Perhaps he is paying us a courtesy call because he could not come to our marriage.'

Aparajita did not reply. There was no need to, for at that moment she could hear the familiar honk of the Tourer at the gate. Kinshuk, her Kinshuk, walked up with measured tread like a successful venturer. He stood by Aparajita's side and looked at Hiranmoy with burning desire in his eyes.

Hiranmoy shook his head from side to side, perhaps trying to classify the sound of the footsteps. Then he raised his hands in a 'namaste'. Kinshuk did not return the gesture. What difference did it make to a blind man?

Hiranmoy smiled. 'Since you have taken the trouble to come, please stay for a cup of tea; there is no hurry.'

Kinshuk frowned. 'Coming here has been no trouble. I would certainly like a cup of tea, but I would also like to hurry back.'

Aparajita, with desperate courage raked from her desire to deny Hiranmoy's lordly courtesy, burst out, 'You don't have to sit here, please come to my room.'

Hiranmoy laughed - 'I am so sorry. I did not realise that there are no chairs here.'

Aparajita said - 'There are many chairs here, but they are all dusty.'

There was a rattling at the windowpanes. The storm had intensified. The people with the live eyes walked down the corridor from in front of the stone eyes.

Hiranmoy continued to stand there whistling to his dog. Where was he? Without his help there was no way this man could find his way. Suddenly this man, who had walked this corridor a hundred times a day, had lost all his sense of direction.

Kinshuk had tea not once, but twice. And he had been there not for an hour, but for more than two hours. He knew all that he had gone there to find out but still he could not leave, and Aparajita also could not bid him goodbye. Her mind was in a whirl; the stormy passion inside her would not subside, and Kinshuk could feel it. There were no more questions. Only trust, and then to leave this house for the night. Not the simple faith of the other day, but a deeper assurance, a chest full of courage, a heart full of commitment. And, of course, the hunger for physical expression.

'Why are you then still sitting on that sofa, Jita?'

At once, as if he had said what was uppermost in her own mind, she left her own place and came and sat down beside him. All her soul reflected her eagerness to reestablish faith, belief and love in the one person who she had betrayed once.

The atmosphere was heavy as if the languid air of that closed room was seeking a definite direction, a decision which would point the way to freedom, which would lift the curtain of darkness, nullify the deathly clutches of the blindly pawing hands.

Kinshuk leant forward. Once again those dreamy eyes neared hers. She leant forward suddenly..

Desire came up against a wall as the music of the spheres became atonal. Kinshuk's eyes quickened, and Aparajita's ears sharpened. There was the sound of very carefully placed steps, somebody orientating himself by blind support from the walls. Steps that came nearer.

Kinshuk said, 'Hiranmoybabu is coming.'

Aparajita said, 'Stone eyes are coming,'

Let him come. He would not see their passion. Even if he sat across from them, what difference would it make? Even if the golden dreams of the two persons in the room became one, right before those stone eyes, what could they ever see?

Aparajita looked at the door. Her glance was an expression of derision, disgust and revenge - if such a thing can be called a glance. 'Let him come. Stay here until he leaves.'

Kinshuk: 'But suppose he doesn't leave?'

Aparajita's eyes were suddenly those of a person who had tasted the forbidden fruit. 'So? Stone eyes do not see.'

Hiranmoy entered the room and in the slightly tipsy way of all the blind, sought support from the back of a sofa. Then he smiled. 'Can you tell me, Apara, how I came to be here?' Aparajita, sitting on the other side of the room, said gravely, 'How could I?'

For some unearthly reason this made Hiranmoy smile. 'The dog was not there. Somehow I figured out the right directions, and after turning through the four corners - well, here I am, right in your room.'

Aparajita: 'Yes, you are, aren't you?'

Hiranmoy sat down on the sofa and asked very concernedly, 'I wonder when Kinshuk left. I would have been happy to talk to him before he went.'

Aparajita did not reply. The windowpanes rattled in counterpoint to the increasing fury of the storm, and the ululation of the wind. She looked at Kinshuk. Kinshuk leant forward again, suddenly ....

Suddenly Hiranmoy laughed. A strange, calm laughter. Shocked, the two separated. Aparajita's eyes now held only frustration.

Hiranmoy said: 'The scent of your hair, Apara - the scent of your hair borne on the wind showed me the way. This is a scent I know. You had this scent in your hair on the day of our marriage. Tell me, am I not right?'

Combined with her frustration, there was now sarcasm in her voice: 'Certainly.'

Hiranmoy continued, smiling: 'Shall I tell you another bit of truth?'

Aparajita frowned, and did not answer.

Hiranmoy said, 'You are wearing the same saree that you wore on our wedding day.'

Aparajita was surprised, 'How did you know?'

Pleased with his achievement, Hiranmoy said, now with a touch of pride, 'I know the whispers that your saree makes, especially this particular one.' He kept silent for a time, and then, as if unable to hold the joy of discovery within himself any longer, continued, 'I can tell you something more.'

Aparajita: 'Yes.'

Hiranmoy: 'You have used my pen at least once.'

Aparajita's eyes now reflected fear. Very quietly, Kinshuk took out a handkerchief and wiped his brow.

Aparajita: 'How ... how did you know?'

Hiranmoy: 'My pen carried the scent of your bosom.'

Aparajita wanted to hide her sinful, proud eyes. She remembered that she had held the pen to her bosom for a few moments.

'Am I not right?' he said.

'Yes.'

'Tell me why.'

Aparajita said, very slowly and very softly, 'You know, and you understand; then why do you ask these questions?'

Her *pallav* threatened to tear her apart. She caught it close to her chest - as if by that gesture she could silence the mad racing of her heart.

Hiranmoy: 'Yes, truly, I do know, Apara, and I understand'.

After a long silence, he said again, 'Where are you, Apara?'

As if shaken from a stupor, she stood up.

Hiranmoy: 'What are you doing?'

There was a quiver in her voice. 'Nothing.'

'Then say something.'

Aparajita : 'You say it. I'll listen.'

Hiranmoy smiled. 'You ask me; otherwise I don't like talking all by myself.'

Aparajita suddenly let go: 'Do you understand my sorrows?'

Hiranmoy: 'Yes, I do.'

Aparajita: 'When did you?'

Hiranmoy's face now reflected an inner pain. 'In this house, that very first evening.'

Aparajita held her breath. 'What did you understand?'

Hiranmoy: 'Your hand touched your forehead in an expression of utter sadness.'

Aparajita's whole body shivered in fear and anticipation. She took two steps towards him and then suddenly stopped. 'You can see. Your stone eyes see everything!' she almost shouted.

Hiranmoy said, 'No, Apara, my stone eyes really cannot see, but I can.'

Aparajita said, 'Tell me truly, what did you see that day?'

Hiranmoy said, 'I saw only that much.'

'But how ... how did you know?'

'There was the sudden tinkle from your bangles.'

'And that was enough?'

'Yes ... Apara. From a little bit of you .... I get a lot of yourself ... but you don't understand.'

Aparajita: 'Tell me, was there any other day when you discovered me?'

Hiranmoy said - 'What did you say?'

'When you discovered the sadness inside me?'

Hiranmoy smiled again: 'Shall I?'

Aparajita also smiled;

'Do tell.'

Hiranmoy: 'One evening, when you were sitting near the window ....'

Aparajita's eyes were now aglow with a new light. 'Yes.'

Hiranmoy: 'Your mind was upset, in pain. Your broken sighs told me ....'

Aparajita blinded herself with her own handkerchief. 'Oh god! You can see so well.'

Hiranmoy's lips quivered in a strange empathetic gesture. 'You felt very lonely on that day, did you not?'

Aparajita was by now leaning forward on Hiranmoy's sofa. A kind of lassitude had invaded her nerves, her bloodstream, her self. The mist was tiring of its own confusion. And, at the other end of the room, the counterpoint to her lassitude, the eyes so full of dreamy passion, were quiet. Kinshuk could not stir, could not breathe, as if a great curse had descended on his soul.

He could not leave, he could not move until Aparajita finally pushed herself away from that blind man's buffer and came to him again. And Aparajita? She was holding on to Hiranmoy's sofa as if in a last bid to keep her sanity. But for how long? Kinshuk sat waiting for the moment when the tunes of that flute would play her false and this girl, this naive sylph of the woods, would come back to him. He did not want to disbelieve her any longer.

However, it was not to be so easily. The blind flute continued playing, 'Do you know how I see you? I see you the way the tree looks at the morning sun.'

'And what an ugly, disgusting face it sees.'

Hiranmoy: 'How beautiful is that face, Apara! Even you do not realise how heavenly you look, what unearthly peace there is your features.'

As if thrown by the force of the stormy wind, Aparajita came to stand right in front of Hiranmoy. The world looked at her only with their eyes. This man, her man, looked at her with sounds, smells and touches. He had looked at her with every part of his being, he had searched her soul with his own. Delirium! Madness! She wanted to break the spell that this man had cast upon her. She wanted to close his mouth. She raised her hand to put it on his lips.

Then she let her hand fall.

Hiranmoy laughed again.'Why did you put your hand down?'

Aparajita's hand was shaking. 'Your eyes, how perceptive they are.'

'I think you had the same lotion on your hand on our marriage day, no?'

Aparajita did not reply. With still eyes and a deep sense of wonder, she continued looking at him. Those calm stone eyes had spread their bitter-sweet magic, the pain and joy of a setting moon.

Hiranmoy said, 'That day I smelt your hands, you had put them in mine. After that, I have not had your hand near me.' His voice, beginning with a bit of self-deprecation, somehow became pained. 'Now all I can smell are cigarettes that I hold in my own hand.'

Impulsively, she reached out her hand and caught his. 'Here is my hand.'

'Yes, the same hand.' He held her hand in both of his.

The brightness of the noonday sun seemed suddenly to vanish from Kinshuk's eyes. In its place was a greater darkness than he had ever known. It was as if there were only those two persons in the room. The pair of stone eyes, and the two deep black eyes, deep as a moonless night, eyes now filled with a mist whose nature no one could fathom. The sweetness of those eyes was casting another spell on Kinshuk, making him feel the crunchy, bitter aftertaste of disbelief. Aparajita seemed to be trying to make Kinshuk deaf to all his own desires; she was almost shouting 'make a streak on my forehead with your nails. Let me feel the madness of it in myself forever. Oh god, why don't you have sharp nails?'

She had taken Hiranmoy's hand and pressed it on her forehead. Two large drops were shining at the corners of her eyes.

Hiranmoy pulled her to himself, held her close. 'I am not at all sorry that I cannot see you.'

'Why should you be? You see three times as much, because you see with all of yourself.'

Mr Nag's adored niece had lost herself in the embrace of a blind man. The thorny rose creeper had shed its thorns and was now only a mass of softness on his chest.

What were they thinking? They had forgotten the world; they were in a deep forest. A deer was looking for its doe in the magic moonlight shadow. They had forgotten that a hungry tiger was nearby. Perhaps, Aparajita had thrown the tiger away as one does a used toy. Kinshuk could see, the blind man's chest was heaving and somehow Aparajita's face had taken on an unearthly colour, she was burning inside with a fire born not of the flesh, but of the soul - a wave getting ready to break herself, lose herself, on the banks at the end of a long journey.

Hiranmoy called softly, 'Apara.'

Aparajita whispered, 'What did you say?'

Hiranmoy continued. 'I do not know what colour your saree is, how beautiful are the pieces of jewellery that you are wearing, but my pleasure is not limited by those things; I see you, I know you ... and you are beautiful.'

There was a sound of tearing off of buttons, as if somebody was throwing off the outer veneer of her beauty. A coloured saree and coloured blouse were thrown off as if torn off by a stormy wind. A small crash of a necklace and a pair of earrings falling on the floor.

Aparajita had thrown off her garments to be feasted upon by the dreamy eyes, and was seeking the beauty of her soul through her naked body. She was looking at her self through the blind eyes. She was at that moment, extraordinary ... she achieved greatness.

A few moments more would perhaps turn Kinshuk into stone. He covered his eyes with his handkerchief and stood up. Walked to the door very very softly and then almost ran away. As if a shy courage had suddenly taken the wings of a wounded bird.

Hiranmoy said, 'What was that? Did somebody leave?'

Aparajita: 'Yes, the eyes have gone.'

Hiranmoy: 'Whose eyes?'

Aparajita smiled: 'A wounded bird's.'

translated by Bappa Chakravarty

Still-born

On this day, the dew had not yet dried on the grass. Banks of fog rose chest high as the four of us carried, through this picture of virgin nature, a reminder of what it is not, an antithesis to the beauty that surrounded us, the autopsied body of Umeshprasad, convicted of fraud, dead by suicide, in a prison cell. Perhaps it was this antithesis that gave us courage, the motivation to carry on with what many would have found disgusting; this sense of being opposed, as if we ourselves represented a reality poised in clear counterpoint to the peaceful world around us. To ourselves, mainly, we perhaps represented a different truth.

People have some funny notions of what constitutes service to society. That, of course, does not make some of them any the less useful. Some of them by their very nature demand - courage? A taste for the unusual? If courage it be then there was an element of tragedy in it. Some might even call it morbid; we certainly didn't. Unusual? That it was, we had all agreed. Anyway, our particular form of Social Service was to arrange for the last rites of the dregs of humanity, the flotsam and jetsam of life who living had had nothing to live by, and in dying had mocked all the rituals of socialised death.

So there we were, committed to an ideal that was not clearly explicable even to ourselves. Kanchanbabu, the President of our Club, was a Commissioner of the Municipality, the motive force behind our coming together. Perhaps he was in a better position to understand the more abstract tonalities of our objectives, but for us the novelty of what we were doing was sufficient. For some reason equally unknown to us, the Kumar Saheb, the prince of Tinpahar Raj Estate, had consented to be our patron, bathing us with his generosity from the huge farmhouse down Madhupur Road.

The land sloped down to where the thin ribbon of the river had tentatively tried spreading out, and man had promptly labelled that effort by siting the burning ghats there. Stark sounds from the bamboo groves magnified by the mad onrush of a mild gale, and the flames of the pyres suddenly fanned into laughing devils intent on devouring the smooth, peaceful blanket of the morning fog. What kind of world is this?

Bholada said, 'Here we are.' Our first acquaintance with the burning ghats would perhaps have been more emotionally tinged, but Kanchanbabu, the eternal realist, brought us all down to earth: 'If we can do our job properly, become a little more popular, and get financial backing from Kumar Saheb, then, believe you me, I shall be the next Chairman of the Municipality. Sudhasindhu won't have a leg to stand on!' He followed up this prediction by suddenly shouting: 'Turn right, turn right, and stop near the office!'

We had never imagined that this of all places, this end to all man's endeavours, would boast one more endeavour, an Office, and inside the office a live human being with a large register and a pen on an office table.

This apparition raised a pair of sooty eyes from behind the blackened chimney of a lantern. Perhaps it was the sound of our tired voices that had shaken him out of whatever dead or semidead world he had been inhabiting.

The man looked at us, and Bholada whispered, 'That ... that man is the Ghatbabu, on duty for twenty-four hours, and a salary of twenty-two rupees and seven annas.'

'Funny kind of man, that one. Peculiar,' Bholada continued. Bholada, amongst all of us, had been here at least a dozen times before. He had seen, no, seen is not the right word - he had experienced, that the man never slept; day or night, the man sat there linking his soul to the register of the dead, staring with unblinking eyes upon the small world of burning embers, white bones and putrefying flesh.

Bholada's whispered comments made us look a little more closely at the man known only as Ghatbabu. Perhaps a shade over thirty, a thin and emaciated body, but the face, the face was somehow different.

Bholada said, 'I believe the man really does not....' Before he could finish, Ghatbabu said in a deep voice, 'Take the body to the waiting room next door.' Before we could respond, Kanchanbabu shouted from behind, 'Excellent, Ghat, excellent! And where, pray, did you learn to order people about like that?'

There seemed to be a transformation in Ghatbabu. The apparition behind the sooty lantern seemed to shrink into itself. Truly, Kanchanbabu had a presence; otherwise how could even such a ghostly being, in its own setting of death and fire, be afraid of the voice of a man from the bright world of the town? However we went into the tin shed door and put down the body there.

The two sheds were side by side, separated by another reminder of the necessities of death, a small mound of wood: deformed, rejected pieces, resembling in their individual grotesqueness a mound of arms, legs, ankles, and joints. And wonder of wonders, there was a jasmine tree also. So flowers bloom even here? Kanchanbabu dispelled our somewhat romantic notions - there is only the tree. Nothing blooms on it.

'Ram, Ram,' somebody seemed to be calling out in a low voice from the next shed. Kanchanbabu smiled - Ghat is waking up the attendant. The actual name of the attendant is Bhalna, but the townspeople call him Ram.

'Why? Why would they do that?'

'Out of fear; don't you know that the chanting of "Ram" is a mantra guaranteed to chase all ghosts away?'

'Funny man,' Bholada had said. A man who chants 'Ram' and stays awake for twenty-four hours for, how many years? five years, no less. Peculiar, to say the least.

Kanchanbabu continues, 'Where will he go? And that fella is a ... I have my own doubts....' Suddenly he stops and says, 'The real thing is: the man's birth, his origin, is unknown.'

Perhaps it was our expression that prompted him to continue. 'One day this fellow turned up in the town, god known from where. Used to stay in a Boarding house like most other people and looked for a job. Found himself a job too, Manager in Radhu Saha's shop. I was surprised, an unknown person the Manager of such a large establishment? I myself went there and challenged him.'

The new manager was sitting right next to the idol of Ganesha in Radhu Saha's shop. When Kanchanbabu walked in and, looking him straight in the eyes, asked, 'Your father's name?' the man was taken aback at first, then mouthed his father's name. But this was not the end of the interrogation. 'Okay, your district is Bankura, but which village, which thana, where do your uncles live? If you are a Brahmin, why can't you say what your Gotra is?'

Kanchanbabu's shouting and intimidating manner seemed to finally break the man. He became totally silent. Even Radhu Saha was surprised. What manner of man is this whom he has permitted to sit next to the idol of Ganesha? His patron saint?

Something had seemed to snap within the man. Without warning he had jumped up and run away.

'But this is not the end of the story,' said Kanchanbabu. 'The man did not leave town. After a few days, god only knows how, he got around that fool of a Municipal Chairman and got a job. I came to these ghats one day and found him sitting there with his register.' Kanchanbabu coughed, and with confidence in his voice, said, 'and I find that even here this scoundrel is messing up everything.'

'What'?

'Yes, on receiving a complaint from the local Police Station, I myself came and checked his register. The complaints were quite correct. The fellow mixes up the names of the parents of the deceased. He had put down "Roy" as the father's surname against Trivedi's dead son's name.'

'Bholada said,' Perhaps he made a mistake.'

Kanchanbabu becomes angry: 'Now Bhola, don't you start speaking like that fool Sudhasindhu. Of course he did it deliberately. There were several other subsequent cases also. I will have that man thrown out.'

Bholada said: 'To what benefit?'

Kanchanbabu said, darkly, 'Of course there are benefits.'

The day was almost upon us. The sounds from the bamboo grove had ceased. The ripples on the water had started reflecting the early light. Kanchanbabu seemed to make some kind of sense. 'And remember a burning ghat is also a place of sanctity; it is not proper to let such a creature loose in such a place.' Bholada said, 'I believe the man is always....' Kanchanbabu shouted. 'Leave your beliefs alone. I am convinced that one man is a ...'

Both of them their sentences unfinished. And we were left more confused than ever. What did Bholada believe, and what was Kanchanbabu convinced about?

By the time the rites were completed it was already noon. On our way to town we noticed in one corner of the grassy field, a tin shack surrounded by a ragged fence of wild bush. From a distance, it looked more like an inverted dustbin than a shack.

Bholada said, 'Those are Ghatbabu's quarters.'

A few days later we were treated to a sight for which we were totally unprepared. In the evening, in front of the neons of the local movie hall, who else do we see but Ghatbabu, that creature of darkness, ash and smoke. We experienced a kind of contextual confusion. We were attracted, as earlier, by his eyes, the sooty cavities which were now staring at a paan-shop; perhaps he wanted a paan.

Adhir Mukherjee, Madhai's grandfather, is normally a calm composed person; spending his days looking at the parade from his bedroom window. Ghatbabu managed to upset him also. Watching him pass by, the old man shut his window with a bang. Not once or twice, but quite a few times we espied Ghatbabu moving about inside the town. But this effort at stepping into the real world, our world, seemed to be rebuffed at every stage. Even the pariah dogs would chase him as he walked down the road clutching a packet of some edibles that he had picked up somewhere. The smell of death seemed to follow him wherever he went.

Kanchanbabu was getting information on the Ghatbabu's movements from us and every time we reported something, he would get angrier. 'The man is getting too big for his boots.'

We did not understand either Ghatbabu or Kanchanbabu. A few days later, at one of our meetings, Kanchanbabu announced, 'I have learnt that the scoundrel has been to visit the Chairman of the Municipality also and asked for four days' leave. I doubt it — I have grave doubts.'

Almost six months passed after this gross declaration of Kanchanbabu's doubts and then, suddenly, we were called upon to perform our own brand of social service once again.

Once more we were carrying the mortal remains of what once had been a living human being. This time, a man once known as Charanbabu, now merely a lump of putrefied flesh, even his inwards eaten away by leprosy. Suddenly Kanchanbabu gave vent to an expression of shock and disbelief: 'Oh, god! what I had feared has happened. The scoundrel has definitely ruined some gentleman's family!'

We all looked towards Ghatbabu's quarters. They no longer looked like a dustbin. Instead, they looked almost picturesque. There were now creepers over the unkempt wild bushes, creepers in bloom. A papaya plant near the well, red and yellow marigolds in their full splendour and, as if lending credence to the positive effort behind all this, a colourful saree drying in the sun. The changes were too stark even for our untutored and unromantic eyes. As if a colourful flag of victory was defying the kingdom of death.

It was all a bit too much for Kanchanbabu. 'The man seems to have really got married. But mark it, he will pay for this ... this fraud on civil society.' Kanchanbabu was really shocked. It was beyond his comprehension that a creature who he had so far regarded as little removed from the dogs that feed on the flesh of the dead ... an *impure* being, could have risen so far beyond himself as to have actually participated in a social, civilised rite. 'I must find out whether he has really got married or is keeping...' he left the sentence unfinished, no doubt with a view to preserving our innocence.

The sound of a motor horn startled us. A large automobile was approaching us from behind and stopped a little distance waya. Kanchanbabu became instantly energised. 'There is our Patron, Kumar Saheb. Stop ... stop, all of you!'

Kumar Saheb was quite a good looking person, fair, slim, clad in spotless white clothes and with a rifle in his lap. He was bound for the jungles some distance away. Kanchanbabu, taking advantage of the proximity of his Patron, stood near the footboard and talked about the coming Municipal elections. The short confabulation over, Kumar Saheb's huge car took a turn by the side of the bushes around Ghatbabu's shack, leaving the imprints of its tyres on the muddy surface. We carried on towards the office of the burning ghat.

Arrived near the office, Kanchanbabu's anger burst out. 'Tell me the truth ... have you married or....'

'I have married.'

'Sure of what you say!'

'Yes, sir, I have been married according to all the proper rites. Do you want to know anything else?'

Ghatbabu was soft spoken and humble throughout in his replies. As if begging Kanchanbabu's pardon for some unknown and undefined affront. Trying, almost, to convince him that in this at least, he had done the proper thing. If something was missing it was not the result of Ghatbabu's leading the life that he led.

Kanchanbabu heard him out and then commented,' But even then, this marriage is no marriage. You understand that, I hope?'

This statement of Kanchanbabu's seemed, in one moment, to destroy Ghatbabu's spark of life. As if the question had raised the ugly spectre of Ghatbabu's whole illegitimate existence in this world.

His eyes turned smoky again, as if an imprisoned soul was crying out for admission to the world of living beings.

Kanchanbabu came out of the office muttering to himself, 'If the fellow had really settled in with a prostitute or somebody. I could have stood it; but to actually marry into a gentle family — god!' He seemed to fall into a reverie and walked off towards the river. We went in and crowded round Ghatbabu.

For the first time, Ghatbabu was looking a little human. He was wearing a clean shirt and there was a kind of shine to his emaciated face. Also, he was wearing a new wristwatch. He called us in a totally alien, *human* gesture: 'Come, sit down.' He began by saying, 'I won't be here long. I am going to leave this job; can't subject my wife and family to this kind of atmosphere.' Suddenly he smiled, 'The wife is carrying. Five months.' Then, 'You won't believe it, but she is quite good-looking. I'll show you her photograph one day.'

'Why don't you show it to us now?' we asked.

'Haven't had it taken yet.'

'When will you do it?'

Our eagerness seemed to melt his last reserves. 'Well you see, another four months before delivery, then another six months for the child's *annaprasan*, then we'll go to Harenbabu's studio in the town and will have a large photograph taken - all three of us together. What do you think of the idea?

Our response was drowned out by the arrival of another cadaver. And then another; Ghatbabu seemed to be tired of it all. 'Put the certificates here, and take the bodies to the next shed.' Very casually he made a pile of the certificates and then continued talking to us. This was a new sensation - Ghatbabu seemed to be trying to break the shackles of the claustrophobic world of death, fire, flesh and bones.

For the first time perhaps, Ghatbabu seemed to be an alien to his world.

On our way back we told Kanchanbabu of Ghatbabu's future plans. He appeared totally unimpressed. 'Don't you believe it. That son of a what-not will never go anywhere. I have grave doubts that the man is a....'

Once again, we were denied the knowledge of Kanchanbabu's doubts - our eyes arrested by a curious sight. Kumar Saheb's huge car was going round and round the Ghatbabu's quarters - as if looking for birds in the fence of wild, unkempt bushes.

Many months passed. This time we were carrying the body of the noted dacoit Inder Singh - death by hanging.

Ghatbabu's quarters were a surprise again. The tin shack had gone back to looking like an inverted dustbin. There were prominent tyre marks around the shack - deep enough not to have been washed away during the rainy season. Where were the creepers and the flowers? The coloured sarėe? Had Ghatbabu really left his job?

We were wrong. He was there, presiding over his register of death like some dark guardian of the nether world. The man was looking, if anything, even worse than when we had first seen him.

Kanchanbabu asked him in his direct way, 'You said you would leave this job and go away. Why haven't you gone?'

'I will.'

'When?'

'Shortly.'

'Good. But you are telling a lie. If you really wanted to go you would have been gone by now.'

On his way to the pyre Kanchanbabu started muttering to himself, 'All right, I know that I have to take steps to remove you physically.' As soon as Kanchanbabu was out of earshot we caught hold of Ghatbabu. 'Where is that photograph you promised to show us?'

'Haven't had it taken.'

'Why?'

'The wife is not here.'

'Where is she then?'

'Gone to live with her parents.'

'And your son?'

'Must have been born by now.'

'When will they come back?'

'I don't know. But they will certainly come back. You see, she was rather upset with me when she left.'

He seemed to have completely unburdened himself. His eyes took on that sooty, smoky expression, searching for some nebulous nothing in the far distance.

The years passed; one, two and then another. Our social work continued. Ghatbabu remained in the office room with his hunched body over his register. Bholada would say, 'I believe the man dreams dark nightmares even in his waking state.' Kanchanbabu would always counter this by shouting, almost: 'Total nonsense!'

Really, the man was not to be believed. Having promised that he would go away, he never did. On the contrary, he seemed to be trying to become a fixture over the years. And where was that vaunted photograph of his? Like his rest of his statements, this also was a piece of fabrication. Something that his limited imagination had told him would gain our confidence. Our repeated questions as to the whereabouts of his family had only elicited evasive answers. There had been no sign of his wife and child these many years.

Then one day we were at the burning ghat building the funeral pyre of a Sadhu. We were all properly respectful. Kanchanbabu was saying, 'I believe Ghatbabu will have to leave his job now.'

'Why?'

'The police suspect him. His name has been put in the register of suspected miscreants.'

Bholada was surprised. 'Why? What has he done?'

Kanchanbabu: 'Our patron Kumar Saheb has filed a complaint against him. He has been seen around Kumar Saheb's bungalow at night. The guards say that he cries and weeps. They think that he tries to scare people by pretending to be a ghost. He was caught red-handed one day; the police beat him up and let him go with a warning. The police have even forbidden him to go near the town at night.'

The Sadhu's pyre was burning brightly. All of a sudden, Ghatbabu arrived near the pyre, hair all awry, torn shirt, and a dirty dhoti.

He made contemptuous remarks at the pyre. 'What kind of a Sadhu is this? So much wood gone waste and this lump of flesh refuses to turn to ashes. Ram! Bring a rod and beat this lump.'

He started making rounds of the pyres, making sarcastic, contemptuous comments all the while. At least Ghatbabu had control of the people of the town in this place that belonged to him, and to nobody else, and was therefore free to express his disgust, his hate, his anger.

'Ram! Who is burning there? Nanda the grocer, perhaps.'

'Yes, Ghatbabu.'

Ghatbabu made a face. 'Once, I wanted credit for a three-anna soap and he wouldn't give it to me.' Nanda the grocer's friends were upset. 'What kind of words are these?'

Ghatbabu whispers into Ram's ear - 'That pyre is burning rather well; take out a couple of burning logs and put my teakettle over them.' Then, turning to another body burning in the distance, 'Who was that? The dancing girl perhaps?' Ram agrees. Ghatbabu: 'What happened to her? Why was she in a hurry to come here? Didn't she accept a contract for the next Holi?' He starts shouting at us: 'What are you people looking at? If you really want to see dead bodies come back in a couple of months. You will really enjoy yourselves then.'

Kanchanbabu could not stand it anymore. 'Ghat, I promise you. I'll make you leave within three days.'

'Yes, yes, of course I shall leave, dust unto dust, etc. etc.' Muttering to himself, Ghatbabu proceeded towards his office.

Bholada said, 'I think the man has had a drink or two.'

Kanchanbabu rejoined, 'Our Kumar Saheb also drinks, but nobody can be disrespectful to the dead as this man is, unless he is ... he is subhuman.'

We peeped into the office room before going back to the town. Ghatbabu seemed to have changed again. There was unrest in those sooty eyes, the register clasped to his chest, as if his very heart wanted to become a past in those pages. Head bowed, acknowledging perhaps that the far horizons held nothing more for him. The nights and days of unsatisfied craving, a desperate desire had made his eyes mere pools of congealed blood.

But how discordant were these ejaculations of this man! In his own way, before his final departure from this place, the man seemed to be deriving a morbid satisfaction from deriding the individual respected memories of the townspeople.

The final hours of the night. We were standing under a banyan tree, sheltering from a short spell of rain. On our shoulders the body of one of the ranees of Kumar Saheb.

That evening we had reached the gates of Kumar Saheb's bungalow as soon as we were summoned by Kanchanbabu. We had seen Kanchanbabu come out of the house with the doctor, had observed the certificate change hands, had seen the Kumar Saheb's huge automobile come out of the gates and take the road towards Tinaphar, had heard the cries of a small child from inside the car. Then, and only then, had we gone up to the second floor of the house and lifted the silk-covered body of the Ranee from a lavish bed. We did not look back.

Once only we had asked Bholada, 'Who was this ranee? Was she Kumar Saheb's wife?'

'No.'

'Then who was she?'

Bholada appeared to be upset. 'The Kumar Sahebs of the world have many different kinds of Ranee. Maybe she was one of them.'

The same grassy slope, the same office and the same Ghatbabu. The same posture - the sooty lantern, the register clutched to the chest. Seeing us, he almost jumped up from his seat and, taking out a piece of paper from his pocket, waved it around. 'Now will you have to believe me. This is my resignation letter.' Kanchanbabu looked hard at him once, then whispered his answer to us. `It would have been better if you had left a few days earlier, then you would not have been punished so badly.'

'What did you say, Kanchanbabu?'

'Why, nothing, just that you get retribution for your sins in this life only.'

The body of the ranee was lying in the waiting room, still covered with a silk sheet. Kanchanbabu said, 'Remove the sheet from her face.' We did so, and saw a face that could belong only to a ranee. The lantern that one of us had hung on a post threw its dim light on that unbelievably lovely face. The discordant note was Kanchanbabu's behaviour; something seemed to have undermined his normal egotistic, abrasive and aggressive self. His flagrant disregard of the fears of the night, his contempt of the phenomenon of death, all, all seemed to have deserted him. His eyes were somehow dimmed.

'How much does the body weigh? How much wood shall we need?' Ghatbabu entered the room, his normal, or abnormal, self.

'You boys come to this side of the room!' All of a sudden, Kanchanbabu was concerned about something.

Silently almost, we went out and stood near the bare jasmine tree, the tree that had turned black from the smoke of countless burning bodies, and had never been in bloom.

We could see, we did see, Ghatbabu standing by the side of the body of the ranee, a reflection in flesh of the jasmine tree. He took a few steps, haltingly, moved the silk sheet down a bit more, and then suddenly, as if his legs could not bear the burden of him any more, he fell to his knees beside the body.

Bholada's soft shout could be heard: 'What was that?'

Kanchanbabu said, 'Leave him be, let him do what he wants.'

The scene had taken on a surrealistic dimension. The beautiful dead face framed by a mass of dark hair. Perfectly contrasted with a small red dot in the centre of the forehead. Sometimes, it appeared as if the thin emaciated hand of Ghatbabu was like a mindless snake, sliding over something that no longer had the capacity to respond to such an impure act, and yet, there was a curious warmth in what he was doing; a last solace, a last farewell. a last assurance to a soul that had forever been in torment. The poignancy of that scene touched even us. Why, why was Ghatbabu showing so much affection for a townsperson? Almost, telling the dead body: 'Life itself is a punishment, come to me'.

And somehow, the ranee's face appeared more serene, as if an escaped prisoner was telling him that this was her last refuge, away from the cruelties of life, this little touch of his rude arms breathing a last breath of peace.

The morning light brought some kind or relief. Ram arranged the pyre. Ghatbabu watched the preparations with calm eyes. Inspected the arrangement of logs himself.

Some more bodies arrived. A change seemed to have come over Ghatbabu. He talked to everyone, ensured that each body lay properly on its pyre.

These burning ghats, far from the town, perched on the wayward sands of the small river, suddenly seemed to acquire a little human touch of their own.

When the fires finally burned down, and nothing remained of the ranee's body, Ghatbabu took the death certificate from Kanchanbabu and went back to his office. Then, when we were about to leave, something, some thought struck him and he said, 'The man has been punished enough.' But we saw from a distance a sight that we had never expected to see - Ghatbabu was asleep. At long last, he was sleeping, with his head pillowed on the register that was as life itself to him.

Kanchanbabu said, 'Bhola, go and get this resignation letter from him. After all, our patron Kumar Saheb himself has filed a complaint against him. We should not allow him to stay here any longer.' Bholada approached the sleeping man and called softly: 'Ghatbabu. Ghatbabu.' At the next instant he glanced at the register and seemed to be shocked. Quickly he came back to us and whispered to Kanchanbabu, 'Please come; the man seems to have mixed up names again.'

Kumar Saheb's ranee has died, the death certificate also says the same, but what is this that Ghatbabu has written? The name of the deceased has been entered as Sumita Ganguly, married with one child, died of a heart attack, name of husband Madhav Ganguly. Ghatbabu has filled up each column neatly. Each square on the register has been filled up with all these strange lies. And the man is sleeping peacefully beside this whole fabric that his imagination seems to have created.

Kanchanbabu looked at us and smiled. Then in a rough voice he said, 'Madhav ... Madhav Ganguly!' Ghatbabu raised his head and said: 'Yes?'

In a moment a year-old story became clear to us. Then this man was Madhav, and the ranee, the beautiful body that we had just consigned to the flames, had been his wife - the woman whose colourful saree had once lent a touch of humaneness to the upturned dustbin of a shack. She had left him to become a ranee, and that is why Ghatbabu never got a chance to get his family photograph taken.

Kanchanbabu repeated: 'Give me your resignation letter.' Ghatbabu laughed, a peculiar, wracking laugh. 'No,' he said. And then took the letter out of his pocket and tore it to pieces. This accomplished, he continued to look at us with eyes that were somehow calm, even laughing.

Another shock seemed to have struck Kanchanbabu. Why doesn't this man want to go? Why does he smile? And is this the picture of a man punished cruelly? Perhaps Kanchanbabu wanted to appeal to reason. 'What will you gain by staying on in this world of burning embers?'

But it failed to depress Ghatbabu. Instead, after a moment's thought, he woke as if from a reverie and made a strange enquiry: 'How is the son of the ranee?'

Kanchanbabu turned his face away. Perhaps even a hard-hearted person like him felt that the man would not be able to stand the next blow. He tried to change the subject. 'You will never receive an increase in salary. It is better that you leave.'

Ghatbabu said: 'The boy must have become older by now....'

'Yes, that is true, but....'

'But what? Please, please tell me.'

Kanchanbabu cleared his throat, and then said slowly, 'But he has a terminal disease; he won't live long.'

Ghatbabu's face registered shock, surprise and a tremendous pleasure: 'Oh! That means the boy also will be coming here, maybe quite soon.'

Somebody seemd to have physically pushed Kanchanbabu back, as if a particularly sadistic apparition had taken its revenge on him.

There was the noisy arrival of another dead body. Ghat stood up and started shouting. 'Ram, Ram, see who has arrived.'

Ram shouted back,'Looks like some businessman.'

'Are you sure it's not a small child?'

'No, no, Babu. I tell you it's a seth, a businessman.'

Ghatbabu continued shouting like a man devoid of all his senses: 'Yes, yes, he will come, where else will he go? He will have to come here.'

The wife has come back, the son will also come; as if the man is picturing a new family in the smoke of these burning pyres. We were all upset at this display, but the worst affected seemed to be Kanchanbabu. It was as if he was going through a particularly private, living nightmare. He stared at Ghatbabu for some more time and then in a couple of steps exited from the office room. We were quickly by his side. 'What, what happened?' But Kanchanbabu didn't wait to reply. A dark fear seemed to have entered his heart.

'I knew it, I knew it all the time.'

Bholada: 'What?'

Kanchanbabu: 'That man. That man is not a man at all, he is a phantom, a particularly malefic spirit.'

Muttering to himself, Kanchanbabu almost ran away from the place. It was now time for us to go too. Before leaving, we asked Bholada, 'What do you think, Bholada?'

Bholada : 'I believe he is a man, but a dreamer.'

'And that means?'

'He dreams while awake; it's a kind of mental disease.'

We looked back at the office room. Ghatbabu was in his position, register clutched to his chest, staring unblinkingly at the horizon, waiting for somebody - or something. Bholada said, 'Can you guess what he is dreaming of?'

We thought about that a little and then said, 'Perhaps he is getting his family photograph taken.'

translated by Bappa Chakravarty

The Impostor

Today is Gaganbabu's youngest daughter's marriage. The largest house on Tarini Mitra Road has, itself, almost become a bride, its normal red colour enhanced by red velveteen covers on the main gate and topped by a live crown of shehnai players on an elevated platform decorated with leaves and sundry other greenery.

The main courtyard now boasts a large carpet, and small bands of guests can be seen reclining in various postures upon it.

For these guests, dining arrangements are on the second-floor rooftop where electric lights have been hung; random noises emanating from there indicate that some guests are already sitting down to their dinner.

There is, of course, a slightly more private, slightly more elevated arrangement for special guests — mainly the groom's party and important social personalities. This second reception area is a random arrangement of about a hundred chairs and a few teapoys. The whole cluster, as if appropriate, is much nearer the main house - near the main hall, in fact - on a kind of raised dais. The teapoys each bear a cigarette tin and the mandatory paans on small silver dishes.

Appropriately enough, one of the first few guests to make use of this exclusive arangement is Mr Dutta, the chief patron and financier of Gaganbabu's business. His status in relation to Gaganbabu's business is matched by his massive physique - draped in a kind of flannel long-coat, secure in the positional charisma of being the director of purchasing of Messrs Stewart and Miller.

The two worlds of carpet-on-the-floor and chairs-on-the-dais are divided - and connected - by a narrow walkway. Astride this umbilical cord are two uncles of the bride. Other than these two senior supervisors there are also a number of lesser watchdogs. Built on a scale appropriate to their role this mobile patrol of Habul, Alok,

Ashesh and Bonku and, of course, Nepal — the real heavyweight amongst them — are also dressed again appropriately in sleeveless undershirts.

The watchdogs reflect the increasing concern and dissecting eye of their supervisors as the crowd of guests entering the house increases in size and density.

The biggest red-coloured house on Tarini Mitra Road has, on this day, divided the world at large more or less into three categories. First, those who are entitled to sit-on-the-carpet and eat-on-the-rooftop. Second, the exclusive minority who will occcupy the chairs and eat in the main hall. And third, those who are neither, who are not guests, for whom the question of dining does not arise, and who, if they have the misfortune to be caught inside the premises, shall justifiably be given a few well-deserved blows to speed them on their way.

This no-nonsense and judicious philosophy has been reflected in the dinner menu also. Second floor rooftop has been allotted specific items - luchi, fried aubergine slices, dry-fish curry, sweet curds and darbesh. Main hall has been allowed, in addition to those plebeian items, several special items - pineapple chutney, sandesh, rice pudding, fish curry and rabri.

This careful attention to the delicate distinction between guests and guests, has resulted in the natural corollary of having to be careful about who is directed where. If a noteworthy personality is directed - by mistake, of course - to the carpetwallahs, and has his dinner on the second floor rooftop, this can very well result in loss of face (certainly), sense of personal insult (conceivably) and even that most terribly tragic of all possibilities - loss of future business.

Alternatively if a plebeian is misdirected to the rarefied atmosphere of chairs and main hall, this can cause quite undue strains on the limited supply of special menu items. And, finally, god forbid, if any member of that terrible third catergory of human beings, the lowliest of the low, somehow manages to enter either this group or that, then of course only calamity is to be expected.

So, the watchword is alertness. A very difficult and demanding task, being executed with dedication and commitment by two uncles. People have to be categorised. The face must reveal all - known or unknown, old or young, dark, or fair, young or old - the face must serve as the index of classification: and such is the task that these two worldly-wise gentlemen have been set. They stand like ticket inspectors astride the umbilical cord and their discriminating eyes sift the evidence - dress, mannerisms, looks - of the incoming guest and accurately place the person. There are no problems. Plebeians are directed to the carpet with a mere wave of the hand, and the 'gentlemen' are welcomed to the elevated world of chairs with folded hands.

After some time a new kind of person - no, a *different* kind of person was seen. Both the uncles had noticed with some trepidation and amazement that a man had peeped around the gateway a few times and then had entered the hallowed premises. Now, the same man could be seen coming towards to the superior world through the proletarian throng on the carpet. What manner of man was this?

A little on the thin side, of medium height, the first impression of relative youth belied on closer inspection by the worry lines on the face. Certainly not less than in his early forties. A head of jet-black hair and a complexion to match. The dress is a different matter. Seldom docs one see such cleanliness - such whiteness. A kurta worn in the latest fashion, a wide-bordered dhoti and white pumps. The epitome of what the well-dressed Bengali Babu is wearing, to take a page out of P. G. Wodehouse.

His very appearence causes confusion and raises doubts. He must be classified - protocol, nay duty, demands it. But neither of the rwo uncles can respond immediately to the demands thus being placed on their social graces. Suddenly however, they observe this, this, *person* being followed by the commando patrol and immediately the whole situation is clear. This creature is one for whom they have all been waiting for a long time.

The joy of detection reigns supreme, of course. This is the person who was standing near the corner shop and had asked Banku himself details about the marriage. The evidence is all there. Thank God that the watchdogs have at last justified their deployment.

The man, meanwhile, has come quite close to the two stern uncles and with a perfectly normal smile made a remark: 'Poor Gagandada, nowhere to be seen; of course, only to be expected on such a day.'

'What did you say? Who is it that you are asking about?' Try as he might, the older uncle cannot remove the shock from his voice, nor the surprise from his eyes.

For a split second the man appeared to be taken aback, but in the next moment, craning his neck towards the chairs, said with a worried expression: 'Oh, oh, our boss seems to have arrived already.' Accompanying his words with a kind of sideslip, the man adroitly brushed the older uncle aside, and seating himself on a chair right by the side of Mr Dutta, enquired: 'How are you?'

And Mr Dutta responded in a deferential tone: 'Thank you, well. And yourself?'

'The man replied, with a fine social grace, 'Oh, quite well.'

The little exchange had already created more confusion and doubts in the minds of the uncles and their minions. To compound the situation, the Man helped himself to a cigarette from the tin on the table, borrowed a match from Mr Dutta himself and exhaled with a great show of being at ease. Only a thin kurta on this winter evening? Will wonders never cease? Nepal gave vent to his state of mind: 'Uncle, what do you think?'

'I don't really know. Seems to me the fellow must be a senior grade employee of the purchasing department of Stewart and Miller; else how does one explain this closeness to Mr Dutta?'

'I would hardly count that as evidence. Very, very difficult to know a gate-crasher.' This from the other Uncle.

'But what do we do?'

The impasse was resolved by Gaganbabu himself who now appeared on the scene and invited the distinguished guests-on-the-chairs for dinner. One by one the guests left their seats and entered the dining hall. The man could be seen seating himself beside Mr Dutta and chatting, apparently quite amicably, with him.

Despondence; watchdogs in the throes of despair; but the horse sense of the younger uncle would not let him give up. 'Don't take your eyes off him. These fellows come in all shapes and sizes. His behaviour will tell all. Don't give up hope, my young friends.' The sequence of menu items in the main hall slowly progressed towards its logical end but still the eyes of the whole watchdog contingent were on the Man.

The object of all this attention, meanwhile, had quietly finished his meal, had paid a left-handed compliment to the cook and had, thereby, caused a few amused eyebrows to be raised. This, of course, had also reaffirmed doubts in the minds of the guardians of Gaganbabu's graciousness.

'Let's catch him by the collar now.' This from the muscular Nepal. 'Otherwise it will be too late. '

'What do you suggest?' The older uncle to the younger one.

'What difference will it make now? He has even had his dessert. All that is left is for him to rinse his mouth.' The younger uncle's voice registers complete frustration.

'But this is unpardonable. To ... to allow this impostor to get away with it all....'

'Wait!' This from the senior uncle. 'Let's not create a scene before the whole crowd. We shall catch him when he thinks he can make good his getaway, and then give him a parting present to remember us by.'

And they waited, and watched. The Man had by now washed his hands. Others had also done the same. Some of the guests went back to the chairs, relaxed, lit cigarettes, chatted with their neighbours. There was a general air of letting down one's reserve.

The Man also looked around, as if trying to become part of the general atmosphere but being unable to, he put on the white pumps and perhaps prepared himself for something, some action, some incident.

The plebeians by now had become energised for the third time, the hungry ones trying to climb the stairs to the second floor simultaneously with the replete ones coming down them.

The Man saw his opportunity: as the melee spread all over the courtyard, his eyes gauged the openings in the crowd and suddenly, like a practised sprinter, he made a fast beeline towards the gate.

But not very far. Nepal and his fellows had been waiting just for this occurrence. They pounced on the Man like a pack of wolves and in a trice had him immovable on the sharp stones of the courtyard. And hard on their heels came the two uncles, exhibiting both their anger and exhilaration.

'Twist his arms hard, Nepal; he may have a knife on him.'

Nepal obediently twisted the Man's arms behind his back; senior uncle raised his arms preparatory to landing a couple of good ones and junior uncle was about to catch hold of the locks of the Man's hair.

However, the working of a perverse fate are beyond everybody's imaginings: and courage and diligence are seldom rewarded. At the climactic moment Mr Dutta appeared on the scene and, casting a contemptuous look around, almost spat out: 'Harassing a gentleman like this; you people should be ashamed of yourselves.'

Nepal stood up and in between taking deep breaths almost shouted: 'He is not a gentleman; he is a gatecrasher.'

The Man had been crouching on the ground, as if offering his back to fate and its minions. Now, as Duttababu approached him, he stood up. Duttababu spread out his hands and said, 'Let him go.'

The noise of the boisterous diners was descending in waves from the second floor roof, was made sweeter by the female voices in their marriage chants, and made odoriferous by the smells from the makeshift kitchens of the caterers.

'What has he done? He has eaten, that is all, isn't it? Let him go.'

They bowed to Duttababu's superior authority, and the Man, seeing his chance, vanished into the languid air of Tarini Mitra Road through a now inviting gateway.

The cold December might has created its own small bouquets of fog and left them to float on the waters of the canal. This is far from Tarini Mitra Road. The streetlights do their best not to see the squalor around them.

The Man walks along the canal. Stops near a small handpump and has a drink of water. Rubs a little water on the back of his neck. It hurts. And with the pain the memory of the beating at Tarini Mitra Road returns.

The Man stands up; with a mental shrug he throws off the pain and the memory of it. Walks. Along the main road and then into a dirty side street, surface almost covered with slime, but he walks comfortably, confidently.

A few shacks - one or two brick houses. The Man walks. Journey's end is a shack down a very narrow lane, its only claim to existence being a charitable attitude on the part of the postal department - Bhairabtala Second Lane.

The Man knocks; the apology for a door opens to reveal first a kerosene lamp and then in its flickering shadows, a thin figure in a red-bordered saree and an ordinary face made memorable by a prominent nose with a nose ring. The woman asks in a worried voice: 'What made you late again?'

The Man gives a big smile, and, in the process of carefully taking off his kurta says, 'There were problems at today's meeting; a lot of chaos; I had to work really hard to keep things under control.'

'Why do you have to go to such meetings?'

'I myself have nothing to lose; but one must keep the larger interest in mind.'

The Man carefully puts his kurta on the ground. Takes off his white dhoti and wraps a towel around his waist. Puts his white pumps carefully in a corner. He looks like an undernourished sparrow, a travesty of humankind.

'Was there any fighting?' the woman asks.

'Fight with me present? When the two sides wouldn't come to an agreement I raised my voice. That put them in their places all right.'

'What was all the disagreement about?'

'Rationing, what else? One set wanted rationing, and the others didn't. Finally I had to step in and suggest a compromise.'

'And what was your compromise?'

'For fifteen days a month there will be rationing, and then no rationing for another two weeks ... you know ... it would go on like that.'

The Man picked up a small piece of washing soap and a small pot. Smacking the pot disgustedly, he remarked, 'You haven't left even a bit of the soda for me; what shall I do now?' Disgust is also evident in the woman's rejoinder: 'Washing clothes at this time of the night - you will be the death of me.'

The Man does not reply. Picks up a bucket and a piece of iron rod. Water had to be brought from the main road. Opens the door and remarks over his shoulder, 'My clothes have become dirty in the melee at the meeting. If I do not clean them now the stains may become permanent. And I have another meeting tomorrow....'

The woman looks unhappy. 'You have a meeting tomorrow too?'

'Yes, I have to attend four more meetings during the month. After that, I shall be free for a month or two.'

The women picks up her courage to rejoin angrily, 'Then get ready to burn my body during this month itself.'

This makes the Man a little nervous, a little embarrassed. A worried note creeps into his voice 'Wife, what are you getting so upset about?'

Wife: 'If you are only attending meetings this month, then when will you go to the club and bring home your part of the commissions?' She becomes angry as she goes on: 'How long do you think I can go on borrowing money? The grocer has refused, even the woman supplying cow-dung cakes refuses to give credit; I don't even have something to burn myself with - and you attend meetings.'

The darkness beyond the door seems to beckon to the Man; the woman seems to perversely hold him back. He turns around and in a very composed manner, says, ' Please, please understand. Somehow we must live through this month. I shall definitely collect my commission from the club at the end of this month - I promise you.'

His voice, his entreaty seems to work some kind of a change in the thin figure in the worn saree and nose ring on prominent nose. Even her look changes to one of warmth. What, after all, is the use of nagging such a person? Look at him now, rib-cage barely covered by dark skin, arms and legs like those of an undernourished bird, a towel around his waist, a single kurta, a single dhoti, and a single pair of pumps his sole means of entering the wide world beyond. So concerned with doing good to others that he has no time to earn money to feed his family. Has practically nothing to eat; and yet, and yet, never complains about fate. Certainly, god is blind; else why should a man like this suffer?

Bare-bodied, in one hand a bucket, and in the other a small piece of iron rod - the Man stands against the door. The flickering shadows play strong games over and round this mute picture; turning him into an ascetic one moment, a piece of flotsam rejected by life the next. The woman, his companion for the last twenty years, tries to understand him afresh. Today, after so many years, he seems to be somebody unknown to her, a man beyond anger, beyond sorrow and beyond greed. The whole wave of sentiments seems to overwhelm her, making stark, uncompromising mental pillars of each instance when she has been rude to this ... this man-shadow; but then God himself must be forced to live the life of a destitute, a ... a ... nothing?

Very slowly, subduing completely her earlier outburst, she said: 'You had something to eat?'

Man: 'No.'

Woman: 'Shall I cook something?'

Man: 'No. Don't do anything at this time of night. You know these meetings completely destroy my personal needs.... In any case I think I shall fall sick if I eat anything now.'

The Man goes out. The woman lies down on the floor, using a bundle of rags as a pillow. Her catharsis over, she falls asleep almost immediately.

Outside, the night looks at itself with dark eyes. The fog on the canal, as if ashamed of its whiteness, escapes upwards towards the stars limned in the reflections of light from the various parts of the city. Sounds die. Only the beat of clothes being washed creates the illusion of life. Bhairabtala Second Lane becomes a mystic whirlpool of sound and life, life and sound.

The Man's total concentration is on removing the last vestiges of dirt and stain from his clothes. As if the very action of cleaning removes a part of his evening.

The hours wend their weary way through the night. Now all that remains is to wash the clothes once more in soap and then leave them overnight in a bucket of whitener. The morning will bring the daily routine of renewing the life of the clothes. And that routine will keep him occupied till the evening. The Man has achieved some kind of expertise in this matter of cleaning his clothes.

Apart from his dhoti and his kurta the Man has one more possession. This is a silk stole. On the days that he has to appear an upper class gentleman the Man spends the whole day bringing the silk stole to a kind of pristine whiteness. The process takes him well into the early evening hours.

The evenings are his operating hours. The mornings and days pass as if in a trance. He really wakes up with the street lamps, the night stars, and the weary trudge of homeward bound people.

The Man can stand the night lights but not the daylight. The harsh glare of the sun blinds him and makes his head spin. The Man has, for all practical purposes, shut the sun out of his life for the last twenty years. The day has become night, and the night, day.

Out in the city, or inside this dark, dark room, the Man is a mystery: to the city and to the room that is only nominally a home.

Inside the room, or outside in the world, the Man is a mystery. The world does not acknowledge him, and this dark room in Bhairabtala Second Lane does not know him.

Perhaps the only one to even remember who the Man really is, his origin, is that thin form lying in a foetal position on the floor of this room. And perhaps even those memories have become overshadowed in the last twenty years by the very nature of the man she has lived with, his undernourished appearance reflecting her own, and the single towel around his waist a counterpoint to her sole red-bordered saree.

How does one deal with such an identity? No, certainly there is no reasoned philosophy behind it; only the perverse product of a life that has changed forms and appearances countless times, generally in order to avoid being recognised as a specific person. The landlord knows him by one name, his neighbours another, and the grocer, a third. And the police have so many aliases for him, that even they have perhaps forgotten what his original name was. After every incident involving himself, the Man has shed his name, behaviour and identity - as if being born anew, and has moved to a completely new place. The government's handcuffs and warrants have vainly searched for him, month after month, and year after year. The Man has consistently eluded them. Who, after all, can chase a wraith? Asansol to Magrahat to Shyambazar to Naihati to Bhairabtala Second Lane. The effect of these twenty years can now at least be seen in the worry lines on the Man's forehead.

The surprising thing is, the person who has been his constant companion all these years, his wife, his woman, even she has been unable to fathom his real self. And the man has certainly not helped her in any way.

Even a few years back when he was somewhat younger and not so thin physically, he would vanish from the home for a few days and would come back with a few clothes, a few utensils, some money, perhaps a gold or silver trinket. The woman thought that her husband was working as an order supplier in the suburbs. The Man had never told her otherwise.

The next phase was when they moved to Shyambazar. This time, the Man used to go out every night and return before the morning. The woman was under the impression that he was doing a night job. But she had been suspicious. Their one and only altercation on the subject had taken place on a festive night. The Man had been getting ready to go out when the woman had stopped him.

'I won't allow you to go out.'

'Why? What's up now?'

'You think that I don't understand?'

'And what do you understand, pray?'

'Night duty means going to the wrong places.'

At this, the Man had started laughing: 'People who have a character lose it by going to the wrong places; I don't have a character - a shadow cannot lose anything.'

And then he had given her concrete proof of his faithfulness - people who go to the wrong places take money with them when they go out in the evenings, and come back empty-handed. I go out empty-handed and come back with money. So, dear wife, don't be worried about my behaviour. The woman had understood and had privately castigated herself for doubting the intentions of such a model husband.

Many, many days ago, during those night duty times only, the Man had once been to an open-air play — not for any aesthetic reasons; his objectives were much more prosaic: the bulging pockets of a few members of the audience, and the gold necklace on the neck of a young girl. He had smoothly accomplished those objectives during the climax of the play. He had chanced to look into the greenroom while making his exit from his own theatre and had seen the erstwhile hero of the play laughing and having a cup of tea. Most of the audience were still wiping their tears.

This incident had left a deep impression on the Man's mind. Like the hero of the play, make the crowd weep and while they are weeping, laugh and have your cup of tea. Perhaps this is the philosophy that the Man has adopted for himself. Every night while people weep because of his actions, he himself is remote, can even laugh, his only concern the appearance of cleanliness.

No, the Man is not sorry. He has no morbid curiosity to discover who has wept, who has suffered or who has been deprived by his actions. For him, what happens is already part of a fleeting past. He has learnt to lay his own ghosts, to live a life unburdened with memories, personalities as impermanent as his activities in a life complicated only by the need to keep moving from one place to another. A heart like ice, or maybe something even harder, something that does not even feel the heat of life.

However, with age, a natural end has come to the night duty jobs and concurrent problems; and now his health also is failing. All that the Man does now is to go to a Club and collect some commission for small jobs. His wife of twenty years knows only this much and has resigned herself to not knowing anything more.

The club is nothing more or less than a place where stolen goods are collected. The Man peddles his commission. That pays for a few handfuls of rice in the dark room of Bhairabtala Second Lane. Nothing in life being easy, even this avenue of income sometimes gets blocked. The club has to change its address fairly frequently in spite of paying protection money to the police.

But what has really started causing complications in an essentially uncomplicated way of life is this new tendency of the Man to attend these meetings. The more frequently he goes to the meetings, the less frequently does he go to the Club, and therefore, the flow of money for the few handfuls of rice trickles down to nothing. Some days, the woman, having had nothing to eat, becomes almost mesmerised by the ash-covered mouth of the oven and then ... and then becomes angry at all the meetings in this heartless world.

The Man's new hobby. As if a belated attempt to establish a new relationship with the world around himself. To be with people, to be able to talk to people who have definite identities, to enjoy a few moments of respectful attention. The Man has enjoyed many different addictions in his life, but this seems to surpass them all, fulfilling some deep need within himself.

Well, it could, perhaps, be called a new kind of business too. The only capital that he has ever needed being the dhoti, the kurta, the stole and the pair of pumps. He accepts that this business will never yield monetary benefits, but what it does yield seems to be balm to the craving heart of an ageing shadow-being.

There are some months in the year when almost every day there are marriages. The lively sound of shehnais, the bright lights, the scent of perfumes and flowers, all these seem to have some fatal attraction for the Man. It transforms him from the bare-bodied, undernourished figure of Bhairabtala Second Lane into a bhadralok, his kurta, his dhoti and his pumps his passport into the world of not-belonging. Perhaps his sense of a stolen life adds piquance to both the food and the welcoming smiles of the marriage organisers. Only the other day, the Man was sitting with a roomful of well-to-do people in the house of a well-known attorney. The master of the house himself approached the Man with folded hands and apologised for any lapse. The Man had been generous, even effusive, in his praise of the arrangements.

There is a kind of inner, objective pleasure in pardoning the small lapses on the part of these well-educated, well-placed, identifiable people. His nominal status notwithstanding, the Man seems to get a genuine satisfaction from stealing their sincere good wishes and welcomes which, to him, are more precious than jewels, being perhaps harder to come by.

The ice in the Man's heart seems to become more flawless as each stain from his clothes is washed away. The sounds of his activities a kind of direct challenge to the silence of the December night. The Man is getting ready for the next day. Another day of marriages.

Suddenly his own noises become secondary to the sound of heavy boots and the rapping of a stick on the pavement. The Man responds in a trice. The sound of the door closing drowned by the barking of stray dogs in the lane.

There were four more days of meetings in the month of December. Of these, the Man had succesfully attended three - one at Bhawanipore, one in Tollygunge and the third at Shobhabazar. There had been no problems.

Today is the last day of meetings this month. The sound of shehnais from every block a little louder, prices of sweets higher and even the taxi ranks are empty. It seems most of the population is in some kind of a mad race to get married.

The Man has been searching for a really good marriage party since early evening, but not to much avail. The one house which had appealed to him he could not get into - they were checking invitation cards at the gate. Another house had a few muscular fellows doing rounds - too uncomfortable a reminder of Tarini Mitra Road. The Man had quietly gone away.

A large display clock on the wall of a music house informs him that it is nine o'clock. The last marriages would be over by ten. The Man must find an opportunity to justify this day. His perambulations carry him to a meaner part of the city. Smaller houses, some with tin or tiled roofs. One of the houses seems to be a little more decorated. There is the lament of the shehnai, and two taxis in front. The groom and about ten other persons can be seen getting out of the taxis. A gang of small children come running. A few housewives in traditional dress appear. A group of persons in dhotis and undershirts also emerge and welcome the groom's party.

The Man stops. Wipes the beads of tiredness and frustration from his forehead and then, finally taking a decision, enters the house.

There is a courtyard. A cow is tethered on one side of it; on the other side the ritual arrangements for the marriage have been made and there is even a priest.

The groom's party has occupied a part of the verandah. There seem to be two rooms in the house, and the smoke and smell of cooking and many bodies in close proximity emanate from them.

The Man walked confidently up to the verandah and sat down beside the groom's party. The groom's party respectfully allowed him more space, and the Man basked in the attention being paid to his clearly very impressive garb.

Among the bride's party is a slightly baldish, ageing man who had been looking at the Man with a calculating eye. The Man had been conscious of this, but not overly worried.

Suddenly Bald-head made a signal to one of the young helpers. The Man became alert, looked at possible means of exit. The young boy appeared with a fan and started fanning the apparition in its pristine white dress. The Man, his relief expressed in a condescending smile, waved away the little extra attention being shown to him.

The priest is ready, the auspicious moment approaches, but the house seems to be subdued: something is wrong. The Man notes that the bride's relatives seem to be afraid. That expression most prominent on the face of Bald-head. Maybe he is the bride's father.

Even the groom's party appears a little grave. And the gravest of them all, the man with a wronged expression on his face, is a person with a black coat and a day's growth of beard. Most certainly the groom's father. The Man starts feeling uncomfortable.

Bald-head slowly approaches the Man and whispers into his ear, 'Would you mind stepping this way for a moment?'

For a second the Man becomes nervous. 'Why'?

Bald-head continues in the same humble vein: 'I have a submission for you to consider.'

The Man puts on an appropriately grave expression and acquiesces.

On one corner of the verandah, slightly away from the groom's party, Bald-head opens up.

'You are, of course, the groom's....'

'Uncle. The groom is the son of my cousin.'

'I knew it. I looked at you and immediately realised that a man like you would never be unreasonable. If you kindly make the groom's father understand....'

'I don't understand anything ... what are you talking about?'

'I won't be able to pay the balance one hundred and fifty rupees of the dowry.'

'All right, don't pay.'

Bald-head is almost weeping. 'Will he allow the marriage to continue?'

The Man looks at the floor for a time. He does not reply and perhaps searches for a way out of this rather tragic set of circumstances. Bald-head continues: 'Nobody knows to what lengths I have gone in order to collect money for this marriage. I have sold one cow, borrowed two hundred rupees on an IOU for four hundred, sold the last bit of gold in the house .... Please. Please,' in his entreaty he presses the Man's hand - 'You are an educated person, you can understand, an ordinary mechanic who repairs fans ... if that man has to pay a dowry of three hundred rupees....'

Man: 'So you paid one hundred and fifty rupees as advance?'

Bald-headed: 'Yes. Yes.'

The Man lets out a prodigious yawn. All that walking since the evening has made him very tired. And there seems to be no guarantee that the food to follow would even make up for all this exertion. On top of this, this new complication. It goes against his basic philosophy, but right now there seems to be no way out. Bald-head repeats his request: 'Sir, we depend on you.'

The Man laughs. 'Why are you so worried?'

'Please tell us what to do. What will happen?'

'The marriage will happen. That is what will happen.'

'The groom will consent?'

'Even his forefathers will consent.'

'And the money?'

'That is my problem.'

Gratitude overwhelms Bald-head. He presses his head to the Man's hand. The Man says very slowly: 'I assure you that nobody will raise the issue of money with you. I shall personally settle everything with them.'

The Man slowly withdraws his hand and putting as much compassion as he can into his voice, says, 'Now, please go and begin your preparations for the marriage.'

Bald-head, overjoyed, rushes off to tell the women; in a moment the house seems to come to life.

Only the groom's father, in a black coat, shouts 'My money, my money is not paid.'

The Man approaches him and with a frown says: 'How much?'

'One hundred and fifty rupees.'

'You shall get it tomorrow.'

'But sir, what is the guarantee? A man who can break his word once....'

'You don't know me, do you?'

'No ... I mean ... not really.'

'Please come outside with me for a moment, and I shall show you who I am.'

Black-coat accompanies the Man outside the house with some trepidation. The Man points to a large house at the corner of the lane. 'You see that house?'

'Yes, sir.'

'Know it well; that's my house.'

'Yes, but....'

'There are no buts. Come tomorrow evening any time and collect your money.'

It is an impressive house towards which the man points. Columns, and a huge grilled gate. Black-coat seems to shrink into himself.

'But will they allow me to meet you?' The man gives a superior smile. 'No, don't worry, just tell the guard at the gate that you want to meet the young master.'

'One more thing, Sir ... we have planned to start at seven from here tomorrow.'

'Come at six and take your money.' And then, as if a new thought has struck him: 'There is no need to repeat this conversation to the bride's father. After all, I am just a neighbour and have no wish to appear as the local do-gooder.'

'Please don't worry, sir, I shall respect your wishes.'

They re-enter the house. The change in the mien of Black-coat is apparent to every one. Men and women become slightly more energetic. Black-coat shouts: 'Let's hurry or the auspicious moment will pass.'

The Man sits down next to Black-coat and befriends him. Black-coat is proud of his son's achievements. Head-peon in an office at this young age. Also, the boy plays football for the office team and reads novels in the night.

The minutes wind their meaningless way. The Man is getting bored. There are no signs of food; certainly, even if it appears, dinner will not be of a standard to which he has accustomed himself.

Suddenly Bald-head reappears and presses his hand, 'Please come inside ... a request from all of us.' Bald-head takes him to the room which is full of women. They respectfully clear a path for him, raising wondering eyes at this character out of a fairy tale, a man who has saved their bride.

A young girl sits in the middle of the room, clad in a cheap red bridal saree, her face between her knees.

Bald-head says lovingly: 'See, my darling, your new uncle is here, pay your respects to him.' The girl looks up - a young face, a child face, made all the more young-old with a dash of kohl around the large, innocent eyes. Bald-head almost breaks down: 'God has brought him to our house today. If he had not been here I don't know what would have happened!' Then, turning to the Man, he says, 'The child has been crying ever since....'

'But why?'

Bald-head smiles, 'She heard that she won't be married.' The Man feels tall. 'Says who? She's going to be married all right; there is absolutely nothing to worry about.'

At that the girl slowly gets up and approaching the Man, bends down over his feet.

Something happens to the Man. He seems to enjoy this new level of play-acting, this unplanned-for journey into a hitherto unknown reality. He almost shouts, 'Go ahead, go ahead with the marriage - what are you all waiting for?'

His urgency infects the people present. The priest gets ready. Black-coat gives final instructions to his son, the groom.

Outside, the Man senses an anticlimactic feeling within himself. He approaches Bald-head and asks to be excused. Bald-head is shocked. 'How can you go without having your dinner?'

'Extremely sorry, but I have people from my office waiting for me.' Excuses don't work. The Man is served sweetmeats by the child-bride herself and she supervises while he partakes of the meagre offering.

Somehow, the minutes pass. The Man rushes out of the main door and does not look back. For the first time in his life, personal devils pursue him through the darknesses of the night towards the small room in Bhairabtala Second Lane.

Next morning found the man again at his ritual with soap and soda-water. The woman asks, 'You have a meeting today too?'

The Man: 'No, no meeting; I sweated a lot at the meeting last night. Must clean the kurta, otherwise the stains will become permanent.'

The last day of meetings for December is over. The only thing to do now is to go to the club and try to get some commission. There is no other pressing work.

The Man never looks back on any incident in his life. But somehow, today, something seems to bother him, some memory perhaps; at one point he even smiles, a small private smile; some memories don't seem to go away.

The sun sets. Today no shehnai laments beckon the Man. But he gets ready anyway. Dust wraps darkness around itself. The man stands, fully dressed, in the doorway of the shack in Bhairabtala

Second Lane. He is thinking, but his thoughts lead him nowhere; there does not seem to be any fixed focus. All that goes round and round in his mind is that shortly, perhaps very, very shortly, there will be a tremendous waste somewhere; whose, how much - all that is beyond his comprehension. Only the nagging sense of impending loss; it makes him weary, and his eyes become unfocused, as if looking at a dream that is only half an illusion. Black-coat will be summarily thrown out by the guard at the large house, he will want vengeance. What will happen to the child-bride; was her smile in vain; will they annul the marriage? Perhaps the groom and Black-coat will go away in a taxi and Bald-head and the others will look on helplessly. The Man gets angry: starts muttering to himself: 'Damn it! I managed to get the marriage through in a few sentences, and these fellows cannot do the rest?' He blames Bald-head, blames the helpless, witless, poor mechanic of a father of the innocent child-bride. Steps out onto the road, then returns and calls 'Wife:'

The woman responds : 'What is it now?'

'Do you have a little gold?'

'Gold! Are you mad?'

'You remember, I gave you a small piece once....'

'Oh my god! That was ten years back!'

'That does not matter. Do you have it, or not?'

'What a memory! You went to Rishra and sold it youself. You have forgotten.'

'Good. Then there is no problem.'

The Man starts walking in circles: the woman, completely bemused, stares at him. He has lost the courage to carry on. But carry on he must. Otherwise there will be a storm that will sweep through the world that is his mind, a storm made horrific by the raving of Black-coat, a storm that will sweep away the innocence on the face of the child-bride.

The Man gets a hold on himself. He turns towards his companion of twenty years:'I am going out on a new job. If I don't return tonight check the hospital or police station tomorrow.' In one large step he avoids both the outstretched arms of his wife and the pleading shackles of her voice. The darkness of Bhairabtala Second Lane swallows him.

Only a few minutes to six o'clock. A guard, clad in a blue uniform and yellow turban, sits outside the gates of the large house.

The Man strides the footpath outside the house like a phantom. All his desperate courage concentrated in this one event in his meaningless life. Only his eyes reveal his tension. Sometimes he stops and strikes an aristocratic pose. What a giant-lie, and a giant-representation, the younger son of this huge house. This phantom knows, one misstep today and this footpath will be wet with his blood. Handcuffs, hospital, court and jail — all the possibilities wait like wolves around the falsities encased in the thin body, with a thinner veneer of clean clothes. One mistake, and all that will remain of the Man will be a live corpse adorned with handcuffs.

Clocks strike six. A greedy and at the same time humble figure crosses the smaller pools of light to approach the larger one near the gate. The picture of a beggar overcome by his need to beg. The Black-coat. A shylock in the garb of an innocent victim.

But the Man is beyond being worried. A new level of desperate courage possesses him. He gives a condescending smile.

'Well at least you are on time. The same, of course, cannot be said of my cashier. He has not turned up today. Come tomorrow, or the day after, and take your money.'

'But...but?'

'But what? You'll leave the girl here? Have a fight with her father?'

Black-coat does not reply. For a moment even the Man's extraordinary confidence falters. But only for a moment. He looks at Black-coat and says: 'Where do you work?'

'In a shop.'

'Clerk?'

'No, guard.'

'Will you work in my bank? Salary of eighty rupees; another fifteen rupees as tiffin allowance.'

Black-coat is shaken. He folds his hands and bending his head, mutters, 'If you are so kind, then ... then ... all I can say is I wish you a long life.'

'Then you promise me?'

'What promise?'

'That you will join my Bank next month and you will not argue with the girl's father.'

'Sir, as long as you yourself are mediating, there is no question of raising any issue.'

'Good. Go back to your son and daughter-in-law and take them home. Remember, you lose the job if you ask the bride's father about money.'

'It will be as you wish, sir.'

Black-coat leaves. The Man has a feeling of having come through fire. He crosses the road and walks down to the main road, smiling to himself. He is free for the rest of the evening.

He goes forward along the main road for a bit, then retraces his steps - back to where the lane meets the main road. He has spent many months stealing the warmth and fellow-feeling from places where he did not belong. For the first time in his life he experiences some kind of an emptiness, a death almost, the departure of an almost loved one. His mind is the mind of a tigress, anxious to smell its young. There are no happy expressions today. From every marriage-house daughters are being bid good-bye. For the first time, the Man feels a great desire to steal a bit of the sorrow, take away with him the charm of separation - he craves the tears of belonging.

The Man approaches the house. Yes, there is the child-bride. They are getting into a taxi. Black-coat is there, and so is Bald-head. The Man approaches and stands very near the bride. His eyes fill up.

Black-coat approaches him with a bundle of clothes in his hand: 'Goodbye, sir, please remember me.'

Bald-head is surprised. 'Who are you addressing as sir?'

Black-coat is upset. 'The person standing in front of you, man. The younger son of that large house on the corner. Don't you know your own neighbours? Have you gone completely blind from crying for your daughter?'

'But, but ... this gentleman is your cousin.'

'What does that mean?'

'It means that he is the groom's uncle.'

A new note is injected by a stocky man from the groom's party. 'Who, who is the groom's uncle?'

Bald-head points to the Man and says, 'Him.'

Something in this exchange seems to mobilise the crowd of onlookers. Shouts of 'Who?' 'Who?' are heard. There is violence in the air.

Black-coat turns to the Man and charges him. 'Who are you exactly?'

The onlookers shout. 'Who doesn't know the younger son of the large house? But who in hell is this fellow?'

The groom's party keeps on repeating, 'No uncle of the groom came with us. Who the devil is this?'

The Man seems to have lost all sense of time and space. He does not utter anything; his very silence lending credence to the accusations being leveled against him.

The trance is broken by a blow that lands on his brow. In a trice, like an animal enraged, he bores his way through the crowd of onlookers and vanishes towards the main road.

The chase failed. The Man is too adroit a quarry, too alike the shades of light and darkness that swallow him.

The morning sun has! not yet lifted the thin covering of fog from the dirt and squalor of Bhairabtala Second Lane. The Man is hard at work washing his clothes. There is a slight bruise over his eyebrow. There are stains on the kurta also.

The Man is smiling. The woman approaches, looks at him curiously and says, 'I am going out for a bit.'

She is carrying a small quantity of rice, a piece of jaggery and a few leaves on an earthen platter.

'Where are you going?'

'To offer prayers.'

'Why?'

'That's my business.'

'Tell me anyway.'

'When you ran out last night, I prayed for your safe return.'

The Man starts laughing. He is overcome by the huge humour of it all. He wipes his eyes and says : 'So finally your god responded to at least one of your prayers.'

'Of course.' The woman is about to leave.

'Listen, wife.'

'What is it, now?' She turns around.

'Why don't you pray for what you wanted all those years ago?' What wish did she have? She has wished for so many things in the last twenty years that it is no longer possible for her to isolate any single one. She asks again, 'Which one?'

'For a child.'

The woman is nonplussed. Today, after so many years, why does this detached individual want new attachments? Whatever it may be, his statement still has the power to make her blush, at least realise her womanhood.

She smiles, and turns her face away. Then follows her action with a physical motion towards the door, as if the semblance of hurry will take away the intimate embarrassment of the moment.

'Wait, wait, hear me out fully!'

'I heard you.'

'Hear some more.'

'What is it?'

'Have you decided what to ask for? A boy or a girl?'

'Whatever you say.'

'I want a girl.'

The Man stares into the unknown. As if the ice in his heart is waiting for a little warmth.

The woman does not wait, crosses the few yards of the courtyard quickly and vanished around the corner.

The Man goes back to his washing. Are the stains really disappearing? Is his sight failing? Is it the loss of emptiness that suddenly makes his eyes see nothing?

translated by Bappa Chakravarty

The Darkness Covered Them

The inhabitants of Dhulgara are Bauri peasants and Vaishnava weavers. The weavers left the loom two generations ago. Now they are also cultivators, only not as good or hard-working as the Bauris. These weavers, however, look down upon the Bauris as boorish, born to till the soil and beneath them in culture. To show their superiority of birth they put a coloured cloth over their shoulders.

Dayaram was the handsomest young man among the Bauris. He died a few years ago leaving behind a widow who was the fairest in the village - Jaba. Jaba's father Kunja Bauri wanted his daughter to marry again and she knew very well that some day she would have to do so. All the villagers wanted Jaba to choose one from amongst them. This was also the desire of her father.

But which young man in the village was a good enough match for Jaba? When compared with Dayaram in looks or accomplishments all the young men seemed quite insignificant. One might consider the marriageable young men one by one - Jaya, Mati, Madhu or Gunadhar; any one of them would suit Jaba in age. They even possessed well-built bodies and were comely looking. Yet everyone thought Dayaram had been far more handsome.

When at work all of them wore either a torn gamcha or an old rag. Elderly peasants would just put a strip of cloth about their loins. These men seemed to take on an earth-brown hue. They could not be distinguished from a distance, as if like the partridges hiding in the fields they had disguised themselves to look like the earth.

Even now when Dayaram was mentioned one could see him. He used to put on a cleaner cloth wherever he was - in his hut or outside or even in the field. From afar he looked like a lily blossoming in the mud.

Dayaram had been neat and well dressed. His gamcha was clean, clothes spotless and hair well kept. He was no more, but his memory hovered in the sky like a swan with outspread wings.

Even after she had become a widow Jaba went sometimes to work with her father in the fields. Sometimes her eyes strayed to the adjoining field where Mati was hoeing. He had on only a loin-cloth. Jaba turned away her face in disgust, for she thought it was unseemly even for a man to be almost without clothes, like cows or horses.

On the way back home carrying water from the ghat Jaba would sometimes see Gunadhar felling trees by the wayside. He was wearing a piece of cloth that hung in such tatters that it would hardly have made any difference if he had worn nothing. Jaba would walk on with downcast eyes. Gunadhar would put aside his axe for a moment and stare at her, panting for breath. His sweating body looked like ebony moist with dew.

Everybody felt that Jaba's marriage should be arranged but the matter seemed to end there. For nobody had the courage to suggest the name of a possible suitor. Who did not know how great had been Jaba's love for Dayaram? The man who would marry her again must surely be as near him in looks and accomplishments as possible. A well-dressed cultured young man was wanted, but where was he to be found?

There never had been such a harvest at Dhulgara within the last seven years. The fields were full of corn; the peasants kept awake at nights to thresh with a song on their lips. Cattle feeding on the new straw grew fat. They sold cartloads of paddy — which was Dhulgara's proud produce — at the market at twice the usual price. But the joy born of plenty began to wane at Dhulgara within the space of three months. The thought of marriages, feasts and festivities vanished like twilight shadows. It took them only two months to understand that nobody was to blame for the turn in their fortune. Like a mad wild boar goring its own belly they had hurt themselves. They had thrown cartloads of gold from Dhulgara at the blackened feet of the rice-mills. All the crumpled paper money tied in torn gamchas round their waists was now worthless.

They would have to eat all the year round but rice was being sold at four and a half seers to the rupee. They would have to go to the grocer's shop at the place like so many beggars. They realised only too well that a handful of clay from the fields of Dhulgara was far more valuable than the dirty rupee-notes, moist with sweat, in their hands.

Not Dhulgara alone, but twenty villages around had made the same mistake. They had asked for a good price for their produce and had got it. In fact the price had been very good — four rupees and two annas per maund. So there was nothing to complain about. They had themselves thrown away their wealth. Before even three months had passed, the whole village was appalled by the spectre of want. To wait for seven months again with eyes turned to the heavens! The weaver-peasants fared no better. Coloured gamchas gradually disappeared from their shoulders. They had hoped to play on their much prized mridangas which hung on the posts of their huts. Some of the older men had thought of taking again to their looms, badly damaged from the neglect of two generations. A small capital, the inaugural rites with an earthen pot, vermillion and panchali music - these were all that were required. The instincts of the artisan, almost extinct by now, might yet gather in strength to inspire them. In every house yarn would be made and the shuttle fly, and Dhulgara would regain the wealth and gaiety of its youthful days. But the dream vanished; the weavers knew they had sadly blundered.

A hush fell on helpless Dhulgara doing penance for its foolishness. But there was still some life left in that part of the village where the weavers lived, and soon the whole village seemed to wake up. Mohan Banshi, son of Dinabandhu, a weaver, had left the village long ago. It was said he was a pedlar in the town. Now he was back in his own village. Mohan visited all Dhulgara. He had a new blue uniform and placed a blue turban lightly on his oiled and well combed long hair. Round his waist he had a leather belt with a brass plate. Mohan had become a watchman — four villages were within his jurisdiction and his pay was seven rupees. With the hatchet hanging lightly from his shoulder and a smile on his face Mohan toured the whole village.

Wherever Mohan went a group of naked children gathered round him. Older men clad in gamchas got over their first surprise and enquired from their verandah after his health. Grown up girls threw a sidelong glance at him and averted their faces, as if they felt Mohan's eye piercing in through the rents in their clothes. The married women reached their hands towards the nape of their necks in a fruitless attempt to veil their faces; but their saris were too scanty for that purpose.

Many girls were standing near the cow-shed in the Bauri quarter gathering cow-dung. Jaba was also there. Walking through quite a number of winding paths Mohan arrived there. It seemed he had got what he wanted after so much aimless wandering.

The girls were collecting the dung in heaps on palm leaves. Every one of them except Jaba looked as hideous as the cow-dung she was handling. One had a kantha on, another had wrapped herself in hessian and yet another had put on the remnants of a very old coloured saree. Perhaps none of these girls were really ugly; it was the dirty things they wore that spoilt their looks. They were certainly better looking than that.

Jaba's case was different, of course. She was wearing a whole sari though it was short. It was of course torn at places through constant use. Clothed in it she seemed to be clinging for the last time to the memory of the neatly dressed good-looking Dayaram, the companion of her youth.

The girls recognised Mohan, the watchman. What did he want, standing there so long? He might have stood there for some more time, but the girls rebuked him in a chorus. Deeply annoyed, they spoke with biting sarcasm so that he might hear: 'Well, well, we know by now you have become a Chowkidar, or a blue pigeon, if you will. Then why stand there and frighten us with your hatchet? Go home now; we don't think you are likely to meet a tiger on the way.'

Mohan hurriedly turned away and went back by a different path.

But Jaba watched Mohan for as long as she could see him. How could these girls abuse him and drive him away like this? It was true he was a weaver, a Chowkidar, and belonged to a different part of the village. Yet he was today the only neat and well-dressed man in the village. Jaba quarrelled with the girls.

Jaba: Why did you bark at him like that?

They: Why not? That man has no shame, why should he stand looking at us?

Jaba: Enough, enough. Stop. You yourselves have no shame. Just look at your clothes.

It seemed that the news of the calamity that had overtaken Dhulgara had spread far and wide. A Christian missionary had arrived at the village; he sang - 'The gates of heaven are open to the poor.' There had come also a doctor who attacked everybody young and old with lymph and knife. An astrologer had come to tell the future. A sadhu offered to appease the planets. Moreover, the special puja was drawing near; there was no escape from sacrificing a couple of goats to Siladevi under the banyan tree.

The resources of the wretched village were almost exhausted to provide offerings for all the gods.

Attracted as if by the blood of wounded Dhulgara, a Loan Office came there to open a branch. Its officers made thorough enquiries for about a week. They surveyed all the huts both in the Bauri and weavers' quarters, sized up the cattle and judged the quality of the land. They appeared to be satisfied. Within a few days a tin shed arose on a grassy plot right in the middle of the village. The Loan Office began to give advances. It advanced loans very cautiously keeping an eye on the weather conditions. All the peasants mortgaged their autumn and spring crops and affixed their thumb impressions to the bonds. Thus not only they themselves, but future crops on the land, were chained to the creditor.

The calamity had strangled enthusiasm in the village. Mohan appeared to be their only hope. If Mohan could move the Union Board with the tale of their woes, and the Board could in some way attract the notice of the Circle Officer, then the District authorities might wake up to the need of the village.

One evening all the weavers and the Bauris met under the banyan tree and respectfully made the proposition to Mohan. The character of this man was fully revealed by this episode. 'No, it can't be done,' Mohan replied, 'I am not a servant of this village. It is my business to catch thieves and bring miscreants to justice. If you really want to approach the authorities, give me five rupees. I shall have an application written and file it at headquarters.'

The weaver's hopes of an easy salvation were thus dashed to the ground. To think of it - Mohan was a boy of their village, the son of their own Dinabandhu! But today he had come back more a foreigner than even the English or the Kabulis. He no longer spoke their language, and the sorrows and injuries of Dhulgara were nothing to him.

Yet the only neat young man in the whole village was Mohan Banshi; he was the only one who had what might be called clothes. Other men in the village made only a crowd like so many cattle; but Mohan's clothes gave him the prestige of a foreigner.

Mohan's appearance had frightened the Bauri people most. Joy, Mati, Madhu and Gunadhar looked vacantly at him from a distance. If they saw Mohan looking at them they lowered their eyes with the consciousness of wrongdoing. They could not claim any intimacy with him, though in their boyhood they had gone with him to the fair at Haranpur and stolen a drink of sherbet together.

All of them again took to the plough. They turned the hard sun-dried soil at the ends of their ploughshares. They broke the clods with difficulty while their women cleared the weeds and levelled the earth with bamboo sticks. They tried to keep a firm grasp on the future in defiance of the conspiracy by hunger, disease, poverty, deception and despair.

Jaba obstinately refused to work in the fields. There was a herd of males working there who were lost to all sense of shame. They had hardly a stitch on their bodies and they did not care.

Old Kunja Bauri pleaded with her over and over again. 'Why think of them? Your work is on the land - and you keep your eyes on the land.'

Jaba - No. I can't.

Kunja - But you must.

Jaba - I can't.

Jaba gave a frank and proud reply. Enraged by her obstinacy Kunja at first gave her a piece of his mind. But soon he turned soft with affection. Really God had not given her such a figure to work in sun and rain. She had some intelligence, and the tastes of a lady. Privations made her cross - moved her to tears. She was not exactly a peasant girl clad in tatters. In fact, her true description was that she had been Dayaram's wife - a fact which she could not forget even now. She would even now put the vermillion mark on her brow, chew paan and dress herself in the few old sarees which were still left.

Sometimes Jaba would sit on the verandah of her hut and comb her hair. Mati would cast a timid glance in her direction as he went by the hedge with a spade on his shoulder. He was wearing a warm coat of foreign wool, which he had procured from somewhere - perhaps begged it of some gentleman in the town. The coat was a misfit; its length covered the torn loin-cloth. Mati was as usual wet with sweat. Jaba looked sidewise at him and turned away her face. Her lips curled in a sarcastic smile. Mati's face turned pale for a moment, his eyes shone in the next.

Early one morning a peddling cloth-dealer set up a booth under a banyan tree. He hung a line from the branch of a tree and placed a variety of sarees on it. He had piled up neatly folded cloths of all sizes - bleached and otherwise. On one side was a heap of cloth for shirting and coating - cambric, longcloth etc. - and on another were a number of readymade garments, slightly faded.

It at first made the pedlar glad to see so many customers. But looking at their clothes he realised his mistake. It was a crowd of half-naked beggars; with their bare suntanned skins they hardly seemed to have the feeling of shame possessed by well clad people. It was doubtful whether they would buy anything.

The excitement of the naked children, the bargaining of the young men, the questions of the women and the keen greedy eyes of the people - all frightened the pedlar. He hurriedly packed up his goods and got up. Charan Bauri, the headman, and some other older men made a request : 'This puja nobody will be in a position to buy your things. Come at the time of Holi. Then we shall buy lots of things.'

'Of course, I shall come - you will take as many as you will.'

The pedlar placed the bundle on his shoulder, gave a crooked smile and took to the road.

On the occasion of the Panchami festival only the land under the banyan tree grew red - for a pair of goats bought with money had been sacrificed. This festivity was not a thing to be seen, only to be heard. The ceaseless beat of the drums sounded like the groans of the hungry wretched people of Dhulgara. There was a crowd of about three hundred persons - old men and women, wives and daughters of the peasants. Rags, strips of cloth and hessian with a dash of yellow on them: their festive robes were as pitiable as the frightened smiles on their face. They seemed to harmonise perfectly with their background of stale and discoloured flowers, dried leaves and the hard grey earth.

But Jaba's case was different. She had put on a sari with a wide border dyed yellow with home-made vegetable dye. She had the usual vermillion mark. She had also darkened her eyes with eye-black.

Indeed she looked a princess! Other girls whispered and smiled with pressed lips. They seemed to avoid the place where Jaba stood. Time was when the girls would eagerly have gathered round Jaba whenever they saw her. They would have tugged at her saree or the ribbon in her hair and everyone would sing her praises. But now they saw an unkind light in the eyes dark with eye-black. Jaba had indeed travelled far from them and seemed to have become a stranger. Today they felt sorry for dead Dayaram and old Kunja Bauri. The girls seemed to avoid the very shadow of Jaba - as if they knew the secret of her pride.

Kunja was a foolish old man. One day he was repairing with his spade a part of the boundary lines of his field when Janaki Bauri asked him - 'Hallo Kunja dada, why has not your daughter come to work?'

Kunja - 'You call yourselves men? You are all naked like beasts and feel no shame. How can a woman come into your midst?'

About ten or twelve men firmly grasped their spades and shouted together. 'What did you say, you old fool? Your Jaba is the only modest woman, you old fool? What about these daughters, wives and mothers of ours who are working here? Are they not as modest? Go to your house and see for yourself. Mohan, the weaver, is putting you to shame; don't you know, you blind fool? Go home and see.'

Old Kunja felt a strange fear clutch at his heart. He shook all over like a leaf. This terrible insinuation seemed to shatter the pride of his fifty-five years to dust.

Firmly holding the spade he jumped up and ran towards his homestead like a wild horse. They ran behind him shouting 'Now, now you stop, old man.'

Jaba was sitting neatly dressed by the sacred tulasi plant in the courtyard. It was now afternoon; soon it would be dark. All the she had to do was to collect a few chips of wood to boil some rice for the old man. Then would come the silent night. Jaba hardly had the strength to resist any more the importunate prayer of a charming well-dressed young man standing in the darkness on the yard. But the wheezing sound of the old man's breath would reach her through the chinks in the bamboo partition. She would not listen to the voice from the dark.

'I am forsaking my caste for you,' - Mohan would say - 'Why do you care for yours?'

Jaba - 'I don't ask you to give up your caste.'

Mohan - 'How can that be avoided? Who will feed you?'

Jaba - 'I am not starving. My father is here.'

Mohan - 'How are you going to clothe yourself? In rags? How many sarees have you left?'

Jaba - 'Only this one.'

Mohan - 'What next? What will you cover yourself with once this one has gone?'

Jaba - 'Well, you could give me a saree.'

Mohan - 'Why should I?'

Jaba - 'All right, don't.'

Thus every night by the sacred tulasi plant in her yard she would see enacted the sweet but deceiving drama in which the man begged her love, promised her things. It was with great difficulty that Jaba had today managed to wrap herself in her worn-out sari. A slight inattentive movement would tear it. A tear half a cubit long already shamelessly appeared above her knee. This was a dishonour she could hardly bear.

Last night Mohan had said, 'The day you appear clothed in rags will see the end of our affair. I shall not come any more. I shall not love you any more.'

Dayaram too had spoken in the same way. If he found Jaba careless about her dress he would threaten her like this. In the darkness the frills of Mohan's turban looked like Dayaram's long curls. Jaba held herself in check. A moment of forgetfulness and she would throw herself into Mohan's arms.

'You are pretty. Why should you not dress well?' said Mohan as he was leaving.

'Stay a little more -'Jaba said.

Her reverie was rudely shattered. A furious uproar suddenly burst on her.

Before old Kunja's spade could come down on her head the other men held his hands down. Kunja trembled all over and sat down heavily. Jaba realised what the matter was from the remarks, words of abuse and regrets uttered by the crowd of people. She knew that her nightly exploit had come to light. This was why they had secretly laughed at her on the day of the festival.

Jaba went to her room and shut the door.

The crowd dispersed. Old Kunja was lying outside in the darkness like a lame ox. Jaba came out and with tears pleaded: 'Come inside, father!'

Kunja - 'No.'

Jaba - 'I swear by our mother earth that I shall never again misbehave or offend you in any way.'

Kunja went to his room leaning on Jaba's arm and laid himself down on his bed. Jaba spread a piece of gunny on the floor and lay there at the old man's feet. She felt she was again in the lap of mother earth from where she had fallen off for the last few days. She slept the deep sleep of peace and satisfaction.

The weavers had come to realise that Mohan was not one of them - he was only the watchman. The Bauris knew that Jaba was an insult to their caste. Both parties began to hate one another, for neither could forget their caste pride. The weavers thought that Jaba had corrupted one of their boys, while the Bauris felt Mohan had brought dishonour to their caste.

At times, of course, the Bauris understood that the blame was not chiefly Mohan's - if Jaba had behaved decorously their honour and prestige would not have been so easily lost. Jaba's father was a strange sort of man. He could not control his daughter and was indifferent, though he saw everything. Was he not afraid of losing caste? However, the Bauris silently bore the insult. Their pride of caste was today as numb as a snake struck with a club.

Old Kunja was again working. People now looked upon him with pity. He had obviously not many days more to live - what was the use of making him an outcast? The poor old man had to work painfully in the field with his bent back though he had an able and grown-up daughter at home. But they would not forgive the impudence of Mohan the weaver. Let the sowing be finished and the crops begin to grow, and when better days came they would judge the strength of that weaver and his axe.

For the last three days old Kunja had noticed something unusual. He had remarked that none of the peasant women were coming to work in the field. Besides, the peasants looked sullen. There had been rain recently and the work of transplantation had to be hurried. But it took all their time to raise embankments. Meanwhile the paddy plants lay nearly submerged in water.

Hriday Bauri being near him Kunja asked, 'Where are your womenfolk? Why don't they come?'

As Hriday remained silent Kunja asked again while his jaw moved with a malicious smile: 'Is Mohan the weaver carrying on an intrigue also with your....'

'You have lost your senses,' cried Hriday. `It's something you can't understand. Better go home and ask your daughter.'

'You might as well speak out.'

'Well, our women will come to work. Else how will transplantation be finished? Now, shut up.'

This cryptic remark baffled Kunja. With a yawn and an ugly smile he settled down to work again.

The pond in the bamboo grove was absolutely deserted even at noon. A long cut from a palm tree was lying in the water near the brink like a tortoise showing its back. Jaba sat on it and was very carefully washing her last sari. The border of the sari was still not absolutely worn out, but its threads had become loose and rotten and it was hardly possible to sew another patch on to it. She did her washing with extreme caution, but still her saree tore in two more places.

Jaba spread her saree in the yard and sat inside her room. She wanted to hide herself from her own self. An uncomfortable feeling of shame oppressed her like a painful fever.

When the saree was dry she found it as rough and stiff as a piece of paper. Try as she might she could not wear it with any decency; it almost broke into pieces like an old mat. In extreme disgust she threw it away. It seemed that the conspiracy of unclothed Dhangara had at last reached her with its malignant purpose.

When the night was a little advanced Jaba came out into her compound. The thrilling sound of Mohan's footsteps could be heard in the dark after many days.

Mohan - 'What was the matter with you, Jaba? Why did you hide yourself these last few nights? Do you mean to kill me or drive me mad?'

Jaba - 'You came every night, did you?'

Mohan - 'Of course. The other day a scorpion stung me, pain all over. Still I waited.'

Mohan's words seemd to throw a spell on Jaba, stilling all her fears and hesitations and anxious thoughts. She collapsed on the ground. As Mohan anxiously tried to raise her a fragment of her sari came off in his hand.

Mohan - 'Why Jaba, you are wearing a rag.'

Jaba - 'Yes.'

Mohan - 'Do you like it?'

Jaba - 'No.'

Mohan - 'Shall I bring you a saree? Will you take it? Say yes. Just for this once.'

Jaba - 'Yes.'

Mohan - 'I will bring you one tomorrow.'

After Mohan had left Jaba sat by the sacred tulasi plant for a long time like one unconscious. To her Dhulgara was lost for ever in the glamour of a new world where clothes, ornaments and toilet articles were plentiful. Her pride of birth, her land and garden, her deity under the banyan tree were now all far away. No tie was strong enough to bind her down.

Shadowy figures passed by the hedge in a group. Jaba came to herself with a start at the sound of their footsteps. After staring for a while her frightened eyes became steady. Then she climbed over the hedge with the joy of a night-bird flapping its wings and joined the receding group.

It was late in the night when Mohan came back from the market-town. During the whole day he had not had a morsel to eat; for he had no money to spare. He had purchased at the shop of the Pal Babu two sarees, one a fancy imitation Benarasi and another a fine one from the mills, paying thirteen rupees cash and keeping the balance of the price to his account. The whole afternoon he had spent at the dyer's shop where he had got the sari dyed for seven rupees. He had dearly wanted to buy a nice towel for himself. But all his money was gone. Today he had reached the goal of his youth, the land of his dreams, and must not hesitate if he had to pay. This was an intoxicating joy, the joy of utterly denuding oneself.

In the middle of the night the jackals stopped howling suddenly. Tiny drops of rain struck Mohan's face. Near the sacred tulasi plant he had placed the carefully folded saris - a gift in which was centred his future happiness. He loitered in the yard. Jaba was still inside her room!

In the corner of the yard the glow-worms were throwing their light on heaps of wet leaves. Mohan at length grew restless. Jaba's assurance had made every moment of the still night precious to him.

As Mohan waited he heard old Kunja breathing like a pair of bellows that had burst. At last Mohan lost patience and removing the bar from the door entered the but. As he struck a light with his flint he saw there was no other person in the hut; only old Kunja was sleeping there. Only an ugly human machine of dried-up bones and tissues, wasting itself out miserably.

A wildness surged in Mohan's veins. He jumped out of the hut, took up the sarees in one hand and with the hatchet gripped firmly in the other vanished into the darkness.

Where was Jaba?

Grasping his hatchet Mohan strained his eyes and ears at every door in the Bauri quarter, at every rent in the bamboo wall and scanned the tops of the mud walls and the darkness below the platforms of the barns. But Jaba could not be traced.

Mohan remembered Moti Bauri - a strong young man he was - to whom it was once proposed to marry Jaba. Where was he?

Moti was sleeping outside the cowshed with a small bundle of straw pressed against his breast.

The sleeping cows and buffaloes were driving away mosquitoes with their tails. Moti alone guarded the cattle. He was as brave as he was poor and had no fear of wolves or hyenas. Only after seeing him with his own eyes were Mohan's doubts set at rest.

For the first time in his life Mohan really kept a good watch. He heard hungry men grinding their teeth in their sleep in every hut. Not a lamp was burning anywhere. Not a word, incautiously loud, of the whispered talk of sleepless lovers could be heard. Only the hungry cries of the babies broke the stillness of the night. How was it that nobody woke up to pacify them?

Mohan grew tired with walking. Jaba had apparently disappeared, yet her invisible presence could be felt like the darkness or the moist air about him. He came to the end of the village, and stood under a karamcha tree.

Mohan had been dozing for some time. He woke up to find himself leaning against the tree. He was so exhausted that he had been clinging to the tree like a dead branch. The night was now about to end.

Some persons were coming along the embankments of the fields. One, two three: many were coming. They were coming towards the village like a herd of startled cows running through the dew.

These were the Bauri girls returning from the fields where, under the cover of night, they had been transplanting their seedlings. The night's work was over, as dawn drew near.

They were coming, the nude daughters of the earth! They had for the night left in their homes their miserable garments - rags, sheets of gunny and kanthas - the garments that the day's decorum forced upon them. Now their bodies were clothed in darkness in the trailing robes spun of countless black threads.

Mohan the watchman was sitting inertly under the karamcha tree staring like one dazed, clutching at his pair of sarees. Mud-splashed figures passed rapidly in a procession before his eyes. Masses of dishevelled hair ruffled against their backs. The muscles of the uncovered bodies seemed to ring like dancing bells with a strange soft music.

'Day is about to break. Hurry along' - It was Jaba who spoke out from their midst.

They cast a look at the eastern sky and sped towards the village along the path under the tree. The world would soon wake to life with the noise of birds, beasts and bees. The women were afraid lest the sun should rise to shine upon their nakedness.

translated by Sanjaya Bhattacharya

A Change of Caste

Mokatpur! That old half-ruined house on a muddy road! The white-ant riddled bamboo trellis below the tiled roof rains an incessant stream of powdery white dust. For three years the house has not even been whitewashed. Full of a crowd of people - grown-ups, children, wet napkins and dirty bedding, this was Sanjoy's sweet home!

The hunger for food and clothes could no longer be met with the limited dole elder brother alone gave every month. Every luxury had already been reduced. Now the stomach was being pinched cruelly. Ghee, sugar, tea — every month elder brother was slicing off bits of the family's hungry tongue. There was no other way. Who knew, that with all his education when it came to learning money Sanjoy would have to sit idle like a cripple? Not for one day or two, but for four long years.

The afternoon's light stormy breeze made the dried beans on the Sirish tree swing with a jingling noise like the sound of heavy anklet-bells. This time of day was always nice. The whole day's store of laziness turned into a sweet lethargy.

Sitting in the verandah with a glass of tea sweetened with molasses in his hand, Sanjoy was re-tasting his daily worries with every sip.

Each one look out for yourself! In season, out of season, elder brother was reminding everyone. But four years ago, this very same elder brother had carried food in a tiffin-carrier on the day of the examination and waited in front of the gates of the college hall. But that was another day. Elder brother's hopes and ambitions were then like a garland of humble desires - blackened with sorrow and want. The weariness of this constant want would one day be washed away; Sanjoy would get a job; the touch of a silver wand would make the Dutt house in Mokatpur shine with plenty. This was the foregone conclusion.

M.A. degree; three certificates for character, health and proficiency in games; three articles on Economics written by himself published in a foreign magazine; medals for singing and acting; a letter of praise for his unremitting services during the earthquake - Sanjoy's varied and versatile genius now lay rotting in a box tied up in a big bundle. For four years, he had sent in innumerable applications without getting a job. Elder brother had lost all hope. Even mother's tongue now overflowed with nagging words.

Sanjoy felt utterly abashed. During these four wretched years, moment by moment, his worries had shattered many of his illusions. In the olden days anyone in his position would have left home and become a sannyasi. But Sanjoy was made of a different metal. Every maxim of the twentieth century's revolutionary economics was known to him.

Sanjoy realised that here affection was only a commodity for sale. Every blessing given was the notice of a creditor's demand. True, if he got a headache, his little four-year-old niece Putul would come and stroke his hair to soothe the ache. But Sanjoy knew that even the tiny little girl's show of devotion hid a shrewd business sense. As soon as her task was over, she would make a straight-forward demand - 'I want a silk ribbon'.

On the surface everything was so lovely. Father, mother, brother, sister, one's kith and kin: home was a nest of affection. What highfalutin' sentiments! But scratch it just a little and the skin would reveal a shameless Shylock's flesh! Sanjoy could not help laughing sometimes. Of course this was nothing new. For millions of years this order had trickled down through the veins of history, beginning from the caveman's family life down to the pattern of domesticity in the household of the Dutts in Mokatpur. Love, friendship, affection, were like chillies, molasses, ginger and pepper; whoever could pay for these was looked upon as the dearest one.

Sumitra too had not been round this side for a long time. Perhaps the wind of love too had changed its course. It was, however, not surprising. Sumitra's father Abhoy Babu too seemed to have changed his attitude completely. He had mortgaged his house. Could it be that a groom had been found even for such a one as Sumitra?

On the last day of the Pujas, last year, she had come to pay her respects. In the Champa-coloured saree even that terribly dark girl had looked so beautiful. Sumitra's sandalwood-decorated forehead had rested languidly on Sanjoy's feet for over two minutes. It fell as if this grown-up maiden's youth was beating its head in mute sorrow. Sumitra had fallen in love.

These memories of past days. It was pleasant to ponder over them, but sister-in-law came and interrupted, 'Have you heard the news about Abhoy Babu's family, brother?'

'No.'

'The Sub-registrar, Nabin Babu and Sumitra are to be — '

'Married. Isn't that it?'

Sister-in-law smiled and went away. That smile was like a taunt. Let it go. The biggest illusion too was smashed, that was the only gain. Those tears, obeisance tendered at his feet, that face blushing with shyness - what a piece of sharp, subtle, pure coquetry it was. While realising this he had pretended not to recognise it; that was his crime.

He must go away, while there was still time, or else, in this auction-house, his whole manhood would be sold away as a counterfeit commodity. He would have to leave behind the hypocritical wiles of this genteel household. Just because of a false illusion about a caste-name he could not mortgage his entire life's ideals and desires, like an absolute beast. Sanjoy realised that his greatest need was Gotrantar - a change of caste.

Sanjoy was going to a far-away place. A job worth thirty rupees in the Ratanlal Sugar Mills; but the question of high or low salary did not arise. Within this thirty-rupee job, he had caught the glimpse of a palace of unbounded freedom.

On the day of leaving, this worn old house in Mokatpur seemed once again to try and exert all its magic with the intent to damp all Sanjoy's enthusiasm. The brothers and sisters were packing his trunk and bedding; little Putul was clinging to him from early morning like a mole on his body, her desire seemed to be - 'I won't let you go.' The sting in his father's conversation had entirely vanished; he was restless and unable to smoke his tobacco in peace. Mother had not yet come out of the kitchen; sitting in front of the kitchen fire she seemed to be trying to make up for her miserliness. She cooked three kinds of fish-curries alone.

Elder brother seemed to be the most upset. He said, 'Go with a happy frame of mind and remember that an enterprising lion among men is bound to receive Lakshmi's favour. One day you might become the owner of that mill. What was Sir Rajendra at one time? Always keep your eyes fixed on future prospects.'

Sanjoy breathed a sigh of relief when he got into the motor-bus.

On one side lay the dried-up river bed, and on the other three - jungle, and in between the 84 Parganas. The Grand Chord line ran like a pulse-beat through the midst of the jungle. A range of chalk hills ran along up to Kodarma station.

The name of the mill area was Ratanganj - a bazaar and far and near, all around, the quarters of the coolies and workers. All over the entire stretch of 84 Parganas were scattered fields full of vegetables and sugar-cane; ugly scare-crows; little huts for the men who drove away the marauding wild swine; narrow, twisting channels of water, and in between big wooden posts hung with buckets to water the fields; like ship's masts they floated in this ocean of green.

The crops of sugar-cane became ripe. Thin sticks standing a foot apart - high as two men. On their heads - banners like strips of green silk. Bustees of the chattries - the warrior caste, and the ahirs - the cowherds, whose bones for generations had manured the earth of 84 Parganas and turned it into gold.

The owner of the mill Rai Bahadur Ratanlal was a very good and polite man. He even addressed a petty pan-man with the respectful 'you' and not as 'thou'. Before his early morning bath every day he went round scattering handfuls of sugar on all ant-holes.

Sanjoy was the cash clerk. The Rai Bahadur assured him, 'This mill belongs to you. If it progresses, you will progress too. Prove your worth. There are plenty of prospects here.'

Rubbing the challan-receipt register and ledger; notes; money and small change, month after month, the tips of his fingers seemed to have become poisoned. In the sound of the crushing machines; mountains of crushed cane husks and the smell of unrefined molasses - there was nowhere the sign of any prospect. Neither did any such impertinence as a futile hope lurk anywhere in Sanjoy's mind. He knew the ways of such honey-tongued money-pots only too well.

It was not the hope of prospects but a far greater and grimmer determination which had brought him here. Like a run-away convict he must completely erase his old self.

The strange character of a particular individual made Sanjoy feel very worried. His name was Neymiar. He was absolute poison in the eyes of the mill officials. He had been working as a loading clerk for the last five years. He started on a salary of thirty rupees and had come down to a salary of fifteen now. Even the man's shadow seemed to possess a terrible contagion of ill luck.

He was ugly; moreover he suffered from pleurisy. Three days in the week, pressing his ribs against the table, he would lie there immobile. To see him one would think that the man must be spineless; otherwise, how could he lie like that, twisted and rolled up like a worm?

Then there was Rukmini - Neymiar's sister. Everyone - the old hands and new, in the mill, had all warned Sanjoy, 'Bengali Babu, keep out of the clutches of that pair - both the brother and the sister!'

Without any encouragement from Sanjoy, Neymiar tried to be intimate with him. Suddenly one day be came and said, 'Don't drink water from anywhere except the number one well. You will get malaria.' Another day he brought several bottles - Iodine, Castor Oil and Quinine pills. 'I brought these from Kodarma hospital for you.'

Sanjoy was just waiting to see where this unselfish friendship would end. In three weeks Neymiar's mask fell off. Sanjoy was writing up a ledger in his office. He looked up and saw Neymiar standing; his two little eyes were burning with a flickering fire.

Neymiar said, 'Now get a gun-licence, Babuji. We will go shooting together. Rabbit roast will go very well with double-brewed mahua liquor every day.'

When Sanjoy showed no enthusiasm, he paused and thought over something and said suddenly in a hurried manner. 'Give me a loan of five rupees, Babuji. Next month you will get six rupees and eight annas.'

Sanjoy gave a straight answer, 'Nothing doing; excuse me.'

When Neymiar had gone Sanjoy smiled to himself. He knew the uttermost wiles of the human heart. He was not to be got at so easily. What was Neymiar after all! But he had yet to know Neymiar.

At night, above the sound of pouring rain someone was heard knocking on the door. As soon as Sanjoy opened the door Rukmini entered with a tray of food in her hands.

'It's Neymiar's birthday today. Neymiar said, you are his only friend, so I brought a little food for you.'

When she finished speaking Rukmini put down the tray of food and sat on one side of the wooden bed and laughed.

Sanjoy saw Rukmini properly now for the first time. The girl was dark and thin. She had bright, intelligent eyes. Dark patches below her eyes spoke of many sleepless nights. But still one realised that if only she was fed properly how charming this face would look! She was wearing an expensive saree and smelt of an expensive foreign perfume. But of all her features the most beautiful were her teeth. When she spoke, they seemed like rows of tiny white pearls. When she laughed, those pearls suddenly burst open like a bunch of flower-buds.

Seeing Sanjoy engrossed in her, Rukmini turned away her face and said, 'Finish your food, I will wait till you have eaten.'

As soon as he finished eating, Rukmini got up and with quick gestures of her hands picked up all the dishes and said, 'It's very late. I am going now, Babuji.'

Sanjoy said in a slightly embarrassed manner, ' How will you go alone?'

'Oh, I'll manage to go.' With a burst of laughter, just as Rukmini put her foot out of the door, Sanjoy suddenly caught her wrist.

Rukmini remonstrated, 'These dishes will fall just now. Wait, let me put them down first.'

A few days later Neymiar came and stood before Sanjoy's table in his office. The spineless creature's eyes were burning again. Lowering his voice he said, 'You love Rukmini?'

The sudden question made Sanjoy start. Neymiar said again, 'But that's something to be happy about. Why feel ashamed? All right, I must go now. Give - '

Sanjoy: 'What?'

'- the five rupees you had promised. Thank you!' Putting the note in his pocket Neymiar continued, 'Whenever you need anything just tell me.'

Sanjoy had really changed his caste. Just as a bird gets his mate by giving the love-call, Rukmini had come to him. This girl of the streets alone had accepted his humiliated manhood with reverence. This was much better than inane domesticity. The first chapter of his revolution was complete.

Letters came from home. Typical letters from a Bengali home: 'How are you? What progress have you made? There is so much want in the household. It would be good if you could send something.'

Letters came, but no answers were sent. In between remained a big distance of sandy waste and quicksands. The letters seemed like bits out of a newspaper. Suffering and want did not reside in the Dutt house in Mokatpur alone. This Neymiar's wife had committed suicide by jumping into a well with three children in her arms. Neymiar carried about cuttings from newspapers containing this news in his breast-pocket. When the sorrows of the world mended themselves so would the sorrows of the Dutt household.

Sometimes the intoxication of strong country liquor set his head on fire and Sanjoy's eyes would begin to water. Rukmini begged him to tell her why he wept.

Sanjoy tore those letters and burnt them with the frenzy of a mad Brahmin who burns his sacred thread.

Thousands of miles away from the 84 Parganas, on the other side of the salt ocean, in the land of the Dutch, the money-goddess became a widow. The gold standard was cancelled and the rate of exchange changed completely overnight. In one stroke the price of the guilder came down and became cheap.

That angry wind of trade navigated the sky and rushed into port in Calcutta. Tons and tons of Java sugar were being landed at a cheap price. The Indian Chamber of Commerce was feeling depressed. Motipur, Champaran and Cawnpore Special sugar lay weeping inside bags at all the depots.

The curse of the Dutch market fell on the Ratanlal Mills and the canefields of the 84 Parganas. In every home of the mill-workers the Manager went round reading out a notice - a forty percent cut in pay and wages.

The peasants crowded round the mill gates. The Manager put his mouth over the megaphone and shouted out the price of sugar-cane: 'Eleven pice a maund! Those who are willing to sell must send in their crops from tomorrow.'

Till evening, the crowd of workers and peasants sat stunned in front of the mill gates. The Rai Bahadur's son, Suraj Babu, had gone to put in a trunk-call to Calcutta to find out the state of the sugar market there,

Rai Bahadur came out himself with folded hands and asked the crowd to disperse. He said, 'What is the good of creating all this trouble, my fathers? All this is a turn of fate, - go and pray to God and ask for better days to return.'

Amongst all the peasants Muniram was a headstrong man. He had the tongue to answer back. He said, 'But the Government have fixed the price at four annas and nine pies, huzur.'

Rai Bahadur replied with a sweet smile, 'Forget all those happy dreams, my brothers. That kingdom of Rama has passed. Goods from Java are committing dacoity now. Everything is on fire. I hope the mill will not have to be closed down.'

Muniram was not the man to give up so easily. He said, 'Tomorrow we will send you our wives and children. Be kind enough to shoot them down, that will be far better.'

Rai Bahadur scolded them most affectionately, 'Foolish mules! Go and cool your heads at home. Oh, Shanker the brave, now close the gates.'

Like a defeated army the crowd turned back from the gates. Workers and coolies turned on their way home. Only Sanjoy walked in another direction. With him were Neymiar, Muniram, Shuklal, Chedi and a few other peasants. They came noiselessly and sat on the steps of the old Shiva temple under the big banyan tree. Sanjoy said: 'We must take our revenge for this.'

Muniram's very soul seemed to have been waiting for this one word of courage. He jumped up and said, 'For Heaven's sake, Bengali Babu, tell us the way out.'

God knows what induced some of the foolish-looking peasants to yell out: 'Har har Mahadev!'

Neymiar turned on them in a rage, 'Shut up, don't make any noise,' he cried.

After a few moments of silence, Sanjoy proposed, 'No one will sell their crop.'

Everyone replied, 'That's right.'

'Don't bring down your price; in the end they will have to buy. Many new machines have arrived. They will have to keep the mill going.'

Shuklal said, 'But supposing they don't buy?'

The problem was nearly settled, but Shuklal's question started arguments all over again.

Sanjoy got up and said, 'They will be forced to buy. Begin the fight, all of you. Take your oath on the banyan leaf that you will fight them.'

There was a strange fervour of hope in Sanjay's words. The little clouds of doubt which had lingered, now blew away in the storm of enthusiasm and oath-taking. With a touch of this holy wind the mute deaf image in the old temple seemed suddenly to wake up.

The meeting ended.

As soon as Sanjoy came near Rukmini's home, he said, 'Neymiar, you had better go now. Begin from today and organise well.'

'All right, Babuji.'

After Neymiar had gone Sanjoy stood silent in the darkness for a long time. Sanjoy, the holder of a M.A. degree, had been turned into a petty cash-clerk. It seemed as if his insulted genius had been counting the days like a snake with hood lowered in futile rage. Now it was time to strike and pour out as much venom as was possible. In the darkness, Sanjoy rigged out all his thoughts in military array and got ready for battle. The chimney of the Ratanlal Mills could be seen faintly. It looked like the raised head of a dinosaur which stared down at the broad cane-fields of the 84 Parganas. Sanjoy knew that somewhere under that monstrous heap of fat, a heart must be hidden; the blow must be carefully aimed there.

Full of elation Sanjay entered Rukmini's room.

The extravagance of his caresses made Rukmini suddenly question him, 'You've got the goods very cheap, haven't you? Still, one day you are bound to leave me.'

'Cheap? Have I anything more left to give? And why should I leave you?'

As if touched with a little remorse Rukmini put her hand over Sanjoy's mouth and said, 'All right ! All right! Forgive me, I won't say it again. But the other day, while you were drunk, you yourself said that I was only the tumbler which held sherbet, but not the sherbet itself.' Then without waiting for Sanjoy's answer Rukmini continued, 'I want a good amount of money. Now, look at me once properly.' Then she removed the end of her saree from her shoulders and stood up straight . 'Do you understand? How am I to manage?'

'Yes! I do understand.' Sanjoy turned very grave.

All the machines in the Ratanlal Mills were closed down. Only a few carts of sugar were obtainable. The last day for supplying orders from the Calcutta market was fast approaching. Rai Bahadur was running round madly back and forth, between the mill and the bungalow of the sub-divisional officer in town.

In field after field the crops of 84 Parganas were drying up. Agents were rushing from bustee to bustee with carts and bags of money. They were saying: release your crops now, for, if once the leaves turn brown, we will not pay even an anna as price. The peasants smiled and remained silent. Neymiar had absolutely disappeared. He did not stay at home nor did he come to office.

He was flying around the fields and bustees of 84 Parganas like a crow, cawing: 'Be warned, don't be frightened by what the agents are saying. Ratanlal Mill is being frozen.'

For the last few days, vultures had been circling over the 84 Parganas. Cattle-disease had broken out. One of Muniram's sons too had died of small-pox.

Moneylenders were knocking from door to door taking round their red cloth-bound ledger-books and mortgage bonds demanding repayment of loans. A labour recruiter got hold of thirty men and disappeared with them to the rubber-gardens of Malaya. On the road leading to Kadamsagar a bullock-cart had been looted. Military police had done a route march.

Cowherds from Kodarma were flocking around like a band of locusts. they were buying buffaloes for five rupees, milch cows for eight rupees and calves for twelve annas. The moneylenders were giving loans on mortgaged silver ornaments, at a high rate of interest. Brass and bell-metal household utensils were being sold at the price of mud. In every home in 84 Parganas wild herbs and leaves were being boiled and eaten. In every home the stores of foodgrain were empty.

It was a nearly a month now. Rai Bahadur was cursing his agents. They must get the raw material however they could. His prestige in the market was tottering. His machines were getting rusty.

The sub-divisional officer came and inspected the mill. His peons had informed the people of 84 Parganas by beat of drums: 'Take heed everyone! Sell your crops now, only one more day's time is being given you! Or else, from tomorrow, crops will be bought from Loyabad Pargana!'

Muniram and Shuklal came in the evening. Their looks were those of mangy dogs. Yet, hope was still burning their eyes, they were only begging for an order - 'Babuji, what do we have to do now? Give us the order.'

Sanjoy replied, 'Wait a few days more.'

Muniram and Shuklal waited without speaking a word for some time and then went away. Probably there was something which they wanted to say, but it remained unspoken.

All the happenings seemed to become suddenly complicated. Rai Bahadur had not yet called upon Sanjoy to render help or advice in the face of such trouble, even though Sanjoy had hinted one day, 'If you like I might try to quieten down the peasants.'

On the other hand, Rukmini too had swallowed a thorn. Something must be arranged now on both sides. But how could one arrange anything without Neymiar? Whenever there was work to be done, he was really a great help.

Neymiar came and stood before him.

The dim dirty light of a kerosene lamp - a dirty khaki pant, a torn shirt, a wild shock of hair - untidy as a crow's nest. That worm Neymiar stood up like a statue made of iron, slim and hard. This casteless man's real image struck Sanjoy with a strange fear; he sat with his head bowed.

Neymiar had come to ask him for the keys of the cash-room. "Like a lizard I will lick up and bring whatever money there is in there and then set fire to the room. The file-register will be burnt to ashes. Who will be able to make you responsible? Who will be able to say how much cash balance there was? Come on, give the key to me!'

Sanjoy raised his head and looked out into the darkness outside. Had the light been a little brighter, one could have seen that his two knees began suddenly to tremble violently with a sudden gust of shivering.

Neymiar it seemed was singing a terrible meaningless ballad. Food, first of all, 84 Parganas required food. Then we would see how they could bring crops from outside down the Loyabad Road. No one would sell his crops. They would rot on every field. they would be burnt to ashes. The peasants had all taken this oath. Tonight in every home long poles were being polished and got ready. They would break their own heads and in return break that of others.

A face pitted with small-pox marks; round marble-like eyes; short, thin; skin the colour of a dung-cake - this Neymiar of whom even a sparrow could not feel afraid, today he had come and was standing before Sanjoy, with the threat of an oncoming revolution in his hands.

Sanjoy's ardour had become suddenly very damp. Neymiar patted his back and said, 'What is all this worry about, comrade-brother? Your peasant-army must be fed. Come, don't delay any more.'

Neymiar slipped out into the darkness with the bunch of keys of the cash-room.

Sanjoy paced the room in a demented manner for a long time. Then he came out and stood there to cool himself with a breath of fresh air. He had never imagined that this little strife would lead to such a terrible end. Who had thought that the tame lion which was brought out into circus arena only to perform his tricks, would with just a little poking, snarl wildly, and turn so disobedient?

'Neymiar!' Sanjoy's cracked voice trembled and echoed in the darkness.'

Sanjoy broke into a run.

From a crack in the window in Rukmini's room emerged a dim light and a moaning sound as of a string instrument. Sanjoy held his breath and stood with his eyes glued to the crack in the window.

Rukmini was rolling on the floor. Her saree had come off. Only the knot remained round her waist. Her hair which dragged on the mud floor was full of dirt. Her glass bangles had broken to pieces and bits of glass were scattered all over the floor. Coiling and uncoiling like a snake which had been hit with a stick, Rukmini was rolling and moaning.

It seemed as if Rukmini's life-breath had gathered into a terrible storm and was trying to burst forth from her body. People do die in such a condition. Was this then what was in store for Rukmini also?

The familiar blue veins on her smooth uncovered knees were swelling up like leeches replete with blood. Her teeth were set hard on her lips. Floods of tears were rolling from the corners of her eyes down to her ears. Her muffled screams of pain rose higher and higher. Her lungs would perhaps burst! Was this then death?

What a cruel disillusion! From behind this mock death the seed of a new life was reaching out its hands towards the earth, turning this pain and agony into a blessing. Sanjoy jumped backwards and stood beneath a tree.

Where was Neymiar? Sanjoy went forward again and looked through a crack in Neymiar's door.

Wearing a pair of black pants with a white belt tightened round his waist, Neymiar was chewing dry bread and drinking strong country liquor from a big pot. A sharp dagger lay in front of him. On his face was a strange look of satisfaction; on his two dry lips, the feline smile of a panther.

In this room the brother, in the other the sister. They seemed like an angry demon and witch from some strange savage world brewing terror with their magic.

Like a fisherman who ran away carrying all his possessions on his back when a sudden flood came bringing in its wake terrific, roaring currents of water - Sanjoy too ran.

Sanjoy was running, not on the road, but crossing fields, slopes and ditches, he ran. The light on the mill gates burned like a will-o'-the-wisp in the fog. It was not very far away now.

And how far was Mokatpur either? If one caught the train towards early morning, he could get there in the afternoon. The beans on the Sirish tree were probably ripe. They rang in the soft breeze of the golden afternoon with the sound of heavy anklet-bells. Elder brother sat on the verandah drinking tea sweetened with molasses. Mother sat in the courtyard cleaning the Goddess Lakshmi's throne. Putul pointed her finger to the sky and counted the flocks of flying kites - one, two, three. Sumitra was perhaps not yet married. Her seeking eyes gazed around the windows of the Dutt house in Mokatpur - towards the road - towards the motor-bus which rushed along.

Rai Bahadur Ratanlal, Surja Babu, the Manager - in front of them Sanjoy sat on a stool, looking like a pale and emaciated invalid. His voice was like a cracked bell. He had been given a glass of hot milk to drink.

Rai Bahadur called out, 'Shanker the brave! Put a guard round the cash-room. Neymiar threatened Babuji with a dagger and took away the keys. Tonight he will come to steal. You must catch the wretched thief red-handed. Make arrangements.'

Then he ordered the Manager, 'Babuji will go the railway station. Quickly have a good horse saddled for him. Open my iron safe, I must give him a reward. What a faithful, honest boy!'

Sanjoy saluted and got up to go. Rai Bahadur told him, 'Go and take rest in your home for a few days. Then come and join my mill at Gorakhpur. You will be paid a salary of a hundred rupees.'

Sanjoy galloped away on the narrow track through the jungles by the side of the range of chalk hills. The breast of the sky flamed red. The peasants had set fire to each of their fields. 84 Parganas was being purified with fire.

One more field to cross, then the railway station. The light of the distant signal was floating in the distance like a blue star. A sudden splashing sound of water. The horse had stepped into a stream. Sanjoy dismounted from the horse and sat by the stream. Filling his hands with water he drank greedily again and again. A jackal which had just finished eating a hen stolen from some household was sitting on the wet sand, licking the blood on his mouth. He, too, came down to drink and put his mouth into the same flowing current of water.

translated by Nilima Devi

Fossil

Anjangarh was a native state exactly eight-and-a-half square miles in extent. A tiger cub, though small, is still a tiger. It was a kingdom. There was a Maharaja. There was an army, a police force, a Keeper of Records, a Nazir and so forth. The Maharaja had more than twenty titles. He was Lord of the Three Worlds, Shepherd of Men, Defender of the Faith and the Subduer of Enemies. Criminals had been impaled on stakes in accordance with the hallowed injunctions of religion not more than two generations ago. Now that was no longer possible. Offenders were stripped naked instead and bees set upon them.

Although the ancient fortress had long lost its splendour the stone masonry was still intact. Two rusty cannons, like the weathered skeletons of a pair of wild elephants, stood beside the great gate. Pigeons had built their nests in the cannon mouth and laid their eggs there in complete security. Tired dogs rested in their shade. Turbans and swords decorated the halls of the castle and brass and iron shields clung to its walls like cakes of dung.

A minister and eight chieftains, the prefect of police, the Amin or Surveyor, the Magistrate and the Keeper of Records formed the administration. The Maharaja looked after the welfare of his subjects with the help of the combined wisdom of his Kshatriya and Mogul officers. The unprecedented oddness of this government made life so uncomfortable for the people that half of them had fled. They were working as coolies on the sugar plantations of distant Mauritius.

The eight-and-a-half square miles of Anjangarh consisted of barren hills, rough rocky uplands and stretches of cactus and wild neem. Kurmis and Bhils brought water in buffalo hide from the hidden springs in the hills four miles away, watered their fields and grew maize, barley and jowar.

Every year there was a dispute between the Kurmis and Bhils and the State revenue department. The peasants were unwilling to surrender their crops to the royal treasury. The State took half. The Maharaja maintained an excellent polo team. The royal stables echoed with the neighing of more than a hundred of the best polo ponies. The Maharaja cherished these divine creatures from Sydney tenderly. They could not be fed on oil cake and bran. Maize, jowar and barley had to be provided.

The revenue officer was forced to call in the police. In the clubbing and spearing by the Rajput police heroes, Kshatriya heroism sparked and flamed. In an hour all protest was silenced. The rebellion was subdued.

Even the wild endurance of the defeated Bhils gave way. They left the kingdom in droves, signing up in the camps of the recruiters of labour. Some went to Delhi with their wives and children, some to Calcutta, others to Shillong. They did not make the mistake of returning.

Only the Kurmis were unwilling to go away. They had lived in this part of the country for seven generations. Their mud huts, large and small, were cool in the shade of the wild neem. Their earth had the sweet smell of mustard. Every throb of their blood bound them to it. They tilled their fields without grudging their labour, rebelled at the harvest and were put down as regularly as the seasons came and went, involving in their course all their days and nights. No alternative seemed possible.

But mercy and piety were not entirely absent from Anjangarh. Every Sunday destitutes numbering a thousand or more gathered in the spacious ground in front of the fortress. Flattened rice and molasses were distributed from the royal storehouses. On the last day of the month the Maharaja himself appeared in all his magnificence, riding an elephant auspiciously painted with sacred signs. He blessed his subjects. and on his birthday the Ramlila was sung in the castle courtyard. His subjects were invited. But as is usual wherever power is displayed to excess, the lathi was present everywhere. In every crowd and with every shout of triumph some unfortunate heads were broken. The flattened rice, the royal blessings and the Ramlila songs were all distributed to the accompaniment of blows. The subjects had grown accustomed to receiving them in that way.

Although the state was administered and revenue collected by big stick methods it was becoming more and more difficult to maintain the dignity of the crown. There were the expenses of the chamber of princes and the maintenance of the polo team. Little by little hands were laid on the royal safes containing ancestral gold and silver.

At this critical juncture a legal adviser who had studied English law was brought into the court. His name was Mukherji. Mukherji had broad, strong shoulders. He quickly became a great source of strength to the ruler both in polo and in the affairs of the state. By degrees he became the *de facto* minister and the minister himself was reduced to signing documents.

Mukherji was an idealist. Still interlaced with his thinking was the dream of American democracy about which he had read in his history books as a child. And although he was young he was extremely cool-headed. He believed that the truly courageous are never defeated and that one who works for good never comes to grief.

Mukherji spent every ounce of his ability in forwarding the best interests of the state. Young and old, in fact everyone who lived in Anjangarh, came to know their Agent Saheb. He was as sympathetic as he was strict. The subjects both loved and feared him. It was at Mukherji's suggestion that the lathis were withdrawn. He caused a furore in the office by auditing the accounts with hair-splitting precision. The boundaries of the state were delimited all over again and a census of the population taken. Even the pair of cannons lost their rust and began to shine with polish.

It was Mukherji the law agent who discovered the hidden subterranean wealth of Anjangarh. Anjangarh held treasure in the bowels of her earth. Layers of mica and asbestos lay in the folds of her granite ribs. He showed them to business men in Calcutta. The rocky uplands were leased for lacs and lacs of rupees. Anjangarh recovered her vanished glory.

A vast palace in the Gwalior style was built beside the fort and decorated with a marvellous mixture of marble, mosaic, concrete and Venetian blinds. Expensive limousines, tourers and a sedan of German manufacture stood in the royal garages. In the royal stables newly imported Irish ponies kicked and frisked.

A power house proclaimed the new life and prosperity of Anjangarh with its day and night drumming.

A fresh tide of life had really come to Anjangarh. The business men formed a Mining Syndicate. Gravel roads were built in the mining area. Coolie lines, tube wells, a club bungalow, a garden with flowers and a gymkhana appeared one by one. The Kurmis crowded into the coolie lines. Their wages were paid to them in cash. They made offerings of pigs to their gods, drank rice wine and pounded their drums in the evening, raising a tumult in the colony.

The Maharaja was contemplating the construction of two new polo grounds. And the palace garden was to be enlarged by the addition of eleven more cottahs of land. He also thought it would be nice to have an Italian band master on a salary.

Mukherji spread the map of Anjangarh on a table and lost himself in plans for his irrigation scheme. Ten canals were to run parallel across the state, from north to south. Here and there he placed large dams with strongly built sluices. All the waters of the Baroka rains was to be caught and cleverly made to flow over Anjangarh's stony bosom, like blood through arteries. Every Kurmi tenant was to have three cottahs of land of his own. There would be winter and summer crops of rice and an extra rabi crop as well. There must be three crops a year. The land on the north was to be turned into a nursery for potatoes and tobacco. On the southern plot he would grow sugarcane, barley and wheat. Then....

Then there would be, gradually, a bank. A tannery. A paper mill. The royal treasury was no longer negligible. This was the auspicious hour. Mukherji would change the face of Anjangarh with each new estimate as though with the strokes of an artist's brush. He would prove that the ruling of a state is not an affair of the big stick; it is an art.

A school. To this the Maharaja gave a plain answer. No. Mukherji stood up. He would see whether or not the Maharaja could be made to change his mind.

The Maharaja tugged fiercely at his beard and pushed a couple of papers over to Mukherji.

'Take a look at these,' he said.

The first paper read:

'All-powerful Court and Lord of the Court,

MAHARAJA!

You are the father of your subjects. We eat because you grant us food. Therefore, let the Court not touch this year's crop of maize, barley and jowar. We shall give the Court as much as is its legal due and take a receipt.

Your obedient servant,
DULAL MAHATO
(Baklam Khas on behalf of Kurmi community)'

The second paper read: 'The Maharaja's men have entered one of our mines and taken away four Kurmi workers after beating up their wives. We consider this a violation of our rights and claim immediate compensation from the Maharaja.' It was signed, 'Yours faithfully, Gibson, President, Mining Syndicate.'

'Just see, Mukherji,' commented the Maharaja, 'how insolent they are!'

'I see,' answered Mukherji.

The Subduer of Enemies struck the table and cried in a dreadful voice, 'Heads!' He was on the point of bursting. 'Cut off their heads and bring them to me! I'll sit here and feast my eyes on them! I'll look at them for two days and two nights!'

Mukherji reassured him. 'Do not worry, Your Royal Highness,' he said soothingly. 'I shall find out what it is all about.'

Old Dulal Mahato had returned to Anjangarh after many years in Mauritius. He had brought with him seven rupees in cash and asthma to comfort his old age. And with his return a change had come into the lives of the Kurmis. A restlessness developed and became noticeable.

The Kurmis learnt from Dulal what cash payment means. You put luggage belonging to a gentleman into a compartment of the train at Faijabad station and receive an anna coin right into the palm of your hand!

'Brothers,' said Dulal, pointing to himself, 'this old man has been cheated once for every white hair on his head. He doesn't trust anybody any more. Cash down. Everything. Pick up your money with one hand before you salaam with the other.'

Dulal spoke with the Syndicate foreigners as with equals. He discussed the wage rates of the coolies, their weekly payments, days off, allowances, medical and other arrangements on behalf of the Kurmis and obtained definite concessions. The Syndicate took pains to humour Dulal. 'Come on, Mahato,' they said, 'We'll build twenty dozen coolie lines for your workers. We'll employ them all.'

Dulal agreed. The foreigners kept their promises to him.

All the Kurmis in the state gathered in the wild neem jungle at the invitation of Mahato. He removed the turban from his white head and stood up. 'Today we have met to found our association, our mandal,' he said. 'Now consider what ought to be done. Learn to know your enemies and your friends. We must not be afraid any longer. We shall never forgive anyone who tries to put a knife into our bellies or into our honour.'

Dulal's thick throat shook like a broken conch with the intensity of his emotion. He spoke, 'Brothers all, from today Mahato's life belongs to the Mandal and the life of the Mandal....'

'To Mahato,' the crowd of Kurmis raised their thousands of lathis and shouted their answer in unison.

They beat their drums and even ran a flag up a pole. Then they went home.

Nothing escaped Mukherji, no matter how secret. He came to know of the event. He understood only that here was a cloud which harboured lightning. Something had to be done immediately while there was yet time. But the Maharaja must not know anything at all about it. A ruler so blinded by feudal arrogance and riddled with so many complexes about prestige would be difficult to manage. Blood might even be spilt, quite uselessly. It was better for him to give fight himself in a gentlemanly way.

Peons informed the Maharaja that the Kurmis had not come to work on his polo field and in his garden, work they were accustomed to do begar, without pay.

The Kurmis now declared it was a sin to work without pay. To do so would bring misfortune to the state.

Mukherji was sent for. Dulal Mahato was summoned. Mahato bowed to the ground before the Maharaja and stood with his hands respectfully folded together. He seemed as timid as a lamb and to be, actually, trembling in every limb.

'It is you who are at the root of this devilry!' the Maharaja hurled the accusation at him.

'I am the dust of your slippers,' answered Mahato.

'Shut up!'

'Yes, Your Highness!'

'Shut up!' the Maharaja thundered. Mahato stood without moving, like a wooden doll.

'Break off all connection with the foreigners instantly! No Kurmi can work in the mines without my permission!'

'I shall communicate your desire to my people, Your Highness.'

'Go!'

Dulal bowed and left. Mukherji was then commanded to serve a notice on the Syndicate. They were not to engage any Kurmi to work for them without the permission of the Maharaja.

The replies came in due course. A signed letter from Mahato stated that, as the Kurmis went without food unless they received wages for their labour and the Syndicate paid them cash they were unable to discontinue their work in the mines. They hoped that the Court would not place obstacles in their way. They, the Kurmis, intended to open a temple of their own in the following month. Would the Maharaja be pleased to grant a thousand rupees from the royal treasury towards expenses? They also requested the Maharaja to permit them to gather wood and burn brush in the jungle without a licence during the coming winter.

The Syndicate, in response to the notice, informed the Maharaja that they were prepared to enter into a new agreement with His Highness's government but it was not possible at the moment. They would, however, be glad to consider it on the expiry of the existing agreement, i.e., after nine hundred and ninety-nine years.

'What do you think of it, Mukherji? It seems to me I shall have to call in the police. I ask you, will you stop dreaming about your canals for once and turn your attention to the maintenance of my prestige?'

The Maharaja spoke slowly but from the expression of his face and eyes it was plain that the wrath hissing in his thoughts was hundred-hooded.

Mukherji addressed him with deference, 'Do not worry about it, Your Highness. Give me time. I shall bring it under control.'

Mukherji surmised that it was the Syndicate which was instigating Dulal's rashness. It was perniciously encouraging the agitation among the Kurmis. Until the link between them was broken there would be no peace in the kingdom. Nothing but misfortune could come of it. What was to be done?

Mukherji went to Dulal Mahato. He stood outside his hut and called him. Mahato hurried out and invited Mukherji to seat himself upon a wooden stool. He took his turban off and, placing it at Mukherji's feet, took his own seat on the ground at a respectful distance. Mukherji explained the situation to him carefully and at the end of his speech broke down emotionally, exclaiming, 'What are you doing, Mahato? You are the children of your king! Sometimes children commit offences, sometimes parents! The Syndicate is feeding you today but they won't look at you any more once their purpose is accomplished. Then, it will be the court that will keep you alive with flattened rice.'

Dulal put out his hand and rested it on Mukherji's feet 'I give you my word, Honourable Agent, I shall do as you say. The

Maharaja is like a father to us. We are prepared to die for him. Let him grant our petition without delay.'

Mukherji left without waiting for a second question or a second answer. No! The symptoms of delirium were appearing, aggravating the symptoms of disease!

Mukherji had to forego his bath, his change of clothes and his meal that day. He drove straight to the office of the Syndicate.

'Mr Mukherji,' Gibson answered, 'We are not money makers only. We have a mission as well. We have always fought for wronged humanity. If necessary we shall fight again.'

'You have turned the Kurmis into coolies by appealing to their greed! How can agriculture thrive in this state? Tell me!'

In his agitation Mukherji disclosed the real reason for his perturbation.

'Whether agriculture survives or not, money will. Can you deny that?'

'Stop arguing and think of co-operation, Mr Gibson. All you have to do is to obtain the sanction of the Maharaja when you engage coolies. The Maharajah will be pleased and that will be of advantage to you in other ways.'

'Sorry, Mr Mukherji.' With a twisted smile Gibson lit a cigar.

Mukherji reddened to his ear tips . He rose, pushed the chair noisily aside and left the office.

McKennon came in and asked, 'What's the matter, Gibson?'

'Mukherji, that monkey of an administrator! I told him a few things to his face. I refused to accept any terms.'

'Good. There's this irrigation scheme of his. Be careful. Fight it at any cost. Otherwise there will be a disastrous shortage of labour. The business is expanding now.'

'Don't worry. We have tamed Mahato. I'll use him to spoil all the plans of the state.'

They exchanged laughter. 'Let me see,' McKennon said, 'Mahato is waiting outside, I think.'

Gibson took Mahato aside. In a secluded room of the office he said to him, 'The petition is ready. Sign it. All the points have been touched. I'll send it to Delhi by today's mail.'

McKennon slapped Mahato on the back as he left, 'Don't be afraid, Mahato, we are with you. If your lands and house are expropriated our lines are always open to you. Don't be afraid.'

Mukherji sat in his office deep in thought. He did not feel like touching his pen. He had nothing more that was encouraging to say to the Maharaja. Perhaps it was no longer possible for him to pilot his affairs. It was time to hand over the reins. Surely the brains of these people had withered in their skulls! Each, in his separate stupidity, was engaged in a game that would lead to suicide. But perhaps it was he himself who had made the mistake!

The Maharaja sent for him. He was received in the ruler's private apartments. The minister and the police chief were present. The faces of both looked shrunken. The Maharaja was pacing impatiently around and around the couch. He began to blaze as soon as he saw Mukherji.

'Take it! Take it! Take the throne and rule this state! I spit on it! I'm leaving!'

Mukherji, speechless, looked at the minister. The minister handed him a letter. It was a note from the Political Agent. Many complaints had been received about the internal administration of the state. More and graver complaints were coming in daily. He hoped the ruler would be able to remedy them without delay, before interference was necessary.

The police chief frowned. 'Your policy of conciliation is responsible for this, Agent Saheb,' he said.

Taking his cue from the police chief the Maharaja cried, 'Certainly. It is true. I know all about it, Mukherji. I am not blind.'

'Know all? What are you saying, Your Highness?'

'Stop! I know everything! How could traders who live by selling the dirt of my kingdom dare to do this otherwise? Who gives them secret encouragement?'

The Maharaja seemed unable to breathe. He sank down upon the couch. A peon fussed about him in an attempt to restore him. The minister, the police chief and Mukherji turned away and gazed silently in different directions.

The Maharaja cleared his throat and resumed the subject. 'My chief of police,' he cried, ' it is you who must save my honour!'

'So be it!' said the magistrate, 'You punish the Kurmis with your police and I shall involve the Syndicate in a civil law suit, Disputable phrases can be found in the contract without much difficulty.'

The Maharaja stole a glance at Mukherji and quickly withdrew his eyes. But Mukherji had seen. The ruler's eyes were wet.

Tears in a lion's eyes! Mukherji divined how much pain there was behind them even though he himself was, by nature, as timid as a rabbit. So? He had not looked at the matter from that point of view. He had been wrong. He went up to the Maharaja and announced quietly, 'I have been mistaken. Your Highness. Kindly grant me leave and permit me to depart. I shall return if you ever send for me.'

The Maharaja softened instantly. 'No, no, Mukherji, what things you say! Where will you go? Of course people are talking but let them! I do not believe what they say! The policy must be changed. It is necessary to be more firm. I cannot put up with the buffets of these toads any longer, Mukherji.'

A weariness like a chill winter cloud, a sense of emptiness and exhaustion, came over Mukherji, slackening his muscles, making his joints weak. He gave up going to office. In the afternoon he dressed in breeches, threw a dozen mallets over the shoulder of a boy and appeared on the polo ground. Throughout the game he kept his pony at full gallop, riding like a storm. He struck right and left, hitting under the pony's neck, taking dare-devil chances. Now and then a mallet would split and the splinters fly in all directions. The flannel on the legs of his black waler and the martingale dripped with the sweat that streamed from the horse's body and the foam of his mouth. Still Mukherji charged, maddened by the desire to score. His opponents were so nonplussed they saved themselves by turning aside as best they could, making off at an easy trot. Even during the intervals of play Mukherji refused to rest. He raced round and round the field at a fast canter. He would lean against his saddle and close his eyes as though drinking in his speed.

Afterwards the Maharaja reproved him. 'Your game is very rough, Mukherji.'

The sun went down that day just as it always did behind the hills of Anjangarh. The Maharaja was dressed to go out on the lawn when a peon brought word that shaft Number 14 had caved in and was still collapsing. Ninety coolies, Kurmi men and women, were entombed.

'The best of news!' The Maharaja rubbed his cheeks and shouted in terrible jubilance, 'Now my enemy is in my power. He must be crushed without mercy. Call the minister at once!'

The minister came but he had a look in his eyes like a dead fish. 'Bad news!' he announced.

'What bad news?'

'Kurmi women were cutting wood in the wild neem jungle without a permit. The forest ranger obstructed them. The Kurmis beat up the ranger and his guard and drove them away.'

'And then?'

'The police arrived and fired. It would have been better if they had used grapeshot. Instead they fired with old muskets and used buckshot. Twenty were killed and more than fifty wounded. The dead are still lying in the wild neem jungle.'

The Maharaja was silent . The Political Agent's inevitable note floated before his eyes like the bright sharp point of a spear.

'Has the news spread?'

'The syndicate certainly knows.'

The Maharaja sent for Mukherji. 'This is what is the matter, Mukherji,' he explained. 'Now show your Bengali brains! Find a solution!'

After thinking a long time Mukherji said, 'First of all get hold of Mahato. Without delay.'

Carrying lathis and lanterns about fifty of the Maharaja's men set out through the dark for Mahato's hut, moving at top speed.

'I am not well, your Highness,' Mukherji apologised. 'Please excuse me. I think I'm going to be sick.'

Shaft No. 14 had caved in. The owners were really frightened. The ceiling of the third seam had not been properly timbered. This was the cause of the disaster. At intervals a great boom came like a cry out of the depths of the earth and with it a shower of dust and gravel. The quartz pillars were snapping like firecrackers under the pressure and crumbling. The pithead had already been cordoned off with barbed wire.

Coolies who ran up from their lines were turned back half way. Go on with your work! Nothing's happened!' they were told, 'Nobody has been hurt. Nobody killed.'

The owners stood in a group at a distance and talked in low voices in the dark. 'There is no way to fill it up,' Gibson said, 'It will keep on caving in for another two days. Burn up the attendance book and make a new one dated as from today.'

'What good will that do?' asked McKennon. 'The Maharaja must already know about it. And there is Mahato. How are you going to explain to him? The papers will know of it by tomorrow morning. They'll splash the scandal for days. Then there'll be an inquiry. One of those awful Gandhi people may be on it. Do you see?'

That night no lights were lit in the club house but a chandelier in a room of the palace blazed with a hundred bulbs. Mukherji was summoned once more.

It was an unprecedented spectacle: the Maharaja, his minister, and the police chief with Gibson, McKennon, Moore and Patterson! Glasses and decanters knocked against each other on the long mahogany table.

The Maharaja greeted Mukherji with smiles. 'Mahato has been taken, Mukherji,' he said, 'It was lucky you suggested it while there was still time.'

'We have been spared a great deal of clumsy annoyance,' Gibson agreed, 'It is fortunate for all of us.'

The police chief whispered to Mukherji briefly the decision that had been taken at the meeting and what they considered it their duty to do. Mukherji sat with his head bowed in his hands, silent.

'Be strong, Mukherji.' Gibson slapped him on the back. 'It is administration!'

About midnight a car once more drove up to No. 14 pithead. People gathered in the dense darkness. Durwans took Mahato's body out of the police van. It was wrapped in a blanket. A truck came up, loaded with the bodies from the wild neem jungle. Throwing the corpses one by one into the hungry mouth of the mine the durwans turned away and sat down to cook their supper.

Mukherji's eyes were wet with the light intoxication of champagne and cigar smoke. Lounging on the car's bumper he gazed at the pithead and dreamt of other things, of a far distant future.

A hundred thousand years after, a party of scientists, sent out to enrich the collection of some museum, would look with greedy curiosity at the fossilised skeletons of their sub-human ancestors, half-animal in build but with straight backs and unbowed necks. And they would examine their implements, some crude iron things. These people had, it would appear, been trapped suddenly by a disaster in the layers of quartz and granite. The scientists would handle the stony bones and speculate. Of the blood stains on them that day there would be no trace.

translated by Lila Ray

Ajantrik

Bimal's taxi seemed ageless. Its longevity matched Bimal's unchanging obstinacy. The taxi was an old Ford. A prehistoric animal of a motor car, it bore all over its body marks of ugly indigence. Unless one was driven by necessity or had never seen a motor car before, no passenger ever went anywhere near it. But although decrepit in appearance it was mighty in performance. It could easily do things beyond the capacity of bigger cars. When on dark rainy nights others dared not carry fares over the frightening broken forest roads of this mica country, only Bimal's hoary taxi was ready to go ahead without a trace of fear. Thus it was that it was engaged when the others had turned tail. Only then.

In the taxi stand among rows of young, gaudy new models Bimal's old Ford dozed like Jatayu, heavy with the burden of age. It really was an eyesore. With a patched-up hood, a broken windscreen, a dented bonnet, bandaged wheels and dirty side-screens, it was a sight. The footstand howled like a trodden dog every time one set foot on it. The seats were so smirched with smudges of engine oil that a well dressed person refused to sit on them even when implored. The doors were difficult to close and, once closed, difficult to open. As soon as one sat inside, Bimal's dirty towel, underwear and the oily, sticky shawl hanging by the rope strung across the hood rubbed against one's face.

The moment the distant roar of Bimal's car was heard each one of the rickshaws fearfully made for the farthest edge of the road. Even the most intrepid cyclists trembled when Bimal's speeding car passed them on the way. You could see it occasionally on a dark night at a distance. It looked like a one-eyed monster uttering shrill screams tearing down the road at you. You would of course know it was Bimal's car. One of the headlights had stopped burning. The body was loose in all its joints and it appeared that at any moment it might explode into a thousand fragments.

Bimal's taxi raised the biggest trail of dust, made the most earsplitting noise and sent the buffaloes on the road into fits. And yet no one dared utter a word of criticism. If someone did, the reply came pat and sharp. 'Don't you go for a shit? Don't you snort and shout? Don't you run? Then what's wrong with my car doing the same?'

Bimal's taxi was a butt of ridicule and called any number of names — the old horse, the lame duck, the blind buffalo and so on. Bimal also called it by a name, Jagaddal. For fifteen busy restless years in Bimal's life this mechanical animal has been his attendant, friend and provider. But did Jagaddal, one wondered, answer to Bimal's calls? It was difficult for others to comprehend that Bimal could instantly follow Jagaddal's moods, turns of fancy and demands.

'Thirsty, aren't you? That's why the strenuous breathing, isn't it? Just a minute, just one minute.' Bimal would park Jagaddal under the shade of a big leaf tree by the roadside, get buckets of cold water from the well and pour it down the radiator. Making a gurgling sound Jagaddal would drink an enormous quantity, feel satisfied and then start again.

For fifteen uninterrupted years Bimal has been the owner and driver of the taxi. At one end of the taxi stand old Jagaddal, bearing the marks of penury and old age, waited patiently for a fare. By its side, reclining on the smooth ash-coloured bonnet of his new taxi, Piara Singh would have a crack at Bimal.

'Why don't you pension off your old woman, Bimal Babu?'

'Yes, and then go in like you for a painted new model whore,' Bimal would promptly reply. It was useless talking any further, Piara Singh wisely decided. For, Bimal would then get angry and Bimal, once roused, could be wild.

Around the temple of the deity Nar Singh Dev, twelve miles from here, a fair is held on the full moon day in the month of Kartik. As usual, a bevy of passengers descended on the taxi stand and taxis drove away one after another with loads of fares. Only Jagaddal was left behind, alone and dozing in the empty stand. Who will want to come near this ruin with its antediluvian shape and primitive trappings?

Govinda came and said a few words in sympathy. 'Well, Bimal Babu. No fare?'

'No.'

'Then?'

'Then what? I'll have my own back in the evening. I'll take a double load, come what may.'

'But how long can go on like this? I'll tell you what. Send Jagaddal to the car exchange and get Maganlal's car from Jharia. A fine six cylinder sedan, believe me. Don't delay.'

'Who's going to take all the trouble?'

'You call that trouble and not this carrying overloads on the sly?'

'Oh, let go! Come on, have a bidi.'

Govinda stopped arguing further. It was better so. Otherwise Bimal might start mouthing obscenities. He never could tolerate others discussing Jagaddal.

Ignoring useless comments Bimal got jugfuls of water to wash the mud and the dirt from old Jagaddal's body. He crawled under the car and, lying on his back, sprayed water vigorously. He examined carefully whether the cowdung smudge on the neck of the tie-rod was still there. He then started polishing the rotund tummy of the differential till it shone. Coming out and giving Jagaddal an all-over he looked at the two big, gaping holes in the worn-out hood and muttered, 'What can I do, Jagaddal? Please make do with the patches this season. If I get a few trips booked in advance during the pujas I'll get you a new rexine hood. Believe me, I will.' It did not end there. Bringing out the last two anna bit from his pocket he bought kerosene oil with it and started removing the rust from the nuts and bolts.

Passing that way Gaur remarked. 'Well, well, what's this, Bimal Babu? A coat of whitewash on a dilapidated temple.' Bimal got wild. His face distorted with rage, he burst out, 'Get lost and fast, will you? Who has asked you to jabber?' Bimal could not understand why anyone should bother about his private affairs. 'Private,' Piara Singh broke out in guffaws of laughter. 'Never knew a car could be a wife.'

Bimal's business was in a bad way but he would not give up his obduracy. Apparently his perverse attachment to the ugly old car confused his business instincts. Otherwise why should he - an unpitying miser who fasted the whole day at Dhanbad because bread was dear there, to return the next day and have a double feed at Gaya where bread was cheap - go on spending without a thought on the car? It was as good as throwing money down the drain. Reminds you of mad Bulaki who had a similar attachment for a broken tinny old pail. Bulaki would often hold his open umbrella over the pail while he got drenched in the rain.

It was evening and the place had grown semi-dark. A few shops lit up their petromax lamps. Puffs of thick smoke from the confectioners' oven spread all over the place and made it darker. The traffic constable, a short distance away, appeared inattentive. A group of villagers with bags and baggage were coming towards the stand, obviously intending to travel to some distant village. Here was a chance.

Bimal shouted in his loudspeaker voice, 'Come on, come on! Ramgarh, Ranchi, Nayasarai, Makudganj, Chitrapur, Jhalda. concession rate, concession!' The words 'concession rate' immediately registered with the intending passengers. but they are fourteen in number! Bimal pushed all the fourteen of them, where normally there was room for only six, inside the cavernous stomach of old Jagaddal. No one outside could say for sure how many lay concealed there as in the tummy of a kangaroo. Bimal gave a few quick turns to the starting handle, and Jagaddal roared like a lion. The bottles of coloured water in the betel leaf shop trembled and tinkled. With a delirious honking of the horn Jagaddal left the stand and disappeared down the road on the right like a burst of the nor'wester. The betel leaf shop keeper muttered. 'Bimal Babu's taxi - fantastic!'

This was Bimal's daily routine. Of late, a suspicion that the entire world was in conspiracy against Jagaddal had become a conviction. He noticed with surprise that flying birds would invariably choose Jagaddal to leave their droppings on. Without hesitation the passersby would use Jagaddal's body to wipe their fingers and rid them of the lime they had taken along with their paan. There were twenty-seven other cars in the stand. But no one dared to treat them with such contempt. What had Jagaddal done to earn such enmity?

'Jagaddal,' Bimal called softly, his voice gentle with emotion. How he wished his love protected Jagaddal, like a talisman, from the collective curse and the daily insults. 'Never mind, Jagaddal, you are here and I am here,' Bimal declared in the reckless manner of throwing out a challenge and pulled hard at his bidi as if preparing for a battle. Whether because of inclement weather or breakdowns or repair work the other cars would occasionally be absent from the stand. But Jagaddal was always there as unfailingly as the sunrise. That could be the reason for the malevolence of other taxi drivers, or so Bimal believed. Which young man will not be envious if he finds a person who should be in his dotage jumping and running about?

Bimal was full of justifiable pride about Jagaddal on this count. Jagaddal had been his constant companion, in joy and sorrow, in good days and bad, and had served him devotedly for the last fifteen years. Other devotees of the god Nar Singh had so many things to ask of their god - fame, beauty and so forth. Bimal, as he placed his humble offering of a few flowers and a penny worth of jaggery, had only one prayer, one modest supplication - 'Oh god, please see that Jagaddal is not incapacitated. Don't make me companionless in these my declining years.'

In the local Bengali club they said: 'The chap is himself a machine. To be obsessed with a motor car night and day for fifteen years. No, it is not human.'

The comment pleased Bimal who confessed to his addiction to the smell of burnt petrol. He laughed to himself and said, 'Bengali Club is right. I am also a machine. What Bengali Club does not realise is that Jagaddal is like a living being, almost human.' In these days of ruthless and cut-throat competition it was old Jagaddal who earned for him at least a couple of rupees a day. and Jagaddal's needs were so little. He could run twenty-two miles on only one gallon of petrol. Jagaddal seemed to understand that Bimal was poor.

Like an Arab stallion Jagaddal was moving at an intoxicating speed on the road to Ranchi. Hurrah, for his breath, speed and capacity to carry loads. Bimal held the shuddering steering wheel hard with his hands, hugging it to his chest. He could feel the thrill of untamed Jagaddal's vibrant heartbeats. The icy wind cut like a steel blade into his skin. Bimal pulled down the woollen muffler wrapped round his head to cover his ears. He was no longer young and the cold affected him badly.

The hill range loomed in front. How many times had Jagaddal crossed the winding, ascending road in the past, racing like an angry leopard, the entire stretch at one go. As he approached the foot of the hills Bimal pressed the accelerator hard with accustomed confidence. For fifty yards Jagaddal moved forward and then gave out a piteous groan. It was as if a few bones in his chest had got dislocated. His ears alert with anxiety, Bimal heard the groaning sound. There was no mistaking it. A disaster. The piston was broken.

A few days later a ball bearing melted as suddenly and damaged the engine. From then on something or other went wrong. No sooner was one mended than something else broke down. One day the fan belt tore apart; the next, petrol would not get to the carburettor; the day after the plugs went dead and the electricals short-circuited.

The solid ground of faith seemed at last shaken. For days Bimal was unnaturally gloomy. He became restless and was all over the place. There were breaks in Jagaddal's routine as well; he was occsionally absent from the taxi stand. Bimal suffered shivers of anxiety. Would Jagaddal give up the ghost at last? 'No. I am there, Jagaddal. Don't worry. I will cure you and see you up and about,' promised Bimal, the expert motor mechanic.

He placed orders and got from Calcutta genuine parts, a new battery, distributor, axle, pistons - he got them all. He started spending recklessly. When he thought it necessary he sent wires to get the materials overnight. He worked at it late into the night - repairing, oiling, changing the parts. Jagaddal was stricken with disease. Bimal became almost mad. the money ran out and Bimal sold his watch, his utensils, and even the wooden cot.

Soon he had nothing left. No matter. Jagaddal, the faithful friend of fifteen years would surely be happy now and get well. It was some job done, wasn't it? A new hood, a coat of paint and varnish - how gorgeous Jagaddal would look! Bimal's fancies took gleeful hold of his mind.

Before closing the garage doors at dead of night Bimal held up the lamp to have a look at Jagaddal. His eyes gleamed with joy. Days of tireless nursing and attendance had completely changed Jagaddal's appearance. He looked like a powerful, muscular wrestler, ready to jump into the ring at a moment's notice.

Bimal washed and went to bed. The last few days had been a period of backbreaking toil. What a soothing comfort it was now to think that Jagaddal had recovered. Tomorrow morning Bimal would startle everybody with the blare of the new horn when he took Jagaddal to the stand. They would be speechless with surprise and suffer again from pangs of jealousy.

Bimal woke up with a start. It was early morning and yet pitch dark. It was raining heavily. Bimal sat up, wide awake. Was Jagaddal getting drenched? The tin roof of the garage was old; who knows how many leaks and cracks there were? It would be a disaster if water somehow got into the engine. It would, besides, scar the new polish on the body.

Bimal lit a kerosene lamp and entered the garage. 'Oh, my God,' he shouted. Rain water was coming down in torrents through a hole in the roof directly over the engine. Bimal ran back to his room and fetched his waterproof overall. He brought along the bedspread, blanket and bedsheet as well. After wiping the bonnet he spread the blanket on it and covered it with the overall. He draped the car with the bedspread and the bedsheet. He then got in and laid himself down on the soft seat. Cramped though he was it was immensely comfortable and his eyelids closed, heavy with sleep.

Next morning the people at the stand crowded round Jagaddal as if a miracle had happened. The vociferous admiring onlookers stood and saw the handiwork of Bimal's extraordinary mechanical talents. Bimal responded with drawn smiles a few times. The smiles appeared half-hearted as if clouded with a grey haze of apprehension.

But why? Bimal felt terribly depressed. Jagaddal was moving all right. But where was the loud announcement of power the moment the engine was started? What had happened to the proud neighing and the speed of the wild antelope?

Bimal took Jagaddal to a field, away from the town and examined him carefully.

'Well now, come on, Jagaddal. Spread your wings like a pakhiraj.' Bimal pressed the accelerator. It was no good. Jagaddal had become infirm. He tried on the gears one after another. At last he got wild. 'Get going or I'll kick you!'

Jagaddal chugged along, panting like a crippled old man at each step.

'The dumb swine, doesn't respond to care, doesn't understand affection, the inert wretch,' Bimal shouted and actually kicked the clutch hard twice. The wild rage grew on him. He would find out the answer today, once and for all. Does Jagaddal want to stay with him or does he not? He had petted and pandered enough. No more.

In his anger Bimal perhaps lost his head. He pushed and rolled down seven or eight huge boulders. The shirt on his exhausted body became drenched in sweat. One by one he loaded the boulders in the car. Load? That was it, and Jagaddal would have to carry it today. Let us see if Jagaddal has the power or is finished for ever.

'Get going.' Jagaddal got going but cried out with pain at each and every joint. It was too much. Jagaddal could no longer carry it.

At last Bimal knew the final answer. Jagaddal was in the grip of his death throes. No doubt about it. Jagaddal's big heart was failing. King Yama had called up his name. Nothing could save him now. The darkness of night would now descend. Bimal had spent his last penny but could not save Jagaddal.

'I will now be alone,' Bimal mused with infinite tiredness. 'My days are also over. My hairs have turned grey, the veins all over my body grown wiry like earthworms. It cannot be very long now before, panting and limping like Jagaddal, I will have to make my exit.'

Lighting a bidi Bimal kept starting at Jagaddal in silence, his mind restless with a gnawing sense of emptiness. 'Jagaddal will go first and then it will be my turn. Goodbye, Jagaddal, good wishes go with you. You have fed and clothed me for a long enough time. What more could you do? It does not matter what happens to me now'. In Bimal's eyes, forever dry and steely cold, came, as had never come before, drops of warm tears.

Returning to his lodging Bimal stationed Jagaddal outside the garage. He went straight in without looking back and sat down in the courtyard with two bottles of mohua liquor.

He had just had his first sip when he heard, Govinda calling him from outside. 'Are you there, Bimal Babu? Govinda came in, a Marwari gentleman with him.

'Good evening, Babuji.'

'Good evening. Which car are you an agent for?'

Govinda introduced him and said. 'He is not a car agent. He has come from Calcutta to buy old iron junk. You have heaps of broken axles, wheel rims and such like. Why not get rid of them for a price?

For a while Bimal stared at them with unblinking eyes. They appeared to him as an apparition of the future. They have come with a hunger that will not be denied. They are here with the begging bowl in their outstretched hands demanding as alms his prized possession. Bimal understood all.

'Yes. I have old iron. Lots of it. What's the price you are offering?'

'Fourteen annas a maund, Babuji,' the Marwari replied eagerly. 'War has broken out. Here's your chance. Sell out everything you have.'

'Yes, I will. That car of mine too, is junk. It has become useless.'

Govinda was aghast. 'What are you saying, Bimal?'

Bimal woke up from his drunken sleep when it was still dark. He drank another bottle and went off to sleep again. But his sleep was disturbed. He woke up several times to doze off again.

It was early morning. To Bimal's ears all the noise and the din of the outside world, now wide awake, were drowned by the only sound he could hear, the clank of the hammer. The Marwari businessman had sent his workmen early and they were fast breaking up the car.

Sorrow and drunkenness. Jagaddal's ribs were being taken out one by one. Bimal's consciousness was floating in some whirlpool of endless silence. It went down in a bottomless swirl and then, light of body, came up again to the surface. In between he could hear the unceasing hammer blows. It sounded to him as if they were digging a grave for dead and dismembered Jagaddal, and the clank, clank, was the sound of picks and shovels.

translated by Kironmoy Raha

The Waiting Room

What train was it that panted its way to the station through the rain and darkness so late at night? Most likely it had brought passengers who had crossed the Ganges on the ferry. One could still hear the siren of the ship. She had ferried one batch of passengers and was now starting for the bank across with another batch.

It seemed that the engine was gasping for breath as it stood by the platform in Rajpur Junction. The waiter in the First Class Waiting Room got busy dusting the tables and chairs and wiping clean the mirror. The sweeper also cleaned up the room with his broom.

The train from the river bank was only a shuttle and the number of passengers few. Most of them were Santal coolies, but there were always one or two who travelled First. Perhaps the proprietor of a sugar mill from Katihar or the Manager of a tea garden in Darjeeling.

The two passengers who hurriedly entered the First Class Waiting Room on this particular night had however nothing to do with either sugar mills or tea gardens. The first to arrive was a young Bengali woman in a fine cashmere coat. Her small emerald eardrops and the stylish hair-do proved her fine taste. A porter lumbered behind her with luggage heaped on his head while she sailed in through the drizzling rain.

The passenger who followed close on her heels had also the inevitable suitcase and bedding piled on the porter's head. He was spectacled and dressed in Indian clothes with a shawl thrown over his shoulders.

A gentleman and a lady travelling by the same train had sought shelter in the same waiting room. This was their only relation, if relation it can at all be called. Perhaps he would wait for a couple of hours and she a little more. Then, when their trains came, each would go his or her own way.

It was strange that in this case the two passengers started as soon as their eyes met. For a moment, they stood still like painted figures. It seemed that both were taken aback and felt shy, awkward and perhaps a little annoyed. It almost seemed that they were afraid to meet. Their plight seemed to be like that of two escaped prisoners who had been captured and put into the same dock. The raindrops glistened on Madhuri Roy's coat. Satadal Dutt looked dazed through his wet glasses which he forgot to wipe.

This waiting room of Rajpur Junction was not the dock in a court. There was no one to ask questions or extort confesions. Yet it seemed that they found this close proximity unbearable. Perhaps they would feel easier if they could part. Satadal moved up to the door and called for a porter.

Satadal could move his luggage and go out. He did not know where, but he felt that almost anywhere else would be better. Perhaps he would go to the Rest House outside the station - it had neither lights nor furniture but neither was it haunted by the spectre of a vanished past.

It was not a porter but the waiter who came at Satadal's call. He stood expectantly but Satadal took no notice of him. Instead he walked up to the door and peeped out. The fine rain blew into his face. He came back into the room and stood by the table. It was as if he was immersed in thoughts of the past. Perhaps he felt that it was stupid to be so disturbed. It would be sheer cowardice and a confession of weakness if he ran away from the waiting room at the sight of this woman.

The waiter was still waiting for instructions. Satadal pulled a chair to the table, sat down and ordered tea. In the other corner of the room, Madhuri took off her cashmere coat, placed it on the bench and sat down.

Satadal Dutt and Madhuri Roy were today only two passengers waiting for their trains in the waiting room. Today there was nothing else between them. Indeed for the last five or six years they had been strangers. This had not however always been the case. There were days when they had not been apart; in fact almost for seven years they had been man and wife. When they first met, she was Madhuri Mitra, a fine looking girl and a friend of his elder brother's wife. It was an April day at Ghatshila and the forests were full of the fragrance of flowers and honey. Their intimacy began on a sudden afternoon when Satadal saw her bathed in the light of the setting sun as she stood in the mahua grove.

There is no doubt that they were soon deeply in love. Their love was legalised and their names joined in the marriage register. It did not however last more than seven years. By mutual agreement, they again went to court and separated.

It seemed that both had realised that there was no longer any life in their love. When they felt that they were drifting apart, they did not wish to keep up the pretence and parted. The love which bloomed one fragrant spring among the groves of Ghatshila did not last seven springs. How was it that their love disappeared when it was out of love that they had married?

Yet there was no doubt that the bond between them had snapped. Satadal felt it bitterly on the day when he was putting his things together with undeft fingers while Madhuri sat in another room reading a novel. He was going to Bhubaneswar for a week in connection with his work. She did not come even once to bid farewell to her husband. He had then felt that the light which poured into the room through the windows was a mockery.

It was not only that winter morning that mocked their love. Equally cruel was a Sunday afternoon in the summer of that year. Madhuri was all dressed up for their usual Sunday stroll. Satadal was however absorbed in sketching a Chalukya temple. He had forgotten all about their Sunday routine and was not even aware that his wife had dressed to go out. She gazed at the purple clouds in the western sky and found them meaningless.

Of such symptoms of declining affection, there was no end. At last they realised that their love was a thing of the past. Or did they think that they had never loved at all? Nobody can tell. Perhaps they could have known if they had talked frankly to one another.

Or was it a case of a new passion that cancelled the old April of Ghatshila? Perhaps the earlier Aprils had become insipid. Satadal and Madhuri suffered in silence and moved in opposite directions. They did not repent for what they had done nor did they blame one another. There could be no blame when either both were right or both were wrong. Their growing indifference was mutual and there was no forgiveness on either side. All this however was undeclared. When their estrangement became intolerable they parted without recrimination. They could no longer bear the burden of their unexpressed misery. Silently they wrote off seven years of married life through an application in the Civil Court.

Within a year and half of their separation, Satadal heard that Madhuri had married Anadi Roy, an engineer. Madhuri also read in the papers that Professor Satadal Dutt had again married. The bride was Sudhakana, sewing mistress in a Calcutta School.

These new marriages must also have been prompted by love. Whatever others might say, Madhuri knew she was happy in her new life. Satadal too was happy with Sudha even though there were people who made unkind remarks.

In the dead of this winter night, when fate brought together Madhuri Roy and Satadal Dutt in the waiting room of Rajpur Junction, it was hardly necessary for them to be excited. They had separated for good and put an end to their relationship.

But if the past was no problem, the present predicament was not so easy to face. Why should two lives be brought so close in a railway waiting room when five years ago the law had cancelled their right to share life? It seemed that their sudden encounter was a mockery of faith, as improper as it was intolerable. If instead of Madhuri and Satadal, any other man and woman had met as passengers in the waiting room, surely there would have been no such sense of constraint. They would have exchanged a few formal words of common courtesy. Madhuri Roy and Satadal Dutt were unrelated today but how could they forget they had been man and wife?

The silence of the room and the burden of his thoughts made Satadal doze for a few seconds. His eyes closed. When he woke, he remembered it was a waiting room. His eyes fell on Madhuri who was sitting on the bench with her face turned toward the wall. Satadal however did not turn away his face. He felt a strange curiosity to watch Madhuri unobserved though he did not know what it was he wanted to see and, in fact, what could there be that was novel in her?

And yet there was something new about her. He had never seen Madhuri in such a fine sari of cloud-dark crepe with a border flowing almost to the floor. In the past, when they went out visiting, she of course put on a handloom sari which rustled as she walked and shed the fragrance of *hasnu hana* all around. Today, nothing was left of the fragrance or music of her movements. She now stood like an image fashioned by another artist. Satadal had never before looked at Madhuri so intently and yet so furtively. Today he really had no right to look at her and that was perhaps why he could not take his eyes off her! The more he looked, the more he realised that she was another woman. Strange and new and a little hard, the proper wife for an engineer!

Satadal shook off these disturbing thoughts and turned to his own immediate needs. He opened his suitcase for his towel and soap. He undid his hold-all and took out a pillow and a bedsheet which he placed on the easy chair.

As for Madhuri, she had no need to look at Satadal directly. She could see his image clearly in the mirror. Perhaps she first did so not because she wanted to but because the mirror was there. Perhaps there was also a furtive desire to look at him unobserved. She watched him in the mirror and saw him take off his watch, wind it and place it on the table. She saw that it was not the watch she knew. The wrist-band was also new. It was black and she had never liked a black band. She saw that he wore a new ring. The pillowcase was coloured and embroidered. She knew that he liked white and plain things and never cared for colour or decoration. Madhuri realised that the sewing mistress had taken him in hand and changed all his tastes.

He picked up his soap and towel and went into the bathroom. It was a welcome chance and she could look at his things closely but what is it that she sought? She carefully inspected every single article but found nothing she could recognise. Everything was new. There was not the slightest trace of what had been five years ago. Perhaps it would have been better if she had not been so curious.

If Madhuri had now looked at herself in the mirror, she would have seen that her eyes were full of jealousy. Her fine eyebrows were curved in envy. Her eyes were however fixed on the three suitcases which were all open. The watch, the purse and the glasses were on the table. The flannel tunic hung from the bracket and its golden buttons glistened against the light. What sort of man was this who could leave all his things scattered so carelessly in a waiting room? It seemed to her that his trust in people was unnatural. Equally extraordinary was her concern about things that nobody had asked her to watch.

As he returned, Madhuri turned her face away but she could still see him clearly in the mirror. There was no doubt that he was much thinner. It seemed that the sewing mistress had hardly any thought for his health. Madhuri had not seen him for five years but she knew he was hungry. His face never looked so pinched unless he was famished.

Satadal was indeed hungry. He took out some food from a tiffin carrier and arranged the plates on the table. As he was sitting down to his meal, he suddenly noticed that he had no water. He took up a glass and made to move toward the corner where there was a jug.

Madhuri had never thought that such an incident would hurt her so much. Since she had not imagined it, she was not prepared. Shaken out of her indifference, she turned her eyes sharply from the mirror and looked directly at him. She was quite visibly annoyed, but this angry movement and the slight frown seemed to be more natural than the pose of indifference she had maintained so long.

'What are you doing?' she asked.

Satadal as he heard the question and looked in surprise at her.

Madhuri burst out, 'Surely the heavens would not have fallen if you had asked me for a glass of water?'

His face broke into smiles as he said, 'Of course not.'

She stood up and came forward to take the glass from his hand. Bidding him sit down, she fetched him water. It seemed she had escaped the burden of silence in the waiting room. His easy smile had broken the barriers between them. It was after all only a waiting room.

She placed the glass of water on the table and started to arrange the dishes. As her bangles clinked against the glass, it seemed that memories which had slept for five years were suddenly revived. Who would say that they were two passengers who had casually met? One would think that they were man and wife and perfectly in tune with one another. He saw that her fingers were thinner, but she took up the food, as though with a prong, as skilfully as before, She stood by his side and their bodies almost touched. He could hear her short easy breathing in the silence of the room. One end of her saree had dropped on his arm but she hardly noticed it. It was nothing so unusual that one need observe it.

'This is all bazaar food, I suppose,' said Madhuri. Satadal did not miss the insinuation in her voice. He knew that she had always had a repugnance for such food. Half apologetically he said, 'Yes, I bought it in the bazaar at Katihar.'

'Where are you going now?'

'I am going to Calcutta,' said Satadal.

She asked again, 'Do you still stay there?'

He said, 'Yes, what about you?'

Perhaps it would have been better if their conversation had not taken this turn. Her hands trembled and she lost her sense of ease. It seemed that his question suddenly made her remember who she was. She moved away a little and softly said that she was going to Rajghat.

The topic ended there. There was nothing else to ask. They were passengers who had come by the same train but now they would travel by different trains along different routes. One would go to Calcutta and the other to Rajghat and yet in a moment of forgetfulness they had drawn rather close,

Perhaps in order to break the sense of constraint, Satadal asked, 'You will then have to take the train for Patna?'

'Yes,' said Madhuri, 'You had better finish your meal.'

It seemed that it required an effort for her to speak these words. However, she got them out and moved away. She remembered that she was waiting for the train to Patna. She could not stay indefinitely in this waiting room. She looked nervously at her wrist watch and went back to her bench.

The glass of water looked like liquid fire in the flash of the electric light. The food she had arranged neatly on the table also seemed full of hostility. Satadal again felt awkward and his feelings were tinged with a sense of shame. He blamed himself that he had run after an illusion knowingly.

He got up from the table and wrapped himself in his shawl. He reclined in the easy chair and lighted a cigarette. He could not touch the food, but did not understand why. In fact he did not even try to understand.

The waiting room was again nothing but a waiting room. Two strangers were counting the moments while they waited for their trains. But the trains were not yet due. Nor was there any sign of a third passenger. Someone at last appeared, but it was only the waiter. He had a tray with a pot of tea and two cups. He placed the tray on the table and left.

Satadal looked at the cup thirstily but turned his eyes away quickly as if he had seen a snake. The two cups on the table seemed to him a mockery of fate. He had not ordered tea for both. Why then had the waiter brought tea for two? No, it was impossible for him to take up the cup.

Madhuri did not look at him directly but she knew that he had not touched his food and it now seemed he would not take his tea either. How stupid of the waiter not to have poured out a cup of tea! But why should Satadal feel so shy? She remembered an old incident, but those days were for ever gone.

The two had gone to Madhupur to spend Christmas with her uncle. It was on the very first day of their visit. He said nothing but spent the whole morning in the garden without taking his cup of tea. The reason for the silent protest was that tea had been served by a servant and not by her. When this was found out, everyone in the house was upset. They all scolded Madhuri. Even her brother, when he heard the story, said, 'When you know that Satadal likes you to serve, why did you send the servant?'

Tonight, they were in a waiting room. It was neither Christmas nor Madhupur nor her uncle's house. Nor was it proper for Satadal to turn his face away and sit silently like an offended husband.

Yet Madhuri could not remain indifferent. It seemed that the scene in the waiting room, like a scene in a well acted play, vividly reminded her of his habits and temper. She almost felt that Satadal had the right to complain. No one could scold her today for not serving him, but she heard a voice within bidding her do her duty. She realised she must also play her part.

'Why are you not taking your food,' she asked. Her voice was tender and persuasive.

'I won't take these things so late in the night,' replied Satadal.

'At least you can have some tea.'

'That is a good idea, but what about you?'

There was a suspicion of a smile on Madhuri's face. 'It was not a part of the contract that I should take a cup,' she said.

Satadal smiled shyly and said, 'Perhaps not, but since the waiter has brought two cups, why not?'

They both turned grave for a moment. It was truly not the waiter's fault. It seemed that there was a tinge of regret in what she said. Perhaps she meant to say that it was not the fault of the waiter, but of their fate. Otherwise, why should they suffer this embarrassment on this rainy night in a waiting room after five long years?

Perhaps she found it impossible to keep on sitting in silence. Perhaps she willingly submitted to the conspiracy to which the waiting room itself seemed a party. In any case, she moved to the table and poured out the tea. She did it with the same old skill and grace. Satadal got up from the easy chair and placed a chair next to his.

Madhuri sat down quietly and found nothing to object to. They both realised that the waiting room at Rajpur was bringing them together. Neither had the heart to check the course of events. When Madhuri sat down beside Satadal, it looked a picture of perfect conjugal life.

Satadal sipped the tea and sighed in contentment. Surely, it was not merely the taste of the tea but because he felt in it the touch of Madhuri's hand.

He smiled, 'You looked so grave that I was feeling uncomfortable.'

Madhuri also smiled. 'For you it was only a slight embarrassment but I alone know what I felt.'

'Were you frightened?'

She lowered her face and said. 'Yes.'

'What was there to fear?'

Their conversation had begun on a light note, but his last words were heavy with an unexpressed sadness. Her words were full of regret. His words had a tone of assurance and intimacy. The past was past. Why should one fear or regret it?

It is easy to judge the dead with sympathy and understanding. We also tend to think of the good qualities rather than the faults of those who are no more. Madhuri and Satadal could look back on their past with sympathy. The fear, the hatred, and the suspicion of the past had been burned up and scattered. Today they remembered the past like the sky of one long night lit up by a thousand stars. It was hard to believe that it was a lost horizon. It would not have been human if they had not longed to capture the spirit of the past. Madhuri looked at Satadal and said, 'You have lost a good deal of weight.'

'What if I say the same thing about you,' said he.

He pointed at her fingers and said, 'Why have they become so thin?'

Madhuri was about to hide her fingers in her saree, but in a mood of forgetfulness, he took both her hands and warmly pressed them. Madhuri did not object.

He looked at her face as if he was seeing her anew. 'There has been no change in your face, no change at all,' he said.

Everything had changed, only not her face. All their past life was cancelled, but the face he had loved remained the same. How could it be? Was it mere fancy or a trick of the eye?

Madhuri blushed deeply. Not like a maiden at the first address of love, nor like a shy bride meeting her lover for the first time in a bridal chamber. She blushed like a wife who had met her man after long years of separation but was sure of her husband's love.

It was not a bower, not a bridal chamber. It was not the house of a newly married pair but the waiting room in a railway station. They were only two passengers but they sat as if they were passengers in the journey of life and had never separated.

As they finished their tea, she asked, 'Where is your uncle?'

'He has built himself a house in Dehra Dun and stays there.'

'And what about Puti?'

'Puti? She has grown up and married. You remember Romesh. He now has a job in Delhi. He married her.'

Her hands were still clasped in his. It seemed he was afraid to let her go. After a long search, he had discovered an image which was lost five years ago. With both his hands, he held her lest she disappear again.

'Could you believe me, Madhuri?'

'Believe you? Why not?'

'I have not forgotten you. I can never forget you.'

'It is nothing strange. I can see you have not forgotten.'

'But what about you? Have you forgotten me?'

Madhuri closed her eyes.

It seemed she wanted to withdraw within herself before she could reply. Her head reclined a little toward Satadal. There was a suspicion of tears in the corner of her eye.

He drew her closer to him and insisted, 'You must tell me, Madhuri; I will not let you go till I have a reply.'

Suddenly Madhuri started as if she had felt the touch of fire. She released herself and stood up. A bell rang loudly and shattered the silence of the winter night. Even the mirror on the wall was trembling. It seemed as if the waiting room was protesting against the impropriety of their conduct. A passenger train had just entered the platform.

Madhuri rushed frantically to the door as she cried, 'He is coming by this train.'

The man who now entered the waiting room was Anadi Roy, Madhuri's husband. His face lighted up with joy as he saw her, like the face of a lonely traveler who had just discovered an inn.

Madhuri's face also lighted up but there was still a touch of sadness in it, like the smoke of a lamp that has burned too long.

Anadi Roy noticed it and asked in an anxious tone, 'Are you feeling all right?'

'Yes, I am quite well.'

'You had to wait for a long time, didn't you?'

'Yes.'

'I could not help it. the trains nowadays never run on time; otherwise I would have been here at least two hours ago.'

Anadi Roy started unpacking to make things comfortable for his wife. As she protested, he only took out a fine shawl, wrapped her in it and said, 'You had better rest for a little while. You will feel much better.'

Satadal was watching them from his chair. He could not stand the scene and got up hurriedly. He walked up to the door and looked out. He returned and rearranged his things. The sight was indeed intolerable for him. The fine shawl clung to Madhuri's body in loving embrace. How proud and happy Anadi Roy looked! To Satadal it seemed that Madhuri was a woman of ancient legend to be won by prowess. Satadal felt like a defeated candidate who could only look helplessly on the scene. He could of course walk out of the room but he still lingered for an answer to his question.

Anadi Roy looked at his watch. It was almost time for their train. Madhuri put on her coat. The porters reappeared on the scene and announced that the train for Patna was coming in.

Madhuri stood by her husband. The porters collected the luggage and started to go out of the waiting room. Satadal feared that there was little hope of getting an answer to his question. It seemed to him that Madhuri had locked him in a house of lac and set it on fire.

Were their seven years of joint life a mere illusion? Was it so easy to forget? Does legal separation so irrevocably divide the heart? Madhuri would never answer that question.

Perhaps it would have been better if with a smiling face she had gone off with her husband, but she did tarry for a moment. The porters had already gone out of the room, but Madhuri paused near the door. It seemed that the bond of past affection held her steps. She turned to Satadal and smiled as she said goodbye. Satadal could not smile. Wounded affection and vain claims throbbed in his heart, but there was no time to give expression to them. He only wanted an answer to his question. He said, 'Of course you will go, but you have not answered my question.'

The smile on Madhuri's face faded. She looked at him in surprise and asked, 'What question?'

Satadal repeated, 'You did not tell me if you have really forgotten me.'

Madhuri kept silent. Perhaps she had forgotten. Yet how was it possible that she could forget a question asked seven minutes ago when memories of seven years were so vivid to her? Satadal was puzzled.

Madhuri said, 'I must go. It is getting late.'

Satadal winced as if her words were like a blow. He remembered that Madhuri had to go and could not be stopped. For seven years he had made her wait, but today he had no right to keep her waiting even for a moment.

Sadly he said, 'Then you won't answer my question?'

Madhuri replied gently, 'It is a question which should not be answered.'

'Why?' asked Satadal.

Madhuri said, 'It is an improper question.'

Satadal got up from his chair and said 'I see.' He turned his face away and said almost rudely, 'Go if you will, but why did you make this show?'

Satadal's words were ungracious. For a moment Madhuri's face became hard. Her eyebrows curved in anger. She brooded for a moment and then her face again beamed with smiles. She looked at her watch and said.' Come and visit us at Rajgir with Sudha.'

Satadal was taken aback and said, 'And then?'

'I shall come to see both of you off when it is time for you to depart.'

'Why?' asked Satadal.

'You will then get an opportunity of paying me in my own coin.' Madhuri smiled and added, 'Why, I would perhaps be as angry as you are today. Perhaps I will ask equally foolish questions.'

For a few seconds, Satadal looked vacant.

Then he burst out laughing and said in a loud voice, 'Yes, I now understand.'

Satadal looked at his own watch. Even though he did not turn to the door, he knew Madhuri had left. The house of lac had not been set on fire. Instead, laughter seemed to be echoing from end to end.

Rajpur Junction suddenly came to life. There was the siren of an incoming train, the train for Calcutta, which entered the platform on the opposite side. Satadal hurried away toward it.

The two trains would move away in opposite directions. Rajpur Junction would become dead and silent after this momentary burst of life. Soon there would be no trace left of the strange encounter between two casual passengers.

Signs of their meeting were however still evident. There was a tray on the table with two empty cups on it. Before the Junction went to sleep again, the waiter would take them, clean them and place them on the cupboard. Perhaps he would place the two cups at two ends of the shelf.

translated by Humayun Kabir

Glossary

adaab : gesture of respect
alta : red liquid used to decorate women's feet
anchal : one end of a saree
anna : one-sixteenth of an Indian rupee, in pre-decimal coinage
annaprasan : ceremony at which an infant is given its first taste of rice
asan : small, homemade rug used as an individual seat
Basanti saree : saree of a bright yellow colour
bhadralok : gentlefolk
bustees : slums
'chalo' : 'come!'
chumki : spangle
darbesh : a sweetmeat
dharamshala : charitable refuge for the indigent or others in need of care and protection
dhuni : censer
Durgabari : a place where the goddess Durga is worshipped
esraj : a stringed instrument
gamcha : a checked cloth, usually used like a towel
ghati : a small metal drinking-vessel
hasnu hana : a flowering tree that blooms at night
jarda : tobacco-based product eaten with betel leaves
Jatayu : the noble, elderly vulture in the epic *Ramayana* who attempts to save Sita from abduction by Ravana
kansa : bell metal
kantha : thin quilt made of old cloth
karabi : oleander
luchi : bread of refined wheat flour dough rolled out and deep-fried; version of a poori, which is made of wholewheat flour
mridanga : two-ended drum
pakhiraj : a mythical winged horse
pou : measure of weight, probably a quarter 'seer'
prasad : food offered already to a god(dess) and then distributed to worshippers; hence also, metaphorically, a gift of the god(dess)

pronami : gift given in connection with a wedding, usually to newly weds paying respects to elders, or by the bride's family to the groom's family
rabri : semi-liquid sweet made from sweetened milk reduced by boiling
sandesh : sweetmeat made from milk
saya : petticoat
sidhe : remuneration in kind
swaraj : freedom
thagini : female confidence trickster
thana : police outpost smaller than a regular police station.